town on which her *Cedar Cove* novels are based) and they
winter in Florida.

Also by Debbie Macomber available in Arrow

Debbie Macomber

Window on the Bay

arrow books

1 3 5 7 9 10 8 6 4 2

Arrow Books
20 Vauxhall Bridge Road
London SW1V 2SA

Arrow Books is part of the Penguin Random House group of companies
whose addresses can be found at global.penguinrandomhouse.com.

Penguin
Random House
UK

First published in Great Britain by Arrow Books in 2019

www.penguin.co.uk

A CIP catalogue record for this book is available from the British Library.

ISBN 9781784758769

Typeset in 11.25/15.5pt Adobe Garamond Pro by
Jouve (UK), Milton Keynes
Printed and bound in Great Britain by Clays Ltd, Elcograf S.p.A.

Penguin Random House is committed to a
sustainable future for our business, our readers
and our planet. This book is made from Forest
Stewardship Council® certified paper.

To Sheila and Norm Crighton
for all the laughter, fun, and Scotch

Dear Friends,

The best ideas for my books come straight from life. My daughter Jody prompted this story about surviving an empty nest. It all started when Jody's youngest headed off to college, and she lamented that she wasn't sure what she was going to do with herself. For years her time had been spent wrapped around her children and their interests, mainly sports. James was a star basketball player, and she drove hither and yon supporting him and his team. Her life was suddenly an empty slate. Now what?

Years earlier Wayne and I faced that same question. I remember when our youngest headed off to college and the changes that took place in our lives. Suddenly, Wayne and I found ourselves parenting our dog, Peterkins. I volunteered to mentor a high school girl who yearned to be a writer, and Wayne took up woodworking. New adventures awaited us at each turn.

Change. Isn't that what happens in life?

With the thought of an empty nest, my creative imagination went to work, and you are now holding the result in your hand. I hope you enjoy Jenna and Maureen's story as they navigate through this new world and the discoveries they make about themselves and their futures.

You, my readers, are my inspiration, and hearing from you is what has guided my career from the start. Every email, website guestbook remark, and handwritten letter is personally read by me. You can learn more on my website at debbiemacomber.com, Facebook, Twitter, Instagram, and every other social media available. Or you can write me at P.O. Box 1458, Port Orchard, WA 98366. I look forward to hearing from you.

Warmest regards,

Debbie Macomber

Prologue

Jenna

Where It All Began

"We need to talk," Maureen said, as we walked across the quad at the University of Washington's main campus. The cherry trees were in full bloom, and the fragrance filled the air.

Maureen and I had met in college as freshmen while taking French classes. We started out as study partners and soon became fast friends. By the end of our sophomore year, we'd made it a goal to travel to Paris after graduation.

Paris. We were dying to see Paris. I'd fallen in love with the city as a young teen after watching *Casablanca* for the first time. When Humphrey Bogart looked deep into the eyes of Ingrid Bergman and said, "We'll always have Paris," I was captivated.

The City of Love had beckoned me. It was the very reason

I'd taken six years of French classes—four in high school and now two in college. I couldn't wait to see Paris. I wanted to walk in the moonlight along the Seine, tour the Louvre, and see the view of the city from the Eiffel Tower.

We'd spent countless hours together planning for the trip over the last two years, and we'd each worked part-time jobs to pay for it. We'd sacrificed our weekends and saved every penny. Finally, here we were in our senior year, and our dream was going to come true.

"Is something wrong?" I asked, holding my thick nursing textbook close to my chest. While commuting to and from my clinicals this semester, I'd spent a lot of time daydreaming about what early summer would be like in Paris. I'd envisioned myself walking along the river, viewing artists busily painting on their canvases, while the sweet notes of a love song drifted through the air from a distant accordion.

"I can't go to Paris," Maureen blurted out.

"What?" Her words took my breath away. I was sure I'd heard her wrong.

"I won't be able to go to Paris the way we planned."

Dumbfounded, I stopped walking and stared at her. Our airline tickets had been purchased, our hotel reservations were made, our itinerary was in writing and on our phones— every last detail had been finalized.

Maureen lowered her eyes. "I'm pregnant. Peter and I have decided to get married as soon as we graduate."

I knew she'd been seeing a lot of Peter Zelinski but had no idea their relationship was this serious. Maureen had taken on the role of tutoring students as a means of earning extra money for our Paris trip. Peter had been one of her calculus students.

I was dating, too. Kyle Boltz was a first-year medical student, and I was beginning to hope we would have a future together. Kyle had a lot of schooling ahead of him, and I would soon be graduating with a nursing degree. We'd met at a party and we had clicked.

"Say something," Maureen pleaded.

That was the problem. I didn't know what to say. I hadn't fully processed that everything—all our plans, our prep work, the anticipation—had changed in an instant. And my best friend was *pregnant*. This changed everything.

"You should still go," Maureen added.

"Not without you." I refused to entertain the thought. It wouldn't be the same without my best friend.

"I've ruined everything," Maureen said, biting her lower lip.

Giving her a big hug, I did my best to comfort her. "You didn't ruin anything. A baby is far more important than a trip to Paris. We'll get there one day."

Maureen's mouth wobbled with the effort to smile.

"And I get to be in your wedding."

"Maid of honor," Maureen said. "I wouldn't have anyone else."

"Deal."

Yes, I was disappointed, but we had our whole lives ahead of us. Paris would have to wait.

Chapter 1

Jenna

I'd waited for this for a long time.

I sat in the small nook with the padded seat in my upstairs bedroom, gazing out the window. The view of Elliott Bay stretched before me. I loved this spot, my contemplation area. I leaned my back against the wall, my knees drawn up as I gazed out over the panorama. The gray skies had threatened rain earlier in the day. Despite popular opinion, Seattle wasn't drenched in drizzle all twelve months of the year. No matter what the weather, my window on the bay never failed to soothe me. In contrast, this afternoon the sky was blue and bright in late September, and the waters of Puget Sound as green as an emerald lawn. The waterfront area of Seattle was filled with tourists, the streets busy with those either departing or returning from Alaskan cruises.

My mind was spinning with the changes about to take place in my life. The day before, I'd helped Allie settle into her dorm room at my alma mater, the University of Washington. My daughter was about to spread her wings at college, just as I'd done all those years ago. Although I'd been looking forward to this day, I worried. Allie was nothing like her older brother, Paul. My son had been the man of the house and was more mature than his years, especially after his father left us. Allie could be overly emotional at times, and I had to admit I'd spoiled her, though not to the point that she was self-centered and irrational. I'd wanted her to commute from home the first couple years of college, but she insisted that she wanted to live in the dorms. Eventually I'd given in, remembering that my parents had given me that experience to let me soar on my own.

This move was big for Allie and equally big for me.

My nest was now empty.

The silent house had never felt louder. It was as if I could hear the hollowness surrounding me. While I had been looking forward to this time, I wasn't completely sure what I wanted to do with myself. I'd spent the last sixteen years as a single mom, dedicating my life, my resources, and my everything to my two children, all the while juggling a full-time career. It hadn't been easy being both mother and father, but I was smarter and wiser, especially in the area of men. I could fix a leaky pipe, clean gutters, and assemble a chest of drawers with instructions written in a foreign language. I was *woman*—and I could pound my chest as hard as any man.

And now, after years of attending sporting events—soccer, baseball, and basketball games, as well as swimming meets—I finally had time for myself. I thought of all the music lessons, the Girl Scout Cookie drives I'd organized, and how I'd been class mother for both Paul and Allie in their grade-school years. The last year Paul was in junior high, I'd been president of the PTA. My kids' teeth were straight, and they both were grounded and obtained above-average grades.

As I looked out my window, I remembered that sense of elation mingled with worries and doubts which nearly overwhelmed me when I dropped Allie off at the college campus. I watched a green-and-white Washington state ferry sail toward Bainbridge Island.

I refused to let my concerns take away this special moment. I let the calming view settle my nerves and I turned my focus onto what this new season of life meant for me.

I'd raised my children, made sacrifices for them, stayed focused on their needs, but now I could look to the future and make plans of my own. Unlike their father, I'd taken my responsibility as a parent seriously. Kyle had proved to be a sorry disappointment as a husband, but especially as a father.

I had an entire list of what I hoped to accomplish in the next few years. For a long time, I'd wanted to find a creative way to express myself. Zumba class, painting. I'd been toying with the idea of creating a Bullet Journal, too. The possibilities were endless. And trips. I longed to travel, to see the world, study new cultures, taste the local cuisines. With France, especially Paris, on the top of the page, of course. Between my work schedule at the hospital and all the kids' activities, I'd never found time to fit any of these things into my life.

But I could now.

Paris. The more I thought about it, the more I longed to make that trip a possibility. Maureen and I had put off that dream for far too long. Like me, Maureen was divorced now, too. We'd been single moms together all these years, and formed our own support group. Both of our marriages had gone down in flames, and Paris was shoved into the black hole called "someday." Well, "someday" was now, finally within reach.

I dropped my legs from my perch and reached for the phone, calling Maureen to invite her over for a movie and some girl time together. She was quick to agree, eager to hear how Allie's move-in at college had gone.

Before she arrived I had the popcorn popping, and for the fun of it, I'd downloaded *Casablanca*, hoping to remind her of our long-ago dream.

The doorbell rang, and I set aside the remote to answer the door.

Maureen came into the house waving a grocery bag. "You'll like what's inside!" She was a petite brunette with deep brown eyes that revealed her subtle wit and intelligence. Her hair was the same shade as her eyes. She wore it shoulder-length, and I envied how thick it was.

Over the years I'd come to appreciate Maureen all the more. We talked often and supported each other through everything that life had thrown our way. She'd been the first person I'd called after Kyle left, and when Allie broke her arm. I couldn't have asked for a better best friend.

She pulled out a container from the bag, revealing my favorite flavor of ice cream: salted caramel, my weakness.

"A perfect addition to a perfect day." I took it from her and headed into the kitchen to place it in the freezer.

Maureen trailed behind me. "How was your hot date?"

My hand paused on the freezer door as I thought back over my dinner with the insurance adjuster. It had been washed from my mind, an evening I was eager to forget. "A disappointment."

"Yellow light?"

Maureen and I had devised our own grading system when it came to men and dating. A green light meant there was real potential. A yellow light meant we were waiting to learn more and would proceed with caution. A red light was a flat no, no questions asked, not happening. No way. No how.

"Red light?"

I gave a sad nod.

"After one date?"

I expelled a lengthy sigh, letting it whistle through my teeth. What was it with men? "He thought dinner at a cheap Mexican restaurant gave him a free license to spend the night."

"Give me a break," Maureen said, shaking her head.

I'd dated off and on since my divorce. My children had always been my priority. Still, there were times when I needed adult male companionship for my own mental health, yet in all the years since Kyle and I had split, I hadn't met a man I felt deserved a green light. Several had looked promising in the beginning, but as we got to know each other better, something always seemed to be fundamentally lacking. I was beginning to think the "lacking" might be me—that I'd set my standards too high.

My marriage to Kyle hadn't helped matters. I'd come out of it with trust issues and with the fear of making yet another mistake. Now, with both kids in college, I'd hoped to seriously look at my relationships with men.

"How frustrating," Maureen said. Seeing the bowls of popcorn on the kitchen counter, she reached for them and led the way into the family room.

I loved my Colonial-style house that was set on a hill overlooking Elliott Bay. Other than my children, it was the best thing I'd gotten out of my marriage. The family room off the kitchen was where we all gathered to watch television, or to sit by the fireplace on a cold, rainy Seattle day on the comfortable, oversized, well-loved leather furniture. One year for Christmas, my dad had a gas line installed to the fireplace, so I didn't need to fuss with building a fire with wood any longer. All winter long, I had that fire going. It added a touch of warmth to those chilly nights while Paul and Allie sank into the big chairs to do their homework.

I had *Casablanca* primed and ready to play.

Popcorn for dinner and ice cream for dessert. Now, that was freedom.

I reached for the remote. Maureen had her shoes off and her ankles crossed on the ottoman as she munched on the popcorn. "You picked the movie?"

"Yup, and you're going to love it." I hit the remote, and immediately the music leading up to *Casablanca* began to play.

Maureen's smile widened. "Is this what I think it is?"

I couldn't keep from smiling. "Yup, and that should tell you what I'm thinking."

"Paris," Maureen cried. "You want to start planning for our trip to Paris." Her eyes shone with enthusiasm.

"At last, our *someday* is here." I could already feel the excitement building inside me. Over the years, we'd never stopped talking about our trip to Paris, but the timing had never been right. "I'm thinking we can go next spring."

"Spring," Maureen agreed with a single nod. She was the trip planner, Lonely Planet in human form. The woman was a hound dog when it came to research. She could find her way around the Internet the way some people could find their way around the Mall of America without a map. Being a librarian no doubt helped. Maureen had majored in library science, and that career was a natural for her. She'd worked for the last twenty years at the Seattle Public Library.

Next spring would be the perfect time to go. Paul was working year-round as a server in Pullman while going through college, and Allie was planning for an exchange program that would take her to Japan for six months, leaving my schedule next year wide open for this trip. Of course, I would need to get time off from the hospital, being certain to get the request in early for my vacation dates. Several months' notice would guarantee there wouldn't be a problem.

"I'll look for our planning notes from when we were in college," Maureen said, showing her excitement.

"You kept them?" That shouldn't surprise me. Maureen was an organizational genius and always had been. She liked her life structured. Everything in its place, and a place for everything. She was a spotless housekeeper. Dust didn't dare make a showing in her home.

"Of course I kept them. Why not? The Louvre is still waiting for us."

"And Sainte-Chapelle." I'd looked at breathtaking photos of the stained-glass windows of the chapel countless times, dreaming of the day I would be able to see it in person.

"Shopping on Rue de Rivoli," Maureen added dreamily.

"Was that on day five?" I asked. If I remembered correctly, shopping had been reserved for later in our self-guided tour.

"Day six."

Naturally, Maureen would remember the minute details. The woman's mind was a steel trap. I sincerely doubted she would need those notes to recollect the details of our original plans. She probably remembered the flight numbers and our seat assignments, if I were to ask. That was Maureen.

She had never remarried after she and Peter split. Like me, she'd dated, too, but not often. Her marriage had lasted only five years. Peter and Maureen had never been a good mix, and they both knew it. To their credit, they'd stuck it out as long as they had for the sake of their daughter, Victoria—Tori for short. A couple years following their divorce, Peter had remarried and had two additional children, both boys. He continued to be a good father to Tori, and had remained an integral part of her life, unlike how my ex had been with Paul and Allie.

I'd always hoped Maureen would find happiness with another man. She deserved it, but I feared she'd lost something of herself in her failed marriage. I understood, as I feared I had, too.

Settling back against the sofa, I brought my legs up under

me and held the bowl of popcorn in my lap as the movie started. I'll never forget the first time Maureen and I watched *Casablanca* in college. The movie had the same impact on Maureen as it'd had on me as a teen. We'd both cried and agreed it was the most romantic movie ever made.

"I love the opening," Maureen said with a sigh. "It's the music."

Surprisingly, Maureen Zelinski had a romantic heart. I suspected she hid that fact from her peers at the library. Only those closest to her would suspect as much.

I munched on my popcorn, relaxing as I got involved in the movie.

"Was Allie able to connect with her dad before she left?" Maureen asked.

I rolled my eyes and shook my head. "No." It hurt me that Allie's father had disappointed our daughter yet again. It demanded effort not to add a derogatory comment about my ex. Even before the ink on our divorce papers was dry, Kyle had basically abandoned the children and me. He'd left Seattle Central Hospital, where we were both employed, him as a surgeon and me as a nurse. He'd promptly moved to another state. It wasn't long before I learned he'd remarried, and, shockingly, it wasn't to the woman with whom he'd had the affair. In the years since, he'd divorced and married two more times. Paul and Allie were his only children.

To be fair, Kyle had faithfully paid child support, and I was grateful he'd held up that portion of his responsibility. What hurt most, other than the fact he hadn't been able to keep his pants zipped, was the way he'd treated our children as nonentities. He would send them birthday cards—if he remembered, that is—and send a check at Christmas. Basically, that was it.

In the last year, Allie had tried to reestablish a relationship with her father. She'd reached out to him, seeking his advice regarding her choice of colleges. I didn't discourage her, and hoped Kyle would take an interest in our daughter. Thankfully, he'd responded, and she'd been thrilled. All the effort, however, had been on Allie's part and continued to be so. She'd phoned him right before she left for school and was told he wasn't available. I hated to see her disappointed yet again.

"Allie has no real expectations when it comes to her father," I said, feeling sad at how true that was.

My phone rang, and I grabbed it off the coffee table. I didn't recognize the number, and ignored the call.

"You going to answer that?" Maureen asked as the phone continued to ring.

"Nope. I've been getting far too many solicitation calls." The numbers that showed up were often local ones that made me think I might be missing a personal call. I'd fallen for that trick far too often.

"I've been getting those calls, too," Maureen said, and seemed as irritated as me with the interruption by robot calls. She leaned back against the sofa, returning to her popcorn.

After five torturous rings, the phone went to voicemail, but whoever had called didn't leave a message. I knew it. Another sales call. If I got one more call from that perky Elizabeth, I was going to scream.

I was about to grab another handful of popcorn when it rang a second time.

Same number.

Maureen glanced at my phone and over to me. "Maybe you should answer that."

"Maybe I should." I paused the movie and reached for my phone, getting it on the fifth ring, just before it went to voicemail.

"This is Jenna Boltz," I stated matter-of-factly.

"Jenna, oh Jenna," an elderly woman's voice returned breathlessly. "I'm so sorry to bother you . . . your mom gave me your number."

I sat up straight and set aside my popcorn bowl. "Mrs. Torres? Is that you?" She was the widow who lived next door to my mother.

"Yes, dear, it's me."

Mrs. Torres was a good friend to my mother, especially since my father had passed. He'd been gone more than two years now, and the two widows looked after each other. Knowing that Mrs. Torres kept an eye on Mom reassured me, and I know Mrs. Torres's children were grateful to have Mom do the same for her next-door neighbor and friend.

"Is everything all right?" I asked.

"Jenna, your mother has taken a bad spill. I'm afraid she's hurt herself."

I jumped to my feet, my heart pounding so loudly it echoed in my ears. "How badly is she hurt? Is anything broken?"

"I . . . I don't know. I think it might be her hip. I hope

I did the right thing by calling nine-one-one. The paramedics are already here. You mother didn't want them to take her to the hospital until I contacted you."

"What?" I asked in disbelief. *My mother is waiting for my approval before she sought medical attention?*

"The paramedics are talking to her now," Mrs. Torres continued. "They're checking her vital signs and suggested I step back. Carol wants to talk to you, but they need a few minutes with her first."

"Of course." I couldn't believe this was happening. My poor mother. She'd already been through so much with the loss of my father. I hated the thought of her being hurt and in pain.

Seeing the concern on my face, and the fact I was on my feet, Maureen was looking at me with alarm. Being a nurse, I immediately went into crisis mode. "Where did she fall?" I asked, wanting as many details as Mrs. Torres could give me.

"Outside, off the back steps. She was working in her garden and started into the house. She must have stumbled." Mrs. Torres lowered her voice, not wanting Mom to hear. "She landed hard on the walk."

I gasped when I heard she'd landed on concrete.

"We'd been chatting just a few minutes earlier," the widow explained. "I was picking a bouquet of dahlias when it happened."

"Thank God you were there."

"I went over to her right away and told her not to move. Carol didn't think she was hurt at first. Although she was in a lot of pain, she insisted she was fine."

That was just like my mother. She wouldn't want anyone to make a fuss.

"After a few minutes she wanted me to help her stand. But I could see she'd hurt herself, and that this wasn't a simple fall."

I closed my eyes with worry. "Please tell me you didn't move her!"

"No . . . oh no. I insisted she stay still until I got help. Even if I'd wanted to, I wouldn't have had the strength to get her upright."

I heard my mother's voice in the background.

"Let me talk to Jenna."

"While I talk to her," I said to Mrs. Torres, "please ask the paramedics to take her to Seattle Central Hospital."

"I'll do that, dear. Now, don't you worry. Here's your mother."

"Mom?"

"I'm so sorry, Jenna."

"Don't apologize, Mom. It was an accident. Mrs. Torres did the right thing to call for help. Let the aid car take you to the hospital. I'm leaving now and will meet you there."

"Okay." Mom gasped for breath as if she was in terrible pain, her voice a mere whisper. My heart clenched.

My mother was a salt-of-the-earth kind of woman. I'd been blessed with wonderful parents who had loved and supported me throughout my entire life. After Kyle and I divorced, I would never have managed on my own without their love and backing. Losing Dad to a heart attack was a blow that had left our family reeling. Two years had gone by, yet Mom wasn't past the fact that she was now a widow. Grief had aged her. She was in her midseventies and in overall good health, but she missed my father something terrible and had given up many of the things they had once enjoyed together.

This past year Mom had stayed home far more than she'd ventured out, tending her garden and working jigsaw puzzles. Maureen had tried to get Mom to join a reading group at the library, but she wasn't interested. I was grateful that she continued playing bridge with a group of ladies from the church.

Mrs. Torres came back on the line. "They're loading Carol into the aid car now."

"Thank you, Mrs. Torres."

"I wish I could have done more, Jenna. I feel a bit shaken myself. Falling is one of my biggest fears. Please let me know if there's anything more I can do."

"I will, and thank you again." Poor woman. Seeing this happen to my mother must have been an ordeal for her. I would be forever grateful that she'd been outside at the time of Mom's fall. I hated to think of how long my mother might have lain on the walk before anyone found her, if it hadn't been for Mrs. Torres.

As soon as I disconnected the call, Maureen was full of questions. "What happened?"

I tossed my phone and my charging cord into my purse as I explained.

"I'm coming with you," Maureen insisted.

"Then follow me in your car." I didn't want Maureen trapped at the hospital because we'd driven in one car.

Depending on Mom's prognosis, I knew I could potentially be at the hospital for several hours.

On the drive over, my mind was working at warp speed, assessing what little I could from the information given me. Mom had fallen, but from what Mrs. Torres told me, she hadn't hit her head, which was a blessing in and of itself. Nor did I know how far she'd fallen. Had she been up one step or two when she'd taken the tumble?

I rushed toward the hospital, then parked with relative ease, thanks to my employee parking pass, although it was at the farthest spot in the parking lot. I trusted that Maureen would find parking in the garage or on the street.

After twenty years working in the intensive care unit at Seattle Central, I'd become acquainted with many of the medical professionals there, but I wasn't as familiar with the emergency room staff, though I did recognize the names of several physicians and nurses as I passed through.

I was directed into the cubicle where Mom had been taken. Relief showed on her face as soon as she saw me. Stretching out her arm, she grabbed hold of my hand as I stepped to the side of the gurney.

"Everything is going to be okay, Mom," I told her, bending over to give her a gentle hug.

Closing her eyes, Mom held on to me as though she never intended to let me go.

We didn't need to wait long for the examining physician to arrive. I wasn't familiar with Dr. Spencer, though I'd heard his name mentioned before, and always in a good way. We spoke briefly, and he put in an order for X-rays.

Patient transport arrived quickly, and my instinct was to accompany her because I knew it would comfort her to have me at her side. However, the woman at the check-in desk came by, asking me to fill out several pages of paperwork. Mom's worried eyes sought me out.

"I'll be here when you get back," I promised, walking down the hallway with her before she was rolled into the elevator.

With a heavy heart, I took the clipboard into the waiting room and called my brother, Tom, to let him know what had happened. Tom and his wife, Louanne, lived three hours away in Oregon. Both of his kids were out on their own now. I told him to stay put until I had more information. I found Maureen pacing in front of the emergency department check-in station.

"How is she?"

"Pale, and clearly in a lot of pain. Her blood pressure's elevated because of that, and her heart rate is fast but steady." I had sneaked a peek at the chart clipped at the base of the bed and scanned the notes left by the paramedics.

Maureen went back to the cubicle to wait with me. Mom returned in a relatively short amount of time, and ten minutes later Dr. Spencer reentered the room. Without a word, he brought up the X-ray on the computer screen for us and pointed out what was quite noticeable, and what I had suspected had happened: Mom had indeed broken her hip. The break was bad, and I knew it would require immediate surgery.

"I've put a call in to Dr. Lancaster," Dr. Spencer said. "He's the best orthopedic surgeon in the state."

I was familiar with Dr. Lancaster's superior reputation as a surgeon. We'd never worked together, so I was uncertain of his bedside manner. All I could do was hope that he would be patient and tender with Mom. For the most part, the surgeons I'd met and worked with had minimal people skills. They were often brilliant, yet found it hard to relate to patients. Because of this, many chose this field of medicine because it had the least amount of one-on-one patient contact. They'd perform the surgery, and the patient would never see them again. In, done, and gone. Yet I knew Dr. Lancaster to be the best orthopedic surgeon in the area, and I was thankful that Mom would be in good hands during surgery, no matter what his people skills were.

Mom's hand tightened around my own. "Everything will be fine, Jenna. Don't you worry."

How like my mother to be reassuring me.

"Yes, it will," I said, although tears had gathered in my eyes. Mom and I were close, and I couldn't bear the thought of losing her, especially so soon after losing my father.

Chapter 2

Jenna

Maureen handed me the cup of coffee she'd brought me from the hospital cafeteria. It wasn't the greatest coffee in Seattle. After working here for twenty years, I should know. I'd downed my fair share of the hospital blend. Starbucks had no competition.

"Thanks," I said, letting the warmth seep into my cold hands. The surgical waiting room was nearly empty. Only two others remained, an older gentleman and a woman who looked like she could be his daughter. I'd observed them and saw that the younger woman was encouraging and comforting the older man.

The volunteer who manned the waiting room desk had left after assuring all of us that the surgeons would be in to speak to us privately after the surgeries were completed. Checking the wall clock, I sighed, noting Mom had been in surgery going on three hours. I couldn't help being anxious. Mom had been through so much already. This was only the beginning; the long road to recovery awaited her. The hospital wouldn't keep her for more than three days before transferring her to a rehabilitation center for physical therapy. I suspected it would be a month or more before she was able to return home.

"Can I get you anything else?" Maureen asked. She'd been a trooper, sitting with me all this time. We hadn't talked a lot, each caught up in our own thoughts. Mine centered on Mom and how grateful I was for Mrs. Torres. While waiting, I'd updated both her and my brother, and promised to phone again once she was out of surgery.

"I don't need anything, but thanks." For emphasis, I shook my head. It was then that I realized it was well past the dinner hour. Maureen must be starving. All we'd had to eat before the call was a few handfuls of popcorn. That had been hours ago.

"I can bring you a sandwich," Maureen suggested.

Again, I declined. I was too worried to be anywhere close to feeling hungry. Besides, by this time at night, the cafeteria selections would be slim.

"You should go," I told my closest friend. "It could be a while before she's out of surgery."

Maureen shook her head. "I'm not leaving you alone."

"I'm fine," I assured her, offering as much of a smile as I could manage. "Honestly, I am." Maureen was scheduled to work in the morning. Luckily, I was off on Monday. I worked three twelve-hour days on and then I had three days off.

I finally managed to convince her I'd be okay. I walked her to the door and we hugged before she headed toward the hospital exit.

Not twenty minutes after she'd left, a surgeon stepped into the waiting area. He briefly talked with the other two in the room, and after a few minutes they departed.

I was left alone.

I'd spent a good majority of my adult life alone, so it didn't bother me. I was strong and independent—I'd learned by necessity. Being alone had been harder for my mom since Dad had passed. She'd always had him by her side, and consequently, navigating the turbulent waters of widowhood had been especially difficult for her. She'd never had to fill the car with gas or take the garbage out to the street or deal with a thousand other tasks that my father had always done for her. At first, simple tasks had felt daunting to her. I was convinced part of her unwillingness to venture out alone had to do with her anxiety over pumping her own gas at a self-service gas station.

As much as possible, I'd tried to be there for her, but I couldn't allow myself to become a crutch. Like I had once been forced to do, Mom would need to find her own inner strength. I had faith in her. But I worried that this hip surgery would undermine Mom's confidence even more.

The minutes passed slowly. I scanned nearly every magazine in the room, and wandered around, moving from one section to another. A few staff members I knew stopped off to chat and offer their concerns. Between worrying about Mom and waiting to hear about her condition, I stewed about everything that could go wrong and prayed for good results and quick healing for my wonderful mother.

When Dr. Rowan Lancaster finally appeared in the

waiting room, it was close to four hours from the start of the surgery. He was dressed in the typical blue surgical gown. The cap on his head was soaked from hours in the operating room.

His eyes immediately met mine, as I was the only one in the surgical waiting area. He nodded, acknowledging me. I guessed that we were about the same age; he might be a few years older. His hair, what I could see of it, was salt and pepper, with more salt. His eyes were a deep shade of brown and told me nothing about what had transpired in surgery. I noted he was taller than me by several inches, with a wide, muscular torso. Orthopedic surgeons needed strong upper-body strength for the demanding physical work required in the operating room. As far as looks went, he wasn't especially handsome; he had sharp, well-defined features.

I was on my feet before I realized I was even standing. My mouth was dry as sandpaper. Worry instantly gripped me and I clenched my hands into tight fists, afraid of what he was about to say. My immediate thought was that something had gone wrong. I knew Mom took medication for high blood pressure and was unsure how her heart would do following a lengthy surgery.

For an awkward moment, he didn't say anything.

"Did everything go okay?" I blurted out.

"It went as well as could be expected. The break was complicated; I needed to reinforce the hip with screws. Your mother's in recovery. She'll be fine."

Again, that skimpy amount of information wasn't enough for me. He seemed to sense my frustration, and lowered himself into a chair, indicating that I should take a seat across from him.

"What do you mean by 'complicated'? I'm a nurse, Dr. Lancaster. I want to know the extent of the injury, the details of the repairs, and how long the recovery process will be. Mom's a widow, and she hasn't adjusted well to life without my dad."

Dr. Lancaster held my look and didn't comment.

His lack of response flustered me. As a result, I started talking more. "Mom and Dad were married over fifty years, and she's lost without him. Now this. I don't know how she's going to deal with being immobilized for several weeks."

I couldn't seem to stop talking. It felt as if the words had been jammed inside of me and I couldn't get them out fast enough.

"I know Mom is going to want to go home, but she can't. She'll be sent to a rehab center and it could be weeks, maybe months, before she's able to return to the house. She has a garden and she'll be upset that her tomatoes won't get canned, but she lives alone, so I don't know why she needs to can thirty quarts of tomatoes."

I kept jabbering, which wasn't like me at all. Even while consciously realizing what I was doing, I kept going.

"Mom loves her garden. She had one zucchini plant that produced fifty zucchinis. It was crazy. No one would take them anymore, so Mom pickled them. Have you ever tasted pickled zucchini? Don't bother; they're not that great."

Dr. Lancaster remained silent. He couldn't have gotten a word in edgewise even if he had tried.

"I—" I stopped abruptly and felt my face heat up. I couldn't have embarrassed myself any more than I had already. I nervously twisted my hands together. Silence filled the room until I spoke again. "I'm sorry . . . I don't know where all that came from; I didn't realize how wound up and worried I was."

"As I was saying, your mother's surgery went well." To his credit, he proceeded to patiently respond to all my pressing questions and assured me that her heart was as strong after surgery as it had been going in. As hard as I tried, I couldn't concentrate fully. My mind was going in ten different directions, and I couldn't get over the way I'd embarrassed myself in front of him.

I didn't notice that he'd stopped speaking for several more uncomfortable seconds. It was then that I realized he was waiting for me to say something, and that he had an inquisitive look on his face. Could I have made an even bigger fool of myself?

"Thank you," I managed, "for everything."

He continued to intently stare at me. "You were at the hospital Christmas event last year," he said.

"Was I?" His observation was out of left field. "Yes, I guess I was."

"You work in the ICU here, right?"

"Yes."

He stood, as if he'd said all that was necessary.

I rose to my feet at the same time and grabbed hold of his hand, shaking it several times, as if we'd completed a long and hard negotiation. "Thank you again."

He nodded, turned, and walked out of the room. Relieved, I sank back down to stop the trembling in my knees.

A few moments after he left the room, a young nurse entered. "Jenna?"

I looked up. "Yes?"

"I'm Katie. I work with Dr. Lancaster as part of his surgical team. He thought you might like to see your mother in recovery before you head home."

It registered that I'd met Katie when she did a rotation in ICU. She was young—a warm and caring nurse—and I'd liked her immediately. "I remember you, Katie."

"I remember you, too. Would you like me to take you to your mom now?"

"Please," I said as calmly as I could.

"Follow me."

I silently trailed after her down the hallway that led to the wide double doors into the surgical recovery area. As soon as I saw Mom, I walked to her bedside and gently took her hand.

Tears gathered in my eyes. I wasn't a woman who gave way to emotion easily. Seeing my mother like this did it to me, though. I raised her hand and held it in mine, pressing it against my heart.

"Love you, Mom," I whispered. "The doctor said you did great. You're a real trooper."

I doubted that she heard me. The thing was, I needed to hear myself. She was at the start of her long recovery process, and I had no idea where that path would take her.

*

By the time I left the hospital it was after midnight. I'd waited until Mom was awake and had been wheeled to her room on the surgical floor. She'd fallen asleep within minutes. I quietly promised her that I'd be back to check on her in the morning.

Before I left, I'd connected with my brother and Mrs. Torres to reassure them that the surgery went well. Both Paul and Allie were night owls, so I waited until I arrived home to tell them about their grandmother. I'd purposely put off calling my children until Mom was safely out of surgery, knowing they'd be worried.

I called Paul first. He was the oldest and my rock in times like these. Allie would get upset, and seeing that I was pretty much an emotional wreck myself, it made sense to contact Paul before calling his sister.

"Mom, it's late. Everything okay?"

I explained to him what had happened, reviewing Mom's recovery time and what it would mean for her.

"She's going to be okay, isn't she?" Paul had been close to my dad, who'd been a father figure to him.

"Yes, she'll be fine; your grandmother is at an age when these kinds of accidents can easily happen."

"I'm glad to hear Grams will be fine. But are *you* okay?"

I smiled to myself. Paul had always been the more insightful of my children. "I think so. I was more shaken than I realized." I didn't mention that I'd made a complete idiot of myself in front of the surgeon.

"You call Allie yet?" Paul asked.

"No, I wanted to speak to you first."

"You know she's going to freak out."

I did. "Why do you think I called you first?" Talking to Paul always calmed me. I could already feel the tense muscles in the back of my neck relaxing.

"You want me to reach out to her?" Paul asked.

"No. Even if you do, she'll want to talk to me."

We said our good-byes and ended the call. I was now better prepared to speak to my daughter. I took a deep breath and called her.

Not even thirty seconds into our conversation, my daughter started to sob. "Grams is going to die!"

"Sweetheart, your grandmother came through the surgery like a pro. She's going to be fine." I didn't tell her about the long recovery process. No need to add to Allie's fears.

"I'm heading to the hospital right now."

"Allie, no," I said as sternly as I could. "Grams is sound asleep and comfortable. She needs her rest."

"Then I'll go first thing in the morning."

"Allie," I said, pleading with her, "you've got a lot on your plate already. Grams would be happy to see you, but I don't want you to skip any of your freshman orientation events, understand?"

"But Grams needs me," Allie protested.

"I'll be there for her," I said. "I'll check in on her regularly throughout the day. Grams would rather have you making new friends at college than sitting with her at the hospital. Call her in the morning; that would mean more to her than you rushing to the hospital like she's on her deathbed."

"Mom," Allie squealed. "Don't even say that."

My choice of words had been a mistake. "Grams is going to be fine. I'll keep you updated, and you'll be able to see her yourself tomorrow evening. That way she'll be able to reassure you herself, which she can't do now because she's sleeping."

The line went silent and Allie seemed to be having an internal debate. "All right," she said, finally agreeing. She hesitated and added, "I finally got ahold of Dad today. He assumed I wanted money for textbooks."

I kept quiet, refusing to let my attitude show. Kyle did only what was required of him in the divorce papers, and not a penny more. When Allie needed braces early in her teen years, Kyle had quoted chapter and verse of our settlement agreement. From that point on, I'd never asked for anything more from the man, and he'd never volunteered. Somehow I'd managed to find room in our tight budget to afford braces for both kids.

"I assured him I didn't need anything," Allie continued. "I wanted him to know what classes I was taking. You know what he said? He told me they sounded pretty basic and that he thought I was smarter than that."

"You're a freshman, Allie. There are certain requirements. Don't let your father discourage you."

"I was going to explain, but he said he had to go because there were people waiting to talk to him."

Clearly other people were more important than his own daughter. I didn't want to discourage Allie from a relationship with her father—she seemed to need his acceptance. I didn't want to see Allie get hurt, though, and was afraid of what would happen once she realized her father didn't give two hoots about her, or, in my opinion, anyone other than himself.

"I'm glad you called, Mom," Allie said, interrupting my thoughts.

"Have fun meeting new people tomorrow and be sure to give your grams lots of love when you see her."

Chapter 3

Maureen

Logan was back in the library. As soon as I saw him, I realized that I'd been waiting for him to show, even though in my mind he was a definite red light. Okay, a yellow light, but a very bright yellow. Why I would even be thinking of him as a potential date was ridiculous. The man was a constant irritation. Furthermore, he'd never shown any interest in dating me, and even if he did, I'd refuse.

When he first started showing up on Mondays, I wasn't sure what to think. Dressed for his job on a construction site, he looked nothing like a normal library patron. He'd come directly to my desk and asked me what people were reading these days. It was a broad question. I asked if he was interested in fiction or nonfiction. He said both. And that was how it all began.

"Afternoon, Marian the Librarian."

I forced a smile. That was an old nickname, and one I'd grown tired of hearing over the years. "My name is Maureen,"

I said, pointing to my name badge. Saying it with a smile proved to be difficult. "How may I assist you?"

"Oh, so formal. Come on, I'm a regular. The least you can do is act like you're happy to see me."

I wasn't about to do that, although I reluctantly admitted to myself how much I looked forward to his visits. I wished I knew what it was about him that got to me. Normally, I was friendly with patrons who stopped by my desk. Perhaps it was the familiarity with which he approached me the first time I'd met him, and every time since. He acted as if we'd known each other our entire lives. He'd been oblivious to the looks he'd generated with his hard hat and work clothes. His self-confidence caught me off guard. The way he talked, you'd have thought we were the best of friends, which sent rumors circulating all through the library. More than once I'd had to assure a coworker that Logan and I weren't romantically involved.

I guessed he was about my age. With men, it was more difficult to tell. His dark hair, which he wore a bit longer than I personally liked, showed streaks of gray. It was tied into a small ponytail at the base of his neck. He wasn't tall or buff—an average-looking man, I'd say. I was drawn, however, to his blue eyes. The color reminded me of robins' eggs. "I finished the Michael Connelly book," Logan said, placing it on my desk. "It was as good as you claimed. What do you recommend next?"

I'd given up telling him where the book return was located. "What are you in the mood for?" I asked, mentally reviewing the books he'd read in the last few weeks. "You've been reading a lot of fiction, so perhaps you'd like to try nonfiction this week?"

"Sure, whatever you think will interest me. To date, you've chosen well."

Hearing him say so was a nice compliment. Unwilling to let him see how much it pleased me, I walked toward the nonfiction section.

"*Hillbilly Elegy* has been a popular choice," I suggested, handing him the book. It was on display, and the book club at the library had it on its list. I'd read it myself recently and felt Logan might enjoy the enlightening book.

Logan looked at the cover, turning it over to quickly scan the quotes listed on the back. "I don't want to appear ignorant. Can you tell me what an *elegy* is?"

"It's like a poem or a speech or a commentary," I said.

"Have you read it?"

"I have," I told him. "That's why I'm recommending it."

He started to read the description written on the flap. "An analysis of a culture in crisis"—his voice faded out and then regained strength—"the social, regional, and class decline." He didn't look overly enthusiastic. "You enjoyed it?"

"Very much. But incase you don't like it, I'll throw in a spy thriller I finished that's back at my desk."

"All right, if you say they're good reads, I'll give them a try. You haven't steered me wrong yet. Thanks, Marian."

"It's Maureen."

He grinned, his blue eyes sparkling with barely restrained amusement. "I know. I like to call you Marian to ruffle your feathers."

"It gets old."

"Ah, but you take the bait every time." He took the book and grinned at me again. "See you next week." And with that, he promptly headed to the checkout desk, then out the main doors.

I'd have another week of peace before he returned. Yet, I watched for him, even studied the clock on Mondays. He most likely came on his lunch break from the construction site near the library. When the project was finished, I was sure he'd move to a new site and a new library, and Mondays would return to what they'd always been. I felt an immediate sense of disappointment thinking about it.

He hadn't been gone even five minutes and I found myself reviewing new arrivals for a book I would recommend to him next week. I instantly made myself stop thinking about Logan and glanced at my watch. It was time for my own lunch.

At least once a week I took a late lunch to meet my daughter, Victoria, who worked for an engineering firm as an administrative assistant. Her office was two blocks from the library. She'd married Jonathan, her college sweetheart, and was doing well. Her husband was an engineer and worked for the state. Our weekly lunches were a good way for us to stay connected. Tori and I had always been close. My daughter was everything to me. I'd mourned with her over a miscarriage a little over a year ago now. We were both bitterly disappointed when she lost the baby.

Tori had already been seated by the time I arrived. She got a tabletop by the window and was reading over the menu. Seeing that I ordered the same salad every week, I didn't need to look at mine.

Sitting down across from her, I saw that she'd already ordered my glass of iced tea. Cold tea in the summers and autumn, and hot tea for winter and spring. If nothing else, I was consistent.

"I heard about Jenna's mom."

My surprise must have shown, because Tori quickly added, "Allie posted on Facebook that her grandmother broke her hip. She asked for prayers."

That explained it.

"I was with Jenna when she got the call," I said, remembering how shaken my friend had been at the news. We'd talked briefly earlier in the morning, and she'd given me the latest update.

"Is Carol going to be all right?"

"I think so. The surgery appears to have been a success, although she'll need to be in a rehab facility for some time."

I could tell by Jenna's voice that she was exhausted. It'd been a long night for her. Although our call was early, Jenna was already back at the hospital checking on her mother. Carol was still recovering from the effects of the anesthesia. Because of the length of the surgery, it could be a few days before Carol was completely herself again.

The server approached the table, looked at me, and said, "The usual?"

"Please."

"And you?" she said, turning her attention to Tori.

"I'll have a bowl of the tomato bisque."

"Is that all?" I asked Tori. My daughter always had a good appetite. She was blessed with a great metabolism and didn't need to watch her weight; she was already too thin as it was, in my opinion.

"That's all. I have a queasy stomach."

I waited until the server left the table before I questioned my daughter. "Your stomach's been acting up? Have you seen a doctor?"

My daughter grinned and shook her head. "It's nothing, Mom, probably just something I ate last night."

A loud boom sounded from the construction site across the street, like something had crashed to the ground. I glanced out the window to see what had happened. To my surprise, I saw someone who looked like Logan, sitting in a circle with a group of other workers. He was chatting with the others and had his lunchbox open. He'd once mentioned that he was a union plumber.

"What was that?" Tori asked.

I shrugged but didn't look away. Seeing Logan made me smile as I watched him interact with his coworkers and saw the laughter they were all sharing.

"You see someone you know?" Tori asked.

I shook my head to clear my thoughts. "No one special. Just a library patron I recognize."

"Across the street?"

"Yeah. See the guy with the hard hat?"

"Mom," Tori teased. "They're all wearing hard hats."

She was right. "The yellow hard hat—the guy in the middle of the group."

When I glanced back, Tori gave me an inquisitive look.

"What?" I asked, still watching Logan. I'd heard him

laugh once in the library and I'd enjoyed the hearty sound of it. He had the sort of laugh that came from the belly, loud and boisterous. By all that was right, I should have asked him to hold down the noise. I didn't, because I'd enjoyed listening to him. He'd made me smile, too.

"That guy stops in at the library?" Tori didn't sound like she believed me.

"Every Monday. He comes to me for recommendations, and I've been selecting books that I believe he'll like."

Tori raised her delicately shaped brows, looking for me to elaborate.

"He calls me Marian the Librarian, which annoys me . . . which is why he does it." I shook my head and unwillingly pulled my gaze away from him. Viewing Logan in his element was a treat. It was easy to see that he was well liked and that his crew looked up to him.

"Mom," Tori said seriously. "Are you interested in this guy?"

"In Logan?" I immediately shook my head, quickly denying any such possibility. It embarrassed me that Tori had seen through me so easily. If she was able to, then perhaps Logan would, too.

"Why not?" she asked.

"Tori, please, be sensible. We're nothing alike. For all I know, he could be married and have a dozen children." Logan didn't wear a wedding band. Okay, I'd looked. That didn't mean anything. I knew men in construction often didn't wear jewelry, for safety reasons.

"You could ask him."

"Of course I could, but I won't."

"Why not? You're an attractive, smart woman."

It was gratifying that my daughter saw me in that light. "Thanks, honey, but it might give him the wrong impression."

"When was the last time you went out on a date?" My daughter wasn't going to let this go easily.

"Two weeks ago. It was a blind date; I should have known better than to agree. Blind dates always seem to end badly."

"Red light?"

"Red light," I confirmed. "I learned early into our dinner that he was separated but still married." Like Jenna, I'd dated my fair share of divorced men. Being divorced myself, I didn't hold a failed marriage against anyone. But I had a hard-and-fast rule that I was unwilling to bend: I wasn't willing to get involved until after the divorce was finalized.

Over the years, I'd learned I didn't need a man in my life. That didn't mean I wasn't open to a relationship. I knew Jenna felt the same way; otherwise, we wouldn't be putting ourselves out there.

One of my problems when it came to dating was my career choice. There simply weren't as many opportunities to meet men at a library. A lot of people had encouraged me to try the online-dating thing. That had never appealed to me, but that didn't mean it wasn't worth considering. I just might.

"You shouldn't let a few bad experiences influence you," my daughter said.

It was more than a few, although I didn't say that. I'd experienced more red lights than I cared to mention. At this point in my life it was difficult; not that I was surrendering to the disappointments. At the same time, I wasn't exactly on the prowl. I'd become complacent, content with my own company. An occasional night out with friends was enough to get me by.

"I'm good, Tori. A few bad experiences haven't ruined me."

"Mom, there're a handful of websites out there to help women your age meet single men."

I wasn't sure how we'd let our lunch get sidetracked onto my love life, or lack thereof. I stared blankly back at her, unwilling to get drawn into this debate.

"Did I tell you Jenna and I have decided to take a trip to Paris next spring?" This was a blatant effort on my part to change the subject.

"Mom, I'm serious," Tori said.

"So am I. Now, let's change the subject." I was more than happy to see my salad arrive.

"Did Dad forever scar you?" Tori asked, frowning.

It appeared my daughter hadn't taken the hint. "Good heavens, no. Your father and I were both too young to know what we were doing. We never should have married. I'm grateful we divorced when we did. His current wife is a much better fit than I was. He's happy. You know that."

"But are *you* happy?" Tori pressed.

"Of course I am." Without conscious thought, I looked across the street again to the construction site. Logan had finished his lunch and was tightening the lid on his steel thermos. He must have felt my scrutiny, because he glanced up and stared directly at me. A ready smile came over him and he nodded, letting me know he'd seen me.

Embarrassed, I quickly looked away, uncomfortable to be caught watching him.

Tori was too busy doctoring her soup to have noticed the nonverbal exchange between Logan and me.

"Maybe you're right," I whispered, surprising myself.

"You mean you'll check out those websites?" Tori said, not bothering to hide her enthusiasm. "I can send you a few suggestions and links, if you'd like."

I reached for my fork and speared a slice of avocado while I mulled this over. "I'll talk to Jenna and see if she's game to give online dating a try."

"You should do this with or without Jenna. I know she's your best friend, but this is for you, Mom. Do it for you."

I nodded, although I didn't totally understand what I was agreeing to or even why. My gut told me it was a mistake, but I wasn't listening to my gut. Here I was listening to the wisdom of my twenty-three-year-old daughter, who had far more dating experience than I'd ever had.

Once I was home from work, I called Jenna, wanting to check on her mother.

"The kids take the news okay?"

"Paul was fine, but as I suspected, Allie was upset and wanted to race to the hospital. I had to talk her out of it."

"How are you holding up?"

"Okay. I was worried about the surgery, but everything seems to have gone well."

I heard Jenna's car door close.

"Listen, I'm at the hospital now. I'll text you later."

"Give your mom my love and tell her I'll be by to see her soon."

"Will do."

"Jenna," I hurriedly said, not wanting to delay her, "I had lunch with Tori today. She had an idea I'd like to bounce off you later."

"Tell me now," Jenna insisted. "I'm curious."

Already, I was regretting that I'd brought up the subject. "Tori suggested I check out one of those online dating sites. I said I'd consider it. Are you game?"

Jenna didn't hesitate. "Nope. I've got an empty nest and I'm not about to fill it up with a man. I can run around the house naked if I want. Have ice cream for dinner. Lounge around in my PJs without worrying one of Allie's guy friends is going to show. You aren't serious about this, are you?"

"Not really," I said, relieved. Like Jenna, I didn't need or want a man cluttering up my life. "That settles it."

Chapter 4

Jenna

I'd made an early-morning visit to check on Mom and stayed about thirty minutes. She remained peacefully asleep while I was there. By the time I returned, it was late afternoon and I felt like I'd been running a marathon all day.

My day had been spent getting the things Mom would want from the house: her robe and other personal items. The feral gray-and-white cat she fed, named Mr. Bones, was at the back door, looking for his breakfast. He was an ungrateful irritation, and hissed at me while I filled his bowl. I canceled her newspaper and mail online.

By the time I arrived back at the hospital it was much later than I'd intended, and my nerves were frazzled. I'd assumed I would be able to join her for dinner, but it was after six and the hospital volunteers had already started clearing the dinner trays.

When I entered her room, I was relieved to find Mom awake. She rolled her head and stared at me blankly. It was as if she didn't know who I was.

"Mom?" I whispered, setting aside the things I'd collected for her. I gently took her hand in mine.

"Jenna?" Her eyes filled with questions as she held my look. "What's happened to me?"

"You fell, remember?"

"Yes, yes . . . oh dear. I lost my balance on the steps and then all those people came and . . . after that, everything is all messed up in my head."

"You broke your hip and had surgery. Don't worry about being confused. It's normal after surgery."

"Is it?"

Being a nurse, I knew anesthesia was hard on everyone, especially those who were older. Mom was disoriented, which, under the circumstances, was to be expected, especially since the surgery had taken several hours. The longer she was under, the longer it would take to clear her mind.

"Are you in pain?" I knew she would heal faster if she didn't have to deal with discomfort.

"I'm tired," she replied, not answering my question. Her voice was barely above a whisper. "They keep wanting me to get out of bed . . . I don't understand all this. It's very confusing." Her eyes drifted closed.

"Rest," I whispered, wishing there was more I could do

to reassure her. Sleep was what she needed most. I patted her hand and sighed when I noticed she hadn't eaten anything off her dinner tray.

Taking a deep breath, I sat down in the chair next to her bed and reached for my phone, answering text messages from my brother and both of my children. I updated them on Mom's condition and answered emails. Before I was finished, Allie texted me back.

When I saw Grams, she thought I was you.

It's from the effects of the anesthesia. She'll be fine in a few days. Don't worry.

The return text message from my son was short and to the point. Typical Paul.

Keep me updated. Give Grams my love.

While she was sleeping, I went down to the cafeteria and got a latte and an apple. Nothing else looked appetizing. The latte disguised the bitter taste of the hospital coffee, and the apple gave me something to snack on.

It was almost seven by the time I returned to Mom's room. She was still sleeping, and I didn't know if I would stay much longer. I'd check on her before my shift in the ICU in the morning. I hoped it would be a quiet day. On my last shift, three victims, all from the same family, were sent to the unit following a car crash. The staff had been racing during the entire shift. We lost the husband and the wife was barely hanging on. The ten-year-old, although badly injured, looked like he would make it.

"Sleep well, Mom," I said quietly, gently holding her hand. "Remember when I was a kid and you used to tell me not to let the bedbugs bite?"

"You had bedbugs?" Dr. Lancaster's voice startled me, coming from the doorway. I resisted turning around to face him until I could find the means to paint a smile on my face.

He wore a three-quarter-length white coat and a stethoscope wrapped around his neck. He was every inch the surgeon. As I'd noted earlier, he wasn't particularly handsome, but I was thankful for his honesty and direct approach after surgery. I appreciated a physician who didn't sugarcoat the truth.

"Nurse Jenna," he said with a nod, acknowledging my presence.

"Dr. Lancaster," I returned.

"I see that your mother is resting comfortably."

"She's disoriented and confused," I said.

"Her mind will clear."

"Yes, I know, but . . . but this is my mother." I'd been quick to reassure my brother and children that all was well. What surprised me was how unnerved I felt seeing my mother incapacitated and in this condition. She'd barely recognized me, her own daughter.

He walked to the computer that was mounted close to the window and typed in his code, then read over the notes the staff had entered that day. "Good . . . she was up and walking and did well. I like my patients to get on their feet as quickly as possible."

"I wish I'd been here to help," I said with regret. The day had evaporated on me.

Dr. Lancaster continued to read the computer screen. "For her age, your mother is in relatively good health. Her heart is in fine shape and her bones are those of a woman ten years younger."

"She walks every day . . . or, I should say, she used to before my dad died. This is going to set her back." I didn't know how Mom would do in a rehab facility. She would hate being away from her home and not having all that was familiar close at hand.

"Your mother has a strong will. It won't take her long to bounce back."

He sounded confident, and it made me wonder how he'd know that. He acted like he knew what he was talking about, but he was the surgeon, not the physical therapist.

As if reading my mind, he answered my concerns. "I was here when she first got to her feet. Your mother has grit. You're worrying unnecessarily."

The fact that he'd been with Mom when she first stood was unexpected. I didn't know of a single surgeon who made a practice of doing anything more than checking the incision after surgery. Dr. Rowan Lancaster had been there with my mother, and I hadn't. Because I felt guilty, I felt a need to explain.

"I wanted to be here, I honestly did . . . but there was Mr. Bones to feed, and . . ."

"Who is Mr. Bones?"

"Mom's cat. Technically, he isn't anyone's cat. He's feral and lets Mom feed him. She's the one who named him Mr. Bones, because when she found him he was skin and bones. My mother is like that. It's remarkable that she's only feeding one cat, not a dozen. She has a weakness for animals."

Rowan Lancaster grinned, and for just an instant I was mesmerized by his smile. It took me off guard. His entire countenance changed; his eyes lit up with warmth, and I realized there was more to this man than I'd suspected. For the life of me I couldn't look away, and neither could he. My tongue felt like it was glued to the roof of my mouth. Rowan—when did I start thinking of him as Rowan, rather than Dr. Lancaster?—was the first one to break eye contact. Instantly, I could breathe again.

The silence grew uncomfortable until he glanced at the robe and slippers I'd brought from the house for Mom. "While you were at the house, did you happen to remember to water your mother's tomatoes?"

"Her tomatoes?"

"Yes, she mentioned she recently canned thirty quarts."

Mom cherished her garden. It was her pride and joy. Not a day passed that she wasn't out watering or pulling weeds—it was the distraction she'd needed after she lost my dad.

With Mom in the hospital, it would be up to me to deal with the huge tomato and zucchini harvest. I had no idea what I'd do with all that produce.

"Do you like zucchini?" I blurted out.

"I beg your pardon?" Dr. Lancaster said, disrupting my thoughts.

"Mom's garden is full of zucchini, and I'm going to need to find a home for them."

That odd, puzzled look of his was back. "Your mother has homeless zucchini plants?"

"Not the actual plants, the vegetables," I explained, smiling at his question. "There will be dozens of zucchinis. I can't possibly deal with all of it. I know Mom would want you to have a few." That might be stretching the truth, but it was worth an attempt to get rid of some.

"I don't cook. Can you eat zucchini raw?"

I never had, not that I could remember, but I was confident one could.

"Sure, everyone does." Another stretch of the truth, but one did what one had to do when it came to hustling excess zucchini.

"In that case, I can give the homeless zucchini a place to hang out."

"Thank you."

"Anything else I can do?"

I couldn't think of a thing. "I don't think so." I was frustrated.

"You sound upset."

"I am," I admitted, reaching for my purse and snagging my car keys.

"Is it about the zucchini?"

"No," I told him, "this has to do with the tomatoes."

"Tomatoes?"

"Yes, you reminded me I hadn't watered the garden. You might end up with a bushel of tomatoes, too. You can eat those raw, no question."

I glanced back to see Rowan Lancaster doing his best to squelch a broad smile.

Chapter 5

Maureen

Although I'd been quick to dismiss the idea of online dating, I found myself considering it that night. In all actuality, what did I have to lose? Sure, I'd met my share of red-light guys over the years, but there'd been a couple men who nearly made it to a green light. Most men were okay, but I'd found a good majority of those I'd met and dated annoying. I was looking for more: a man who would enhance my life, and I his.

My marriage hadn't been horrific. Peter wasn't a terrible person or even a bad husband or father. We simply didn't mesh. Ultimately, the only thing we had in common was our daughter. In retrospect, we were both too young to know what we were getting ourselves into when we said our vows.

Because I was pregnant with Tori at the time, getting married had seemed like the right thing to do, and so we had. Neither of our parents were especially pleased, but we did it for the sake of our unborn child.

The divorce didn't devastate me as much as it convinced me of my inability to have a solid relationship with a man. I accepted my part of the responsibility for my failed marriage. I hadn't opened up to my husband the way I should have. My natural tendency has always been to be an independent and private person. I'd learned early in life that the only person I could completely trust was myself.

What Tori said over lunch resonated with me all night and I didn't sleep well, tossing and turning, mulling over what was wrong with me. My mind drifted to my childhood. I was a teenager when I'd inadvertently learned that my father was having an affair. My mother knew. She couldn't help but know, and yet she chose to pretend that her husband wasn't involved with another woman. I'd wanted to shout at them both, confront them, force them to be honest with each other and to fix whatever was wrong with their marriage. I longed for them to stop putting on their happy, "everything-is-wonderful" front for the world to see, when below the surface their marriage was a disaster.

Perhaps this was what led to my own inability to have a long-term relationship. I didn't feel that I could trust a man to be honest with me. At the end of all my musings, I decided that I'd let life take me where it would. I wasn't necessarily looking for a relationship. If I did meet someone and I gelled with them, then great. If not, that was fine, too.

On Tuesday, I left the library at quitting time and intended to walk to the same bus stop I always did, planning to visit Jenna's mom at the hospital.

Only I took a detour.

Don't ask me why. I can't explain it. I'm a woman of habit, of discipline, and I rarely deviate from my pattern. But rather than take the familiar route as I did every working day, I decided to stroll past the restaurant where Tori and I had shared lunch the day before.

Okay, the truth. It wasn't the restaurant that interested me, it was the construction site. I was looking for Logan, hoping to catch a glimpse of him. The truth is sometimes difficult to admit. I blamed Tori. That was easy enough to do. She's the one who'd hounded me about Logan, making more out of his Monday library stops than was warranted.

Tori knew me all too well. Although I hadn't openly admitted it, she sensed I was curious about this plumber. When she mentioned the idea of dating, the first person I thought of was Logan. As difficult as it was to admit, he'd been in the front of my mind the entire night while I internally debated the online dating issue, wondering, if I did sign up, if I'd meet someone like him.

This was silly; I was silly. Logan hadn't so much as hinted that he was interested in me. He liked to tease me, he sought me out for book suggestions, and he asked my opinion on a variety of titles. That was it. I was forced to ask myself what I hoped to accomplish by walking in front of the construction site. It was a difficult question to answer and one I preferred to avoid.

As I speed-walked past the restaurant I heard someone shout my name.

"Hey, Maureen!"

Not just someone. It was *Logan*. If an earthquake had split open the sidewalk in that moment, I would have gladly allowed myself to be swallowed up by the crevasse.

"Wait up!" he shouted.

My steps reluctantly slowed. I glanced over at the construction site and watched, with my heart pounding at an unhealthy rate. Logan looked both ways before running across the street.

I bit my tongue to keep from hollering that he was jaywalking. I stood frozen, terrified that he would realize I'd purposely walked this way with the hope of seeing him. This was bad. Very bad. I was a woman in my forties and behaving like an adolescent who didn't have the good sense that God gave a goose. I straightened my spine, put on my demure librarian façade, and did my best to look surprised.

"Logan," I said politely and with a fake calmness, my entire body as straight and stiff as a telephone pole.

"I was hoping to see you," he said.

I waited silently, too embarrassed to encourage conversation. In fact, I pointedly looked at the time so he'd think I was on a tight schedule.

"I started reading that book you recommended."

"*Hillbilly Elegy*?"

"Yes. It's good. I'm enjoying it."

I nodded again, stiffly but politely. "I assumed you would, which is why I suggested it." Again, I checked the time. "I need to be somewhere, so if you'll excuse me."

"Sure."

I started walking away, and to my surprise he joined me, matching his much larger stride to my shorter ones.

"I'm headed in that direction," he explained, as I nervously looked his way. "My truck is parked in the lot a couple blocks from here. You parked around there yourself?" he asked, trying to start a conversation.

I could only imagine the picture we made. Logan in his hard hat, holding on to his lunch pail and steel thermos, and me in my pencil skirt and navy-blue cashmere sweater with black pumps. If ever any two people were opposites, it was us.

"I take the bus," I explained. "It's convenient."

"Do you drive?"

"Of course I do." I didn't mean to sound defensive, and feared that it came out that way.

"Just asking," he said, continuing to walk at my side.

We'd gone half a block in silence when he asked, "Do you like beer?"

"Beer?" I repeated, although I'd distinctly heard him the first time. "Not really."

"What about wine?"

I wasn't sure what my drinking preferences had to do with anything. "Why do you ask?"

He shrugged and made a small gesture with his hand. "I don't know. I thought we might have a glass of wine together one night after work. Talk books, that sort of thing."

The invitation was enough to make my step falter. I paused on the sidewalk as people flowed around us like we were a boulder in the middle of a fast-flowing river. "We, as in you and me? I mean . . . you want to have a drink with *me*?"

The minute I asked the question I wanted to groan. Tori would be disgusted if she could hear me. Men had asked me out dozens of times over the years. It shook me how badly this one man unsettled me.

"The truth is, I'm not sure why I'm asking. Well, I like you . . . I like the books you've recommended. Coming into the library that first day was something of a fluke."

He held my look, waiting for me to respond. "Why's that?" I asked, while I considered his offer.

He grinned again. "I had time to kill and I thought to myself, *Why not?* I've always enjoyed reading, but I was in a rut. I'd read seafaring historical novels for years and wanted to expand my horizons. That's when I decided to go to the library . . . That's when I met you."

I vividly remembered the first time he stepped into the library. He looked like Chip Gaines gearing up for demo day. He'd paused, glanced around as if waiting for someone to point the way. Then he'd approached me. I'd asked him a few questions, and steered him toward something I'd recently enjoyed myself. He read it so fast that I was stunned when he returned it two days later and asked for a second suggestion. Since that day he'd been a regular, coming every Monday, and sometimes more often.

"It shouldn't be a difficult question. If you'd rather not get drinks, it's fine." He shrugged, like it made no difference either way.

Although he made it sound as if a refusal was no big deal, I could tell that it was. Men and their fragile egos. I was married long enough to be able to recognize it in his voice. He'd taken a leap of faith by asking me, and I'd left him dangling off the edge of a cliff as he awaited my answer.

Good grief. I didn't know why I hesitated. It wasn't like Logan was proposing marriage. We weren't moving in together. Yet I paused, unsure of how to respond.

"Like I said, no pressure," he added. "I mean it."

The heat invaded my cheeks and left me feeling like I'd developed a sudden fever, the kind that comes on quickly and takes over the entire body. My tongue seemed to have swollen to twice its normal size. This shouldn't be such a difficult decision, but for reasons I had yet to understand, it was. It felt as if my entire future was hanging in the balance with this simple decision.

"Would it be terribly rude of me to give you my answer tomorrow?" I asked.

"Rude, yes, but not terribly so," he said, and laughed before adding, "I'm teasing. Sure, tomorrow will be soon enough. Should I come into the library or would you rather meet me after work, like you did today?"

"Ah?" I prayed he wouldn't mention our meeting hadn't been accidental. I'd been looking for him, hoping to see him. He must have seen through me as easily as reading a road sign.

Logan made the decision for me. "I'll come into the library tomorrow on my lunch break."

"Okay, sure. That would work."

We'd rounded the corner. I pointed out my bus stop down the street.

"I'll walk the rest of the way with you," he said.

"Okay." My heart was pounding. I wanted to tell him that

wasn't necessary, but my tongue had twisted into knots. I felt it was best to say nothing more.

We reached the bus stop and I stood apart from the regulars, who were staring openly at Logan and me. I was sure to get questions once I boarded the bus, as many were people I was friendly with from our daily commute.

Logan grinned. "Good to see you, Marian. I'll catch up with you tomorrow."

I offered him a weak smile, which was all I could manage. Logan seemed to notice the attention we were getting, and to make it worse, he winked at me.

"See you soon, Cupcake."

Cupcake?

Initially, I was upset, until I found myself smiling, as were all those around me. On the short ride to see Jenna's mom, only one of the regular commuters questioned me about Logan, and for that I was grateful.

Once at Seattle Central, the volunteer at the information desk told me the room number for Jenna's mom. I took the elevator to the surgical floor and walked down the hallway until I found the right room. Jenna was with her mother, and I had to assume she was on a dinner break, because I knew she was working today.

Jenna turned when I entered and smiled when she saw it was me. The last couple days had drained her emotionally and physically. She looked tired and concerned. It went without saying she had a high-stress job. I couldn't imagine dealing with life and death the way Jenna did.

"How's Carol doing?" I whispered, because her mother was sleeping.

My friend briefly closed her eyes, trying, it seemed, to find the best way to explain what was happening. "Physically, Mom's doing great. Two days postop, and she's up and walking. In a couple days, she'll likely be transferred to a rehabilitation facility, one of the best in the city, according to Dr. Lancaster."

"That's a good sign, isn't it?" It shocked me how quickly patients were moved in and out of the hospital. On Sunday, Carol had been working in her garden. Now she'd had major hip surgery and would be headed to rehab.

"Yes, but Mom remains disoriented and unsure."

"Isn't that normal following surgery?" I asked.

"It happens. Dr. Lancaster didn't seem overly concerned. It was only the first day and Mom had been through so much. Then today it was the same thing. Mom didn't seem to know who I was," Jenna said, expelling a lengthy sigh. "You know my mom—she's usually quick-witted and alert. I don't know anyone else who does the *New York Times* Sunday crossword puzzle in ink."

I didn't, either.

"Enough about Mom," Jenna said. "How are *you* doing?"

I should have expected her question. Jenna could read me like a novel. "What makes you ask?"

"Your cheeks are red. Either you've hoofed up the four flights of stairs or there's something you're hiding from me." Jenna tilted her head to one side. "Don't tell me you actually went on one of those dating websites?"

"No, although I toyed with the idea for a bit." Drawing in a deep breath, I squared my shoulders and plunged ahead. "As it happens, I've sort of met someone."

"How do you 'sort of' meet someone?"

"There's this guy, a construction worker—a plumber— who stops by the library . . . His name is Logan. He's a regular."

"And?"

"And . . . he asked me to have a drink with him."

Jenna's smile was big enough to make her mouth ache. "You *are* going to accept, aren't you?"

"I . . . I don't know."

"Maureen, of course you are," she insisted. "Why would you refuse?"

The list of reasons building in my mind was longer than my arm.

Jenna didn't wait for an answer before she blurted out, "You should go. What's holding you back?"

"But . . ."

"What would it hurt?" she continued. "The door is open. Walk through it. Stop overanalyzing this."

Jenna was right. I routinely overthought everything.

"You make it sound easy."

"It *is* easy. All you need to do is say yes. If Logan asked you out for a drink, he's telling you he's interested. He has a library card and he's gainfully employed. What more do you want?"

"Fine," I said, growing weary of this discussion. "I'll accept Logan's invitation."

"Good. It's our time. We can do with it what we want now. We both need to get back in the game."

Jenna was right.

"Do you have another date lined up?" I asked.

"No, and I won't for a while. Not with Mom incapacitated. It'll be a while before I can seriously consider dating again."

"Your mother isn't going to need you twenty-four/seven. Didn't you just get done telling me she's going to a rehab center?"

"Yes, but . . ."

"Your nest is as empty as mine. Like you said, this is our time. Get out there, Jenna. Have some fun."

"Fine," she grumbled. "And just who do you suggest I date?"

The sound of someone entering the hospital room caught us both unaware. It was a physician, and I had to assume it was the surgeon that had done Carol's surgery.

"Excuse me, ladies, but I couldn't help overhearing your conversation."

Jenna and I stared at him like we'd been caught shoplifting. He looked from Jenna to me, then back to Jenna.

Grinning, he focused on my friend. "Jenna, if you're in need of a date, I'd be happy to volunteer."

Chapter 6

Jenna

"What?" I wasn't sure I'd heard Rowan Lancaster correctly. It sounded like he was offering to date me. This had to be a joke.

Rowan stepped into the room, filling it with his presence. He arched his brows and appeared to be waiting for my answer. I couldn't have said a word if my life had depended on it. I stood there, looking like a prize-winning bass with my mouth hanging open.

"I said if you need a date, I'd volunteer."

I glared at Maureen. This was her fault. She might be my best friend, but in that moment, I could have throttled her. "I appreciate the offer, but I don't need a date," I insisted.

"Forgive me, I must have misunderstood," Dr. Lancaster returned.

"I can't . . ."

"Why can't you?" Maureen demanded, ignoring my

panicked look. "Especially when you have a handsome doctor willing to wine and dine you?"

"Yes, why not?" Dr. Lancaster seconded.

I inhaled deeply, hoping to compose myself enough to explain. I didn't want to insult Rowan. "I appreciate the offer, but . . ."

"She's flattered," Maureen translated, nodding toward the surgeon.

This was payback, I realized. I was the one who'd insisted accepting Logan's offer should be easy. It was a simple drink. No big deal. This was a reminder of how uncomfortable this dating business could be.

"Yes," I repeated, "I'm . . . flattered." My mouth felt dry. Nevertheless, I needed to explain, and hoped I didn't come across as insulting. "I should clarify . . ."

Before I could continue, his name was called over the loudspeaker system. Rather than wait for my explanation, Rowan lifted his hand and stopped me. "I have to go. There's no need to explain further." He turned and, without another word, left the room.

My heart sank. Rowan had been nothing but professional and caring when it came to my mother's surgery. I was afraid I'd offended him, and that was the last thing I wanted to do. He was nothing like what I'd expected. While highly respected, the rest of the hospital gossip said he was distant and aloof, but I think it was because of his quiet and intense personality. I was left to wonder if any of what I'd heard about him was true. I was afraid I'd offended him, and that was the last thing I wanted to do.

"Jenna," my mother softly rebuked me with her tired voice. "I can't believe you were so rude." Apparently, she had woken up during the awkward exchange and had heard me stumble all over myself to refuse the good doctor's offer.

"Mom, I can't date Dr. Lancaster," I said, hoping she would accept that excuse and drop the subject. Knowing my mother as well as I did, I should've known better.

"His first name is Rowan," Mom told me between pinched lips. "He asked me to use it, and if I use it, you should, too." This was followed by the look. It was one I recognized from my childhood when I'd displeased her.

"Yes, I know . . ."

"You were rude."

I couldn't disagree. Rowan had been wonderful with my mother, discrediting my assumptions about surgeons.

"He *likes* you, dear," Mom continued, gentling her voice.

I sincerely doubted that, as I barely knew the man. I stared at my mother, happy to see her mind had cleared enough to carry on an intelligent conversation, a first since her surgery.

"Now tell me what the problem is," Mom insisted.

"Yes," Maureen repeated, "what's the problem?"

No need to pause—my reasons were multiple. "First off, he's a surgeon."

"That doesn't make him a serial murderer," Maureen pointed out.

I shot her a look I normally reserved for my children and imagined it was an exact copy of the very one my mother had just given me.

"Second, we work at the same hospital," I added. Surely my mother and my best friend were wise enough to see the inherent problem with that.

"You're thinking of Kyle, aren't you." My mother tossed this out more as a statement than a question. "Well, your excuses are just that—excuses. Rowan is nothing like your ex-husband."

"Perhaps not," I willingly conceded, "but none of this matters."

"You're right," Maureen was quick to agree. "Weren't you the one to tell me no more than ten minutes ago that when a door opens, you should walk through it?"

"Yes, but—"

"Well, now that a door has opened for you, it isn't as easy as you thought, is it?"

I'd been wrong, blinded by my own insecurities. I'd been married. I'd lost my husband to another woman. To several women. After I'd divorced Kyle, I'd made the decision to focus on the kids, to push my needs aside until they left home. I didn't want to bring a stepfather and/or stepsibling into our small, tight circle. This was a personal choice I'd made; I had many friends who'd decided differently and who had remarried to create blended families.

This didn't mean I wanted to live the rest of my life as a recluse or a hermit. I had dated plenty, but I'd never allowed a relationship to stand between the children and me. All my energy and devotion had gone into raising them.

Paul and Allie were grown now, starting their adult lives. Both were in college and basically on their own. There should be nothing holding me back. Only there *was*, and I was currently running through that long list of insecurities in my mind. I'd been quick to say it was my turn to live my life, without understanding that it would mean lowering the walls I'd erected around my heart.

I had looked forward to this time after the children left home. When the kids were teens and hormones were bouncing against the walls like Ping-Pong balls, I longed for the days when I would be free from the burdens of being a single parent. Now that the time had arrived, I found myself afraid to open the door to this next stage of my life. Sure, I looked forward to doing all the things I'd put off for years: the crafting classes, being part of a book club, getting more involved at church with the outreach ministry. What I hadn't considered was finding that special someone to share my life with and what that would mean.

"You're looking thoughtful," Mom said, breaking into my musings.

I wanted to explain when I noticed the time. My break was over; I was already late. I had to get back to work. Heading in the direction of the door, walking backward, I gestured with my hands. "You're right, so right." Pointing at Maureen, I added, "Let's talk."

My friend smiled and nodded. Even without me explaining, she knew what was in my mind. This didn't mean I would take Rowan up on his offer. I was convinced it was a pity invite, despite my mother's claim that he was interested in me.

*

The remainder of my shift passed in a blur. After twelve hours on my feet, the first thing I did upon arriving home was fill the bathtub with scalding-hot water. It was how I relaxed after dealing with the life-and-death issues of my patients in intensive care. I'd lost a sixty-year-old man following heart surgery. Although I dealt with death almost daily, I'd never grow accustomed to it.

As soon as I'd divested myself of my uniform, I slipped into the bathwater and leaned back, resting my head against the edge of the deep tub. Closing my eyes, I released the pent-up tension and attempted to relax.

Only I couldn't.

My mind returned to Rowan Lancaster and the look that came over him when I'd hesitated at his offer. I hadn't been able to read him. I didn't mean to be rude. Nevertheless I feared I had been. After Kyle, I'd made it a hard-and-fast rule to avoid all romantic interest from anyone involved in the medical profession. Surgeons were an automatic red light.

Dating another surgeon. No way. Nohow. Not happening.

That didn't mean I wasn't open to a relationship with someone inside the medical field, although admittedly, I would need a bit of mental adjusting. If I was going to bring a man into my life, it would have to be one I genuinely liked and respected. A man I could fall in love with every single day. The thing was, I'd gone all these years without a relationship, and quite honestly, I didn't need one. My life had always been filled with work, the kids, and family; there had barely been room for anything else. Paul had been involved in soccer, and I'd attended countless games, carpooled to his practices, and been the team manager. Allie loved all forms of dance, with ballet and tap being her favorites. At about age ten, her interest drifted to the piano. That lasted three years before she joined the high school swim team, resulting in carpools and meets that took me across the state.

The last bit of my bathwater was circling the drain when the phone rang. I recognized the ringtone as that of my daughter. I knew she was calling about her grandmother, wanting to know how she was doing.

"Allie!" I was anxious to hear how things were going for her.

"I didn't catch you in the tub, did I?"

Allie knew my routine. "I'm out and getting dressed."

"Good. I didn't get up to see Grams today, and I feel awful. How's she doing? She's not upset with me, is she?"

"She's doing great. She asked about you but remembered it was your second full day of classes. She would have been upset if you'd skipped any of them." I didn't mention her continued confusion, since it seemed to have magically cleared up when Rowan stopped by her room. "She could be released tomorrow to a rehab facility."

"Grandma in rehab?" Allie gasped.

I grinned. "It's a rehabilitation facility where she'll get full-time care. She's going to need physical and occupational therapy before she can return home."

"Oh." Allie's relieved sigh drifted over the line.

"How was your day?" I asked, knowing her head must be spinning with everything she had going on.

"Great, although I'm not so sure about my roommate."

This didn't sound encouraging. When Allie and I had arrived on campus and unpacked in her dorm room, her assigned roommate had yet to arrive. Allie and Kristen had been in touch over the summer and had been texting the entire time, and they appeared to be a good match.

"What's the problem?" I asked.

Allie sighed. "Kristen has a boyfriend. I heard about him all summer. It was Mark this and Mark that."

"And?"

"They broke up yesterday," Allie said with a disgusted sigh. "Kristen blew up when she heard that a friend back home saw Mark kissing another girl. That started the phone calls at all hours of the day and night, followed by endless shouting matches, concluding with long bouts of sobbing. I didn't sleep all night."

"Poor Kristen."

"Kristen?" Allie bellowed. "What about me?"

"You have my sympathy, too. But give her time. She'll recover and meet someone else before you know it."

"Speaking of which," my daughter added enthusiastically, "I met this guy at lunch today and found out we're in the same psychology class. I swear he looks like McDreamy. He's gorgeous."

"What's his name?"

"Wyatt, and he asked me to a party tomorrow night."

"He's a freshman?"

"No, a junior, and he's part of a fraternity."

"Where are you two going?"

"To a house party."

I bit down on my lower lip, refusing to lecture her, although the words were on the tip of my tongue. "Remember the rules."

"Of course. I'm not stupid. I promise not to accept a drink from anyone. Only accept unopened cans."

"Good girl."

"I convinced Kristen to go with us. She'll cover my back and I'll watch hers."

That helped ease my mind. "Mackensie might come, too. She's a transfer student I met in one of my classes and she's friends with Wyatt."

"Good. The more, the better." I was pleased to see that my daughter was quickly making friends.

"Give Grams my love and tell her I'll stop by tomorrow if I can," Allie added quickly, as if eager to change the subject. My mind started racing with what she might possibly be trying to hide from me.

"I'll give Grams your love. Call me in the morning, okay?"

"Bye, Mom." She disconnected, and I noticed she didn't say anything about us connecting the following day. I wanted my children to spread their wings and soar on their own. That was one of the reasons I'd agreed to let Allie live on campus, even though she could've commuted easily from home. I wanted her to get the full college experience. Now I was left to wonder if I'd made the right decision. I heaved a sigh and decided that time would tell.

Letting go was far more complicated than I'd ever dreamed it would be.

Chapter 7

Jenna

When Thursday morning came and went without the normal morning text from Allie, I became concerned. Generally, I left personal issues at home while I was at the hospital. Today, however, I couldn't help fretting over the fact that I hadn't heard from my daughter. When we'd talked, I'd tried to appear nonchalant about her attending a frat party. I'd given my daughter the opportunity to make adult decisions, to live on campus and choose her friends. All at once I was faced with a beehive of doubts. I hadn't felt nearly as nervous when Paul went off to college. The fact that he was a young man shouldn't have made my concerns that much different, but as the man of the house, my son had always been mature for his age. Allie was a bit flighty and somewhat of a follower. Granting her freedom wasn't turning out to be as easy or as comfortable as I'd thought it would be.

This frat party and the fact she hadn't checked in worried

me. I wasn't naïve. I knew what those parties were like. I'd attended a few myself as a freshman in college. But the party wasn't my only concern; this was the first time in my daughter's life that I hadn't been able to meet her date.

I didn't know a thing about Wyatt. I hadn't set eyes on him. I'd had no opportunity to get a feel for what kind of person he was. That troubled me. Allie, my sweet, slightly spoiled, fairly innocent, and newly-turned-adult daughter, had gone to a frat party, and neither I nor her brother were around to protect her.

At break time I couldn't wait any longer. I hurried to collect my phone from my locker and called her. Allie didn't answer until right before the call was ready to go to voicemail.

"Hello." Her voice was groggy, as if I'd woken her.

"Are you sleeping?" I checked my watch and saw that it was late morning. I didn't give her time to answer. "Don't you have classes?"

"Not until this afternoon. What time is it?" The question came on the tail end of a yawn.

"What time did you get in last night?" I asked, doing my best to keep the irritation out of my voice. Allie knew better than to stay out late on a school night.

"Late."

"Obviously."

"Why are you angry?" my daughter asked, clearly not understanding the angst she'd put me through.

"I'm not angry, I'm concerned."

Allie exhaled loudly, as if losing her patience. "Mom, get real. I didn't call because I was asleep."

I was convinced my daughter had lost all sense of priority. "Are you making your bed?"

"What? I'm still in bed. So no, I haven't made my bed."

Her sarcasm wasn't helping. "I meant in the mornings."

"You're serious? You actually want to know if I'm making my bed?" She made it sound as if that was the most ridiculous question anyone had ever asked.

"Yes, tell me you're making your bed."

"What has that got to do with anything?" Allie demanded, fully awake now.

"It tells me everything." If she'd let go of this one simple discipline, then it told me that within the first week of her leaving home, she'd abandoned everything I'd ever taught her.

"Mom," Allie said pointedly. "Do you know how ridiculous you sound?"

Hearing how calm Allie was and how wobbly my voice had gotten, I began to see her point.

"Is this about Grams?" Allie asked. "Is this inquisition because you're worried about her and transferring all your stress over to me?"

She could be right. "Maybe. I was worried, Allie. I can't stop thinking of you as my baby girl, even though you're technically an adult."

"I'm fine. Nothing happened at the party. Kristen, Mackensie, and I hung out with Wyatt and his friends. We had a good time."

"You drank beer?"

"Yup, but it was from a can. And no worries. I opened it myself."

I heaved a chest-deep sigh. "Good."

"And, Mom?"

"Yes?"

"I've made my bed every morning since I arrived on campus."

Another sigh of relief.

"Aren't you at work?" Allie asked.

"I'm on break." I felt foolish now for making an issue out of something that wasn't. "Have a good day, sweetheart."

"I'm going to be fine, and you will be, too," Allie said, assuring me.

I did feel better. Returning to my shift, I worked straight through until it was time for my dinner break. I had my phone close at hand and saw that I had a text message from Maureen and another from my son.

I did it.

Maureen didn't add any other details, so I phoned her. She answered on the second ring.

"Hey," she said with a happy lilt to her voice.

"What did you mean by that text?"

"I told Logan I'd meet him for a drink."

I could hear the barely constrained enthusiasm in her voice. This was big for my friend.

"He stopped by the library just like he said he would, wanting my answer, and I agreed to meet him."

"When is all this happening?" I had to admit I was surprised. When it came to men, Maureen had high standards.

Not that she was a snob, she just liked to be in control, while I was comfortable going with the flow. She was highly organized. Even the spices in her cupboard were alphabetized. I teased her that she had devised her own Dewey decimal system for her shoes, categorizing them by style and color. As a spotless housekeeper, Maureen had a place for everything. I doubted there was even a crumb in her carpet. The fact that she'd agreed to this date told me there was something special about this guy.

"Logan suggested we meet Friday night at the sports bar close to the library. I've never been there. Do you know anything about those?"

"Not a thing." I held back from saying that I didn't think Maureen would be comfortable in a sports bar. I thought of her as more of a wine-and-piano-bar kind of girl.

"I guess I'll find out," she said, and then added, "I probably should've suggested somewhere else. I briefly thought about it. But it's right after work on Friday, and Logan says it's near the construction site. I guess that's where he usually heads on Fridays."

"You seem to like him," I said, pleased that she was willing to give this attraction a chance.

"He's a yellow light."

"With green potential?"

She hesitated. "Could be."

"Go for it," I said, hoping Logan was the one for her. He'd piqued her interest, and that spoke volumes.

"The thing is," Maureen started to say, then halted. She sounded introspective, pulling together her thoughts before she spoke. "The older I get, the better I've come to accept myself. I have more confidence and I'm less worried about others' opinions of me. I'm more willing to take chances."

I understood what she was saying. I was comfortable in my own skin, too. I felt good about myself, and I was eager to move forward. Although I wasn't on a manhunt, I hoped to someday find someone with whom I could share my life, but a man wasn't no end all.

I was getting ahead of myself. Way ahead. For the last couple days, I'd been cleaning out Paul's bedroom. My son was basically on his own now, and it was unlikely he'd be moving back home. With a bit of reorganization, I'd managed to shape a creative space in his room for my own pursuits. I'd signed up for an art class, which was something I'd always wanted to do. In my enthusiasm, I'd nearly bought the store out of supplies and assembled an area to paint in Paul's old room.

Maureen and I chatted for a few minutes more. When she asked about my mother, I told her Mom had been released to a rehab facility. Parkview was one of the best in the Seattle metropolitan area. I was pleased they had a room available for her.

As I made my way into the belly of the hospital to the cafeteria, I checked on the text from Paul. My son was good about keeping in touch, which I appreciated. I could count on hearing from him two or three times a week.

I read through his text. He asked about his grandmother and mentioned that he was enjoying his job. Paul had worked over the past two summers at a restaurant in Pullman,

Washington, and continued part-time through the school year. I'd worried that the hours during the semester would distract him from his studies. Paul, however, had maintained a good GPA, so I had no reason to complain. The spending money came in handy for him. His classes had started a month earlier than Allie's, and I was glad he got home for a long weekend before they began.

Once in the cafeteria, I picked up a salad and banana and headed toward the cashier. Usually I pack a meal from home and eat in the break room, but I'd been running late this morning.

I was about to return to my floor when I saw Rowan Lancaster sitting alone in the corner of the room. He'd apparently finished his meal and was staring down at his phone. His face was twisted into a thick frown; it appeared that what he was reading had upset him. I hesitated, unsure if I should approach him or not.

After our embarrassing conversation the last time we'd seen each other, I felt I owed him an apology. This wasn't going to be easy. Yet, I found I was curious about him. I'd made a few more subtle inquiries and discovered there wasn't much more to learn about this private man. While highly respected, no one seemed to know much about him.

My steps slowed as I approached his table. As I neared, he glanced up, and when he saw it was me his eyes briefly widened. I stood on the opposite side of the table with my tray in my hand.

"May I join you?"

He gestured toward the chair across from him.

I placed my salad and banana on the table and pulled out a chair. Rowan set his phone aside as I took my seat. Avoiding eye contact, I peeled away the cellophane from the plastic salad bowl.

Stumbling upon him wasn't something I'd planned, but I didn't want the opportunity to pass. The longer I waited to explain myself, the more awkward it would become. "I wanted to explain about . . . you know," I said.

Apparently, he didn't know, because he said nothing.

This wasn't off to a good start. I swallowed hard and hoped that by rehashing yesterday evening, I wasn't going to make things worse.

"My mother said I was rude."

Again, he remained silent, holding my gaze, as if trying to gauge my sincerity.

"I sincerely didn't think you were serious with your offer of a date. I thought it may have been a joke on your part, speaking up the way you did. You weren't serious, were you?" I asked, giving him an out.

He considered my question, and after an uncomfortable silence, he replied, "I don't know."

He doesn't know?

"You don't know?" He could have taken the easy out I had just given him. After all, it was what I expected him to do, and we could both laugh it off.

"It seemed like a good idea at the time," he added. "In retrospect, I can see that it wasn't."

"Because I made a mess of it." I wished I'd handled the situation differently. "I apologize if I offended you."

"Is there something about me that concerns you?"

"No," I quickly assured him. That was the last thing I wanted him to think. "I tend not to date doctors from the hospital. I don't think it's a good policy to mix work with my personal life."

"Was your ex a physician?"

I nodded. "A surgeon."

He frowned in much the same way he had when I first saw him looking down at his phone in the cafeteria.

"I can't say that I blame you," he said, accepting my explanation.

"Thank you for understanding," I said.

"Of course. I've put it out of my mind. You should, too."

He was right. As a means of distraction and because I was uncomfortable, I opened my dressing and poured it over my salad. I assumed, seeing that he'd finished his meal, that he would leave.

He didn't.

"Mom got moved to Parkview," I said, hoping to fill the silence.

He nodded. Of course he knew she'd been moved to the facility. He'd arranged it.

"Your mother will do well there," Rowan said, leaning back in his chair.

I agreed. "From what I understand, I have you to thank for her placement there."

He didn't confirm or deny it. He reached for his tray, scooted back his chair, and stood. "Thank you for stopping by, Jenna. Have a good day."

"You, too, Rowan."

As he left the cafeteria, my eyes followed him, and I felt a sense of disappointment, like I'd missed an opportunity. I'd wanted Rowan to stay and wished that we could have talked longer.

Instinctively, I knew there was more to Rowan Lancaster, and deep down, I realized that I wanted to find out what it was.

Chapter 8

Maureen

Tori called as I was leaving the library Friday afternoon. We chatted as I walked toward the sports bar where Logan had invited me for a drink. My daughter was full of advice on what I should and shouldn't do or say. I listened, or at least pretended to listen. I found it amusing that my daughter seemed to think I needed advice on men.

Okay, so it wasn't so far from the truth. Tori had much more dating experience than I'd ever had. Her father was the first and only man I'd given my heart to, and I'd been wary ever since. The bottom line was that I'd done a spectacularly poor job of choosing a life mate, so bad that I'd built a thick wall around my heart. Any man would need to scale that barrier, and I wouldn't make it easy. Yet for reasons I barely understood, I found myself interested in Logan. He was intelligent and opinionated, and he didn't back down easily.

I admired his wit, and beneath the hard hat was a man as solid as any I'd ever known.

"Wouldn't it be best to be myself?" I asked Tori, humoring her.

"No," Tori's voice blasted through the phone. "Mom, listen. I love you. You're my mother and you're wonderful."

"But?" I could hear it coming.

"But," Tori echoed, "you're completely naïve when it comes to men like Logan."

I wasn't sure what that meant. "If I can't be myself with him, then who should I be? One of the Kardashians?"

Tori choked on a laugh. "Funny, very funny."

She tried again. "Think back to the time you dated Dad. What was it that attracted him to you?"

"Calculus." No need to exaggerate the truth. "Your father was flunking; I was his tutor."

"It was more than that, Mom," my daughter insisted.

I closed my eyes and tried to remember what it'd been like between Peter and me. The truth was hormones. Lust, pure and simple. Peter liked me, paid me compliments, and gave me attention when I felt frumpy and unattractive. I was a classic nerd. In high school, I was too shy and brainy for boys. I'd attended only one dance—our senior prom—and I'd gone with a group of girlfriends, without a single dance with a boy the entire night. While in college, Jenna kindly insisted that I'd intimidated the boys, and she was probably right.

"What your father found attractive about me was my brain," I explained, without mentioning that Peter wasn't exactly the brightest bulb on the Christmas tree. "In the end, my intelligence wasn't enough to keep him in the relationship."

My daughter sighed heavily, her voice coming through the phone like a rush of wind. "Mom, the reason you haven't attracted a man is because you haven't tried, not because you don't have anything to offer. You give off the vibe that you aren't interested. Pay attention to Logan. Laugh at his jokes; let him believe he's witty and fun, even if he isn't."

"I can't do that." I hated to disappoint Tori, but Logan was smart enough to see through that in a heartbeat, and he'd be insulted. Even if I tried to do as Tori said, I'd come off looking like an empty-headed buffoon.

"Why can't you?"

"Tori, listen," I said, exhaling sharply to keep from laughing. "I appreciate your advice, I really do, but I can't be anyone else—I can only be me. I'll sink or swim with Logan. Time will tell. Either way is fine with me. Furthermore—"

"Mom, stop, please," Tori said, cutting me off.

I snapped my mouth closed.

"You've already agreed to meet Logan; all I'm asking is that you make the most of this. I can tell how much you like him and that he has potential. What is it that you and Jenna say? The green-light, yellow-light, red-light analogies? Just think. Logan could be your green light."

"It's far too early to tell," I told her, yet secretly I was beginning to wonder the same.

"I don't know what it is about Logan, but for whatever reason, you're drawn to him. All I'm saying is don't ruin it by being too quick to judge him. Give this evening a shot. Enjoy yourself."

We spoke for a few minutes longer before we said our good-byes, and I found myself in front of the sports bar. As hard as it was to admit, my daughter was right. I would never have agreed to this if I wasn't interested in Logan. I was the one who'd gone past the construction site when it was out of my way. And while I might like to think Tori and Jenna had bullied me into accepting Logan's invite, I was the one who'd told him I'd be there.

I opened the door to a cacophony of noise. The bar was packed, and everyone seemed to be talking at once. Televisions blared on multiple walls. I immediately felt completely out of place. Drawing in my determination, I stepped inside with my head held high, refusing to be intimidated.

Two burly construction workers glanced briefly at me, silently telling me with their looks that I'd better get moving or get out of the way. I stepped to the side as they barreled past. It took a moment for my eyes to adjust to the dark setting, after coming in from the bright outdoors. The room was filled mostly with men who looked like they'd stepped off a construction site. I'd never seen more Carhartts in one place in my entire life. After a few moments, my ears acclimated to the noise. A baseball game blared from the biggest screen, and when I say big screen, I mean *big*. I'd seen smaller-sized swimming pools. I couldn't tell you the name of the team. My knowledge of professional sports could be carved on a grain of rice.

Logan had apparently been waiting for me; he sat at

the bar. When he saw me, he smiled and slid off the stool. He walked over to where I stood, carrying a mug of frothy beer. I remained focused on his face, and a small, happy feeling curled inside my stomach.

"You're right on time."

I offered him a shaky smile. "I'm always punctual."

He grinned and looked almost boyish. "It figures."

"What does that mean?"

"It means I wouldn't have expected anything less from you. Being on time is a good thing."

He hadn't made it sound like that, but, determined to make the best of this, I decided to let it slide and do as my daughter had suggested. No matter how out of place I felt, I was here to be with Logan and have a good time.

"Do you mind if we sit someplace besides the bar?" I asked, before he led me back to where he'd been waiting. I'd never sat at a bar before, and I'd prefer a table, hoping we could talk and get to know each other outside of sharing our opinions about books.

"Sure," Logan said, agreeable. "We can sit wherever you like, Marian." He added a wink.

I smiled back, refusing to let him see how much that pet name annoyed me. Looking around, the only table with two seats was close to the giant television screen. With no other option, I motioned toward it, and Logan hesitated before he nodded. I understood why as soon as we sat down. The speakers were close to the table, and the baseball game blared loud enough to cause permanent hearing loss.

"You want a beer?" Logan leaned across the table and shouted.

"I don't drink beer, remember?" I said loudly, the table pressing against my torso. "I prefer wine."

"Red or white?"

"Red."

"I'll be right back," he shouted as he pushed back his chair.

I cupped my ear. "What did you say?" I asked.

He shook his head and stood. "We need to move."

I agreed. Unfortunately, the only seats available were at the bar.

Logan sent me an apologetic look. "I should've gotten a table sooner."

The place was hopping, which was understandable, seeing that it was Friday night. The game was only one distraction. Pool tables were set up in the back, and several rowdy games were taking place.

We approached the bar and Logan effortlessly slid onto the stool.

I tried to do the same, but I didn't have the leverage to climb up with my tight pencil skirt, and no way was I hiking it up and exposing God knew what. That would be awkward and demeaning. After several unsuccessful tries, all I'd gained was unwanted attention and a couple cat calls. My face was flushed with embarrassment.

Logan hadn't even noticed. He was busy talking to the bartender, ordering my drink.

"This isn't working," I said, tapping his shoulder.

He glanced at me and quickly recognized my problem. I

wasn't sure what I expected, but it certainly wasn't him taking matters into his own hands. He slid off his barstool, grabbed ahold of me by the waist, and effortlessly hoisted me up. Taken aback by the unexpectedness of it, I gave a small cry of surprise. Once the shock had passed, I secured my purse strap over my shoulder and twisted the barstool around to face the bar.

The man sitting to my left looked at me like I was a freak of nature. I chose to ignore him and turned my attention to Logan.

"What kind of red wine do you want?" he asked. Apparently, he'd been discussing the different choices with the bartender, which is why he hadn't noticed my predicament.

"The house red would be fine."

Logan gave my order to the bartender, who promptly poured me a glass, placing it in front of me. I raised the wineglass and Logan raised his thick beer mug, touching the edge of his mug against my glass.

"Here's to books and librarians," he said with a grin.

I tasted the wine and immediately made a sour face. It was awful and left a bitter taste in my mouth.

"You don't like the wine?"

"It's a bit heavy for me," I admitted. "And it's chilled." Red wine was best served at room temperature.

"Would you like something else?"

"How about a Cosmopolitan?" I suggested. That was sure to loosen me up and take the edge off my uneasiness. I didn't need anyone to tell me that I was getting more than a little unwanted attention. I tried to ignore the way the two men on the other side of me had put their heads together, pointing at me. They weren't the only ones, either.

The incident with the barstool hadn't helped. Nor did the fact that I was one of only a handful of women in the bar. Most of the others looked like they were familiar with the men. Very familiar, in some cases. A few seemed to be part of the crew, while a couple others were dressed more for an outing at the beach than a sports bar, in stark contrast to my business casual.

Logan got the bartender's attention and asked for the cocktail. The guy looked at Logan like he was speaking a foreign language. "We don't do those girly drinks here."

The last thing I wanted was to create a fuss. I gestured to Logan. "It's fine. I'll finish the wine."

He looked uncertain. "You sure?"

Before I could respond, a couple men stepped up to the bar and slapped him across the back. "Logan, great to see you. Heard you were foreman on that municipal job. How's it going?"

The three of them got into a lengthy conversation. From what I could make of it, they'd all worked together on another job and hadn't seen one another for a while. Caught up in the conversation with his friends, Logan seemed to have forgotten I was sitting next to him.

Ten minutes into their reunion, he suddenly remembered me. He looked apologetic as he gestured toward me and made an introduction. "This is Maureen," he said, nodding in my direction. "Maureen . . ." He paused momentarily, seeming to have forgotten my last name.

"Zelinski," I supplied.

"These two are Marv and Ed. We've worked together on a number of other jobs."

"So I gathered," I said, and smiled in their direction. They nodded politely at me but sent questioning looks to Logan.

"She's with you?" Marv asked.

"Maureen's been recommending books for me to read. She works at the library."

They burst out laughing. It was as if Logan had delivered the punch line for the funniest joke they'd heard in years. I'd had it. His friends were right on the money. This entire episode was one big joke.

"Thanks for the wine," I told Logan, setting the wineglass back on the bar.

He looked shocked, his mouth sagging open. "You're leaving?"

I couldn't get out of this place fast enough. Unfortunately, I'd forgotten that I was perched on the barstool. Worse, my legs were too short to reach the floor. I pointed my toes toward the ground and attempted to slide off. All I succeeded in doing was yanking my pencil skirt halfway up my thigh.

Logan's eyes focused on my leg, and he wasn't the only one. A couple men leaned over so far to get an eyeful that they nearly fell off their stools.

"I could use some help here," I snapped at Logan. I had no interest in providing a striptease for his friends.

Logan immediately helped me down. He tossed money

on the bar and followed me outside, trying to keep up with my ten-minute-mile pace to get as far away from that place as possible.

"Hey," Logan shouted after me. "Wait up."

Reluctantly, I slowed, and he quickly caught up with me.

"Did you do that on purpose?" I demanded.

He looked bewildered. "Do what?"

"Choose the one place in town where I'd stick out like a polar bear at a beach resort?"

"No," he sputtered, taken back.

"I don't believe you."

"Fine, don't believe me." He rubbed his hand down his face as if at a loss for what to say next.

"I don't, and furthermore, I don't appreciate being the brunt of some joke." I started walking faster and prayed Logan would let me leave with my pride intact. My prayer went unanswered. His steps matched mine, although he didn't say anything for the next half-block.

"Would you like to go someplace else?" he asked, after an uncomfortable few minutes.

The man couldn't take a hint. "No."

"Some other time, maybe?"

"No." I didn't understand how he could even ask me that. Apparently, he hadn't had a good enough laugh the first time. "In case you haven't noticed, we're not a good fit."

Logan slowed his steps. "I guess this is it."

"This is definitely it," I stated, more than eager to make my escape.

"You sure?" he asked.

"More than sure." The evening couldn't have gone any worse. I continued on to my bus stop without looking back.

I barely remember getting on the bus. I took a window seat and leaned my head against the glass as the disappointment and regret flooded me. By agreeing to see Logan, I'd exposed myself, making myself vulnerable.

I knew both Tori and Jenna would be waiting to hear from me. Reliving the experience was more than I could bear. I reached for my phone to turn it off. Before it shut down, I saw two messages. One was from Tori.

Have fun. I have a good feeling about tonight. This is a whole new beginning for you.

Yeah, right, I thought to myself, *a good feeling*. The second message was from Jenna.

Call me when you get home. I want to hear every single detail.

I didn't know what I was going to tell my daughter and my best friend. One thing I was sure of: I would put it off as long as I could.

Chapter 9

Jenna

I didn't hear from Maureen on Friday evening, and when I tried calling her, the call went directly to voicemail. Not a good sign for the first date with Logan.

I spent the majority of Friday night reviewing my conversation with Allie from the day before. She'd brushed aside my concern. Despite her reassurances that all was well, I couldn't keep from worrying. It didn't help that she hadn't called me when she'd said she would. Before she'd left for college, we'd talked about this very thing, the temptation and risks of drugs and alcohol. I'd been convinced she was smart enough to avoid these pitfalls. What I hadn't taken into consideration was how hard it was going to be for me to let go. I must have sounded like a helicopter mom when I demanded to know if she made her bed.

Late Saturday morning I decided to reach out to her, hoping to repair any damage from my frantic call from Thursday.

Allie didn't answer.

I sent her a text. Again, no answer.

The lack of response immediately concerned me. Was she all right? I was tempted to try calling and texting again, but thankfully, common sense prevailed. I set down my phone, although I couldn't keep from pacing from room to room.

When I couldn't stand it any longer, I called my son, knowing he would give me the pep talk I needed.

"It's Mom," I said the instant he picked up.

"I know, Mom," he said, humoring me.

I could tell I'd woken him. Glancing at the time, I noticed it was after eleven. He'd never been a late sleeper until he'd taken the job at that restaurant. His employer had him working the closing shifts. I didn't think it was a good idea for him to be taking all these hours. He knew how I felt and had ignored my concerns.

"What has you all twisted in a knot?" he asked. "You sound upset."

"I am upset. I didn't think it would be this hard."

"It's Allie, right?"

He knew me far too well. In as few words as possible, I explained the situation with his sister. It didn't take long for Paul to talk me off the cliff. Before I'd reached out to Paul, I'd had to stop myself from hopping in the car and driving to the university to check on Allie myself.

Paul listened calmly while I spewed out my worries.

"You raised Allie," he said, reasoning with me. "She has her head on straight. Now let go, Mom, and trust her."

His words gave me pause.

Let go.

Trust.

No one told me it would be this hard. "But—"

"Allie's perfectly fine. My guess is she was out with friends last night and got in late. This is the first time in her life that she isn't living under a curfew. She's going to revel in that freedom for the first few months. Let her. She knows what's important and will settle down soon enough."

"You think I'm overreacting?"

"She hasn't been at school long. Trust me, if there's a problem, you'd be the first person she'd call. Relax."

Paul was right. As the tension left my shoulders, I exhaled a long sigh. "When did you get so smart?" I asked him.

He chuckled. "I don't know that I am," he said, yawning out the words.

He sounded beat, the way I did after a long shift at the hospital. "You worked last night, didn't you? What time did you get to bed?"

"Late."

I noticed he didn't mention how late. "I don't want this job interfering with your studies," I reminded him, using restraint. I understood that the tips were good and that the job helped pay for his books and extracurricular activities. He was studying for an engineering degree, the same as my father. This job shouldn't take him away from what was important—his studies.

"Don't worry," he insisted. "I'm good." This was followed by another lengthy yawn.

I wasn't convinced.

I was taking Paul's advice when it came to trusting his sister, so I hesitated before calling him to task. He was three years older than Allie and had basically been on his own for two years now.

I'll admit I felt better after expressing my concerns to Paul. I was grateful for his level head.

Chapter 10

Allie

"What?" Allie groaned into her phone as she rolled onto her back and stared up at the ceiling. Her head throbbed, and she pressed her hand against her forehead.

"Hey, is that any way to greet your big brother?"

"Paul," she said with a groan, "why are you calling so early?"

"It's noon."

"Already?" Allie grumbled.

"You hung over?"

"Do you have to speak so loudly?" She tried to sit up but got an immediate headache and fell back against her pillow. "A little." It was more like a lot, only she wasn't willing to admit it. She'd been out until dawn with Mackensie and had had Jell-O shots as well as beer. They'd laughed and flirted the night away. It'd been the most fun she could ever remember having. She didn't need to report to anyone, didn't need to be home and in bed by midnight. Her mother, God love her, had been a stickler about that curfew. It was ridiculous. Allie wasn't a child, although her mother continued to treat her like one.

"You're freaking Mom out," Paul scolded, sounding very much like the big brother.

"Why?" Her mother didn't have a clue what she'd been doing the night before, which was a good thing.

"She called and texted you, and you didn't answer."

"Mom tried calling me?" And Allie had been so out of it that she hadn't heard the phone. "Then she called you when I didn't answer." It was just like her mom to overreact and turn to Paul for help. He had been her go-to person for every little problem. Her brother who could do no wrong. When Allie hadn't picked up the phone, naturally her mother would have gone all freaky.

"If you don't want her showing up at your dorm room, then I'd suggest you call her back."

"You've got to be kidding. I'm not a child," she protested, and then grimaced at the sound of her own voice.

Paul was the peacemaker in the family and he sounded calm and reassuring. He asked about her night and then advised her what to say to calm their mother.

"Who was that?" Mackensie asked, after the call ended. She'd spent the night in Allie's room, as Kristen was gone for the weekend.

"My brother."

"Is he cute?"

"Not to me. He's a dork, but he is my brother. Girls think

he's hot. I don't. He called to let me know my mother has gone ballistic. She tried to reach me earlier, and when I didn't answer, she freaked and called my brother."

"What's the deal?" Mackensie sounded puzzled.

Allie was mortified and embarrassed, but she tried to downplay it. "It's just my mom. She's like this. She always needs to know where I am and who I'm with and what time I'll be home. I thought it would be different when I left for college, but apparently it isn't."

Mackensie sat up in bed and brushed her thick, sandy blond hair off her face. She looked pale and her eyes were red-rimmed.

"Did we do anything stupid last night?" Allie asked, hardly able to remember what happened after the third shot.

"Define *stupid*."

Allie was afraid of that. "Did I stand on top of a table and toss my bra into the crowd?" She vaguely remembered that happening and wasn't entirely convinced she wasn't the one going braless.

"No, that was Heather."

Heather? Allie couldn't remember meeting a Heather, but she was relieved it wasn't her.

"Paul suggested I call Mom and play it all down the same way I did about the frat party." Two parties over three days. No one told her college was going to be this much fun.

"Best get it over with now," Mackensie suggested. "It will only get worse if you put it off."

This all seemed ridiculous to Allie. "Is your mother like this?"

"No. Thank God. She's cool with whatever I do."

Allie was jealous. If only her mother would let loose and give her the space she needed. All the talk about letting Allie become her own woman. It meant nothing if her mother was going to constantly be on her case.

Chapter 11

Jenna

While I waited to hear back from Allie, I cleaned the house and put in a load of laundry before I headed off to visit my mother. On my way over, I took a detour and drove to Maureen's house. She still wasn't answering her phone, which concerned me. Given time, I figured she'd resurface sooner or later. When she did, I had the feeling there would be copious amounts of tea involved. Maureen and I always drank tea when we unburdened ourselves to each other.

Like the time when I learned Kyle was having what I thought was his first affair. We'd gone through two pots as I wept my eyes out. Only later did I discover that my husband had been unfaithful almost from the moment the preacher declared us husband and wife. I ended up forgiving him for that one affair, determined to save our marriage. When I learned of the second affair, it had devastated me. Maureen was the first person I'd gone to, even before I told my parents.

Another pot was poured when Maureen had her split with Peter, although it'd been an amicable divorce. I hadn't known there was such a thing. It was an oxymoron as far as I was concerned, seeing how bitter my own divorce had been. Both Maureen and Peter had been civil about their separation. Peter had been a disappointment as a husband, but he was a decent father, unlike Kyle.

Maureen didn't appear to be home, so I drove on to Mom's house to check on her garden. By the time I headed to see her at Parkview, the backseat of my car was loaded down with tomatoes and zucchini. The hospital staff would gratefully take them, and what they didn't I'd donate to the local food bank.

The afternoon was lovely, and there were two or three patients in wheelchairs sitting in the sunshine on the patio on the east side of the building. The front porch had a sitting area, and I was pleasantly surprised to see Rowan Lancaster on an outside bench.

I didn't know if he was at the facility to visit my mother or if he had other patients there. He was looking down at his phone again, his face a dark mask. It was the same look he'd had the evening I'd seen him in the hospital cafeteria. I wasn't sure if I should approach him, but then he looked up and saw me. His face slowly relaxed as he set down his phone.

"So, we meet again," I greeted him, glad to get the chance to talk with him. He'd been caring and encouraging with Mom. He'd gone above and beyond what she'd needed. His attentiveness to the surgery and her aftercare couldn't be questioned, but to my frustration, his personal life remained a mystery.

"I have some tomatoes from Mom's garden with me." I motioned toward my car in the parking lot. "Would you like some? I know Mom would want you to take however many you'd like."

"No zucchini?" he asked, appearing to tease me about my chattiness the night of Mom's surgery.

"As many as you'd like," I responded, trying to hide a smile.

He grinned and shook his head. "Thanks anyway. I don't cook much."

"Okay." I started to leave when my phone rang. I'd been expecting to hear from Allie and wasn't about to miss the call. I turned away to answer.

Sure enough, it was my daughter. Before she could say more than two words, I blurted out, "How late were you out last night? Why didn't you answer my call?" I demanded, forgetting Paul's advice.

"Mom, please," she said, with what sounded like a grimace. "Don't yell."

"I'm not yelling." I wasn't. My voice was raised but I wasn't yelling, although I felt like giving her the third degree.

"You are yelling, and my head hurts, so please stop."

Closing my eyes, I inwardly groaned. I knew what that meant. "You've got a hangover?" This was too much. I needed to sit down. It felt like my knees had lost their strength.

"It's not a hangover," Allie insisted. "Everyone in college drinks."

Not *my* perfect daughter.

"Everyone?" I cried. "I don't think so, Allie." I bit my tongue, afraid if I came down too hard on her we'd end up arguing. "You were careful, I hope?" She knew what I meant. I'd heard too many horror stories of young women raped after being slipped a roofie. Or considering themselves invincible and choosing not to go to and from parties with a group. Working at a hospital was not the best environment for a worrying mother, because I'd dealt with far too many tragedies.

"Mom, I'm not stupid. Yes, I drank the beer out of a can I opened myself."

"And you got drunk." Every fear I had was bouncing around inside my head. I don't know why I went to the worst-case scenario. Suddenly I could see my daughter becoming an alcoholic and flunking out of college.

"If you must know, all I had was two beers and a couple of Jell-O shots. It went to my head fast because I'm not used to drinking. It wasn't a big deal."

It was to me. Before I could give her my opinion, she continued talking.

"I was back in the dorm early. The reason I have a headache is because my period's due."

I didn't believe her. This wasn't the best time for calling her out, so I bit my tongue.

"I'm sorry I didn't answer when you called." Allie sounded genuinely contrite. "I was asleep."

"It's okay. I made more of this than I should have."

"You think?" Allie said.

Despite the fact I was convinced she wasn't telling the whole truth, I was relieved to hear her voice.

"How's Grams?"

"I'm at Parkview now to check in on her, and I'll call you after I leave." I had a few more questions I intended to ask, too.

"Okay. Love you."

"Love you back," I whispered, ending the call and sitting down.

I realized I'd chosen the bench where Rowan Lancaster was still seated. "That was my daughter," I said, briefly closing my eyes. Her call had done little to reassure me. Rowan seemed to be waiting for me to continue. "She's a freshman at the University of Washington. Her brother said it was time to let go and trust her. I know I should, but it's harder than I thought it'd be. Funny thing, I'd looked forward to an empty nest, and it's nothing like what I expected."

"How long have you been divorced?" he asked.

"Sixteen years. Allie was only two." It felt weird to be discussing our private lives like this. For the most part, I'd kept my home life and my job separate. "Do you have children?" I asked. If I was divulging information, he could, too.

"One. A daughter. She's twenty, and starting her junior year of college."

"Then you understand."

He shook his head. "Sorry, I don't. My ex-wife . . ." He paused and shook his head as though he'd said more than he intended. Rising, he avoided eye contact. "Have a good day, Jenna."

"You, too."

With his shoulders slumped as though bearing a heavy weight, he started toward the parking lot. I sat in the warmth of the afternoon sunshine and watched him. Emotional pain radiated off him. I could sense it as keenly as if he'd spoken of his loss.

Rowan's car was parked in a space in the front of the lot that was reserved for physicians. I was curious as to what kind of car he drove. I knew Kyle took pride in his expensive cars.

My ex had the nerve to email Paul a photo of his red Ferrari soon after Paul had picked up a part-time job at college. I'd been furious. Outraged. But because I had years of practice, I was able to hold my tongue. I was convinced Kyle had done this on purpose, just to show me how well he'd done without me. Well enough to afford a fancy car, but not well enough to help his children with college expenses.

Rowan stopped in front of his car, a Volvo SUV, and squatted down to look at the driver's-side tire.

It was flat.

Chapter 12

Jenna

Rowan's tire instantly brought back the memory of a time when Kyle and I had gotten a flat. My husband, with both children in their car seats, had thrown a temper tantrum worthy of a two-year-old. Kyle had kicked the tire as if to punish it for having the audacity to cause him to dirty his hands with a menial task far below his dignity. He'd thrown down his car keys and jumped on them like he was putting out a brushfire. I'd been shocked at his behavior and embarrassed that a grown man could act so juvenile. I'd sat in the car, stunned, while Paul and Allie cried in fear, not understanding what was happening. I did my best to calm them and tried to reason with Kyle.

Now here was another man facing the same circumstances. Granted, he didn't have little ones in the backseat. I held my breath, watching for Rowan's reaction to the inconvenience. Calmly, he examined the tire and, without a single display of temper, walked to the back of his vehicle to open his trunk. I couldn't see him for a couple minutes, although I suspected I knew what he was doing. Sure enough, when he returned, he had a small replacement tire and tools in his hands. He intended to change the flat himself.

Kyle had refused to do any manual labor that might put his hands at risk, because he was a heart surgeon, and his hands were his livelihood. I understood his concern and had encouraged him to call for help. He took my advice, but we had to wait more than an hour for a Triple A truck to respond. In the meantime, Kyle paced back and forth, shouting at the dispatcher, complaining about how long it was taking for help to arrive. Several times he informed them that he was a doctor, and that this was an emergency. It wasn't, but lying was never beneath my husband. The memory of that awful afternoon had been burned into my memory. The incident spoke volumes to me about the kind of man I'd married.

As soon as I saw what Rowan was about to do, I felt I had to stop him. Changing the tire himself could be dangerous, especially when there was help a mere phone call away.

"You don't need to do that," I said, stopping him.

Rowan glanced up, his eyes widening with surprise.

He, too, was a surgeon, and should proceed with caution, rather than risk injury to his hands.

"I have Triple A," I explained.

"I do, too."

"Then let them change the tire."

Rowan continued looking at me, as if he had trouble

deciphering my words. He remained in a squatted position by the tire as though undecided. He had the jack out and was about to use it to elevate the front of the Volvo when I stopped him.

"Rowan, you're a surgeon," I said, reiterating my concern. "You shouldn't take this risk."

He half smiled, as if he found my concern humorous. "You don't need to worry, I can change a flat without doing myself bodily harm."

"I'm sure you can."

"I appreciate that you care, but it isn't necessary. I've done this before plenty of times. It's not a big deal."

I crouched next to him so we were at eye level. He did have nice eyes, although now they looked more puzzled and slightly amused by my insistence to call for help. "Please, Rowan, let me call them."

"Why would you care?" he asked.

"Because you're a good surgeon, and highly respected. I don't want to see anything happen that might prevent you from helping someone else like you did my mother."

He hesitated, considering my plea.

I placed my hand on his forearm. "Please, Rowan, let me call Triple A."

He slowly exhaled. "All right. Ask how long I can expect to wait."

"You mean you'll let me call?" I'd expected more of an argument.

He sat down on the curb, his hands gripped together and resting between his bent knees.

The number was programmed into my phone. I waited for the customer service representative to pick up, quickly explained the situation, and groaned when I learned it would take forty-five minutes before anyone could reach our location.

Rowan awaited my answer.

I ended the call and repeated what I'd been told. "It's a Saturday, and there's a pileup on I-5, so it will take longer than usual." I didn't have high hopes that Rowan would willingly be detained that long.

"Will you have a cup of coffee with me while I wait?" he asked.

My fingernails bit into my palms. I had a long list of items I wanted to take care of this weekend. I wasn't eager to take forty-five minutes out of my day, but it didn't seem fair to ask him to twiddle his thumbs alone after I'd been the one to make a fuss. And if I was being honest with myself, and I was, I wouldn't mind getting to know Rowan a bit more. All I knew about his personal life was that he'd been divorced and had a daughter who was a young adult. I couldn't help being curious as to what else I might learn about him.

"Sure," I agreed. "I'll wait with you."

"There's a Starbucks less than a block away," Rowan said, coming to his feet. He brushed off his backside.

"There's a Starbucks a block away from everywhere," I joked.

Rowan grinned. That he would welcome my company was unexpected, and I intended to take full advantage of it in order to learn more about him. However, the reason I'd stopped off at Parkview was to check up on my mother. It seemed unnecessary to leave and then return, so I offered another alternative.

"I think there might be a place for us to have coffee here at the facility," I said. I seemed to remember the staff mentioning it when I'd first visited Mom.

"There is."

We went inside the rehab facility. The nurse manning the front counter seemed familiar with Rowan and looked confounded to see him back so soon.

"My car has a flat," he explained. "Will one of you let me know when Triple A arrives?" He placed his hand at the small of my back as he escorted me down the wide hallway. While walking away, I noticed the woman looking at us, followed by her leaning over to whisper something to the nurse at her left.

We found the room where patients greeted family members. It had several tables and padded chairs. Against the wall was a table with three large dispensers for regular coffee, decaf, and hot water, plus a large bowl of fresh fruit.

Rowan stepped up to the coffeepot and handed me a cup and a sleeve, allowing me to go first. I doctored my coffee and chose a table. Rowan quickly joined me. At first neither of us spoke. The lack of immediate conversation felt awkward. It was as if neither of us knew where to start. I knew he was a private person and reluctant to discuss anything outside of the hospital. The gossip mill there was always rife with news, and I avoided that.

"You mentioned your daughter," I said, hoping to learn a bit about him. Most everyone took pride in talking about their children. "You said she's twenty?"

"Yes."

"Does she live in the area?"

"She lives in California." He shifted in his seat and appeared uncomfortable. "With her mother." This last bit of information came with some reluctance. I could see he wasn't comfortable discussing his ex, and decided it would be best to avoid anything in reference to her.

"This is my daughter's first year at the U-Dub. She wanted to live on campus, and I agreed. Now, I'm having second thoughts."

"Why's that?"

I hesitated, unwilling to share too much of what was happening, and answered with a halfhearted shrug. "When we talked about her living on campus, I was unsure, but she convinced me she was ready to be on her own. I thought she was and now I'm having doubts."

"Something happened, then?" he pried gently.

"A frat party on Wednesday and another party last night. I couldn't reach her this morning and I panicked. She said she was out with friends and home around midnight. Frankly, I don't believe her. I can always tell when my daughter is lying."

"Did you call her on it?"

I was reluctant to explain that I hadn't. I'd wanted to, but I would have come off as a total basket case because of my last overreaction. "Letting go isn't nearly as easy as I assumed. I'm sure you understand."

He didn't agree or disagree.

"I don't want Allie to make a decision that could affect

the rest of her life. She's young, naïve, strong-willed, and can easily be led astray, especially when she's working so hard to fit in with others. I can't help but worry." Already I'd said more than I'd intended to.

He nodded, as if he shared my concerns.

"I called her brother. Talking to Paul helped. He reminded me Allie is smart and able to hold her own. He thinks I'm worrying unnecessarily." Looking down at my untouched coffee, I took a sip and mulled over my morning, the worries buzzing around my head like pesky flies. I hated flies. When one got in the house I didn't stop until I had either killed it or shooed it out of the house. Worries were like that for me, too. I had this driving urge to do everything within my power to find peace of mind.

"The idea of having an empty nest appealed to me. All these years as a single mother has worn me down," I said continuing. "I was looking forward to the freedom to explore new interests. I didn't stop to consider how alone I'd feel with the house empty. It was nice the first week or so . . . and then there was my mother and her accident, so I haven't had time to do much of anything that I'd hoped to start. Well, I did set up my art room in Paul's old bedroom and move some clothes around. Once everything settles back to normal, I hope to start painting."

It was then that I realized that I was the one doing all the talking. To avoid the temptation of dominating the conversation, I sipped my coffee.

"What's your daughter planning to major in?" Rowan asked.

"I'm not sure. She isn't, either. I have a feeling she'll eventually go into social work. She has a caring heart and wants to help people. Although I'd rather she worked for Social Services here in the United States than some faraway third-world country."

"Those countries need help, too."

"True." I agreed, only I wasn't willing to send Allie that far from home.

"As for her major, kids often don't know what they're best suited for right out of high school," he commented. "Did you always want to be a nurse?"

"Yes, from as far back as I can remember. My mother was one, so going into medicine felt natural for me. What about you? Did you always want to be a doctor?"

He looked down at the cup in his hand. "Science and medicine have always interested me. It was only later, once I was in medical school, that I felt drawn to surgery."

"How did you decide to specialize in orthopedics?" I knew that upper-body strength was a necessity to specialize in that field. The thought brought my gaze to Rowan's muscular chest and arms. He was one fine male specimen.

"I felt the draw during my rotation. Orthopedics suited me."

"Well, I, for one, and for my mother's sake, am grateful that you did."

A hint of a smile came over him. He wasn't a man who smiled often, and it pleased me immeasurably that he would smile for me.

"What about your son?" Rowan asked. "Is he interested in medicine?"

"No, he's into engineering. My dad was a nuclear engineer and Paul was close to him." Paul hadn't declared his major until his junior year. He'd always had top grades, although I was concerned about this part-time job he'd taken.

"That's a good field."

"I think so, too. Paul is outgoing and friendly, with an aptitude for numbers. He'll do well at whatever he chooses in life. Allie, too." I was extremely proud of both my children. They were amazing. I don't think Kyle realized all that he'd missed as their father.

"You're frowning," Rowan observed, breaking into my thoughts.

"Sorry, I don't mean to be," I said, embarrassed that I'd allowed my thoughts to travel down that negative path. I didn't usually mention Kyle. There wasn't any reason to now, either. The incident with the flat tire was what had brought him to mind.

"What were you thinking about?" he asked. "Your daughter?"

He would have to ask me that. "My ex-husband. Sorry."

"You're still angry with him after all these years?"

How was it this man could cut right into the heart of the subject? I wanted to deny my feelings, put on a cheerful smile, and change the subject. The intensity of his look convinced me it would be best to speak honestly. I found it curious how interested he was in my marriage and my dealings with Kyle.

"Yes, I suppose I do sometimes still feel angry. Not often these days, but every now and again a memory will surface that brings it all bubbling back up."

"Was it something I did?"

"Not at all. The thing I've come to accept about forgiveness is that it's an ongoing process. Letting go of the hurt hasn't happened all at once. I'd like to think I've forgiven my ex, and for the most part I believe I have. That doesn't mean I've forgotten the hurt, though. Forgiving and forgetting are two separate things."

Rowan's eyes looked deep into mine, concentrating hard, as if delving into his own past. "You're a wise woman."

His praise flustered me. "It's kind of you to say so. I have a long way to go when it comes to wisdom."

"Don't we all?" he asked.

A shadow fell across the doorway, and both Rowan and I looked in that direction. A distinguished, handsome man came into the room with a warm, eager smile.

"Rowan, I heard you were in the building," he said. He was tall, with wide shoulders, and impeccably dressed in a sharp, custom-tailored suit.

Rowan stood up from the table and the two men exchanged handshakes. "Jenna, this is Rich Gardner; he's the CEO and director of Parkview and several other of their facilities. Rich, this is Jenna Boltz. Her mother is a patient here."

Rich took my hand in both of his and focused on me as if he was spellbound by me. His eyes were the deepest, darkest shade of blue. A woman could drown in those eyes.

"Nice to meet you, Rich," I said.

"The pleasure is all mine. If there's anything I can do to help your mother while she's here, please don't hesitate to contact me personally."

"Thank you."

"I mean it, Jenna." He reluctantly let go of my hand and reached inside his suit jacket. He took out a business card and handed it to me.

"Thanks," I said again, looking down at the card. I could feel his eyes roam over me. He was interested. Very interested, and I was flattered. Men who came on strong like this were a yellow light to me, but I tried not to prejudge. I glanced toward Rowan, wondering what his reaction was to Rich's attention. As best I could tell, he had none.

"Here's my personal number. Just give me a call." Rich took back the card from my hand, collected a pen from a pocket inside his suit coat, and scribbled down the number.

When he'd finished, he returned his attention to Rowan. "I heard you're having car trouble."

"It's minor. Triple A will be here any minute."

"If you need anything—"

"It's all taken care of," Rowan said, abruptly cutting him off, his tone not nearly as friendly as it had been at first.

"I'll leave the two of you, then." Rich's eyes connected with mine again, and before he walked away he asked about my mother and her room number, which I shared with him.

He left, and I noticed Rowan studying me, as if to gauge my reaction to the handsome director.

I fingered the business card in my hand. "He seems nice."

"He's good at his job," Rowan admitted.

Our coffee had cooled considerably, and so had our conversation. It was then that I realized that I'd learned next to nothing about him, as I had done most of the talking.

We'd spent a good portion of that forty-five-minute wait discussing me and my concerns for my children. He had continually refocused the conversation back to me, avoiding any discussion about his background or his life. Disappointment settled over me.

"What were you saying?" I asked Rowan, hoping to pick up the conversation.

He appeared to have lost track also. "It must not have been important."

I took a drink of my lukewarm coffee and looked up when the receptionist from the front desk approached.

"Triple A just pulled into the parking lot, Doctor."

Rowan looked up. "Thanks." Taking his empty coffee cup, he pulled away from the table, stood, and tossed it in the recycling container. "Thanks for waiting with me, Jenna."

"Sure, no problem." And then, before I could stop myself, I added, "Maybe we could do this again sometime . . . you know, have coffee."

"I'd like that."

"I would, too."

I wasn't entirely sure why I'd made the offer, but I chalked it up to curiosity. Rowan Lancaster was a man with secrets, and I was determined to learn what they were.

Chapter 13

Maureen

I shouldn't have been disappointed when Logan didn't stop off at the library the way he normally did on Mondays. I thought that he would at least return the latest book he'd borrowed, but if he had, I didn't see him, and I always saw him.

After the disastrous date on Friday, the weekend had dragged by. I'd spent two miserable days rehashing what had gone wrong.

I blamed Logan.

I blamed myself.

I even went so far as to blame my daughter for her pep talk, which had only confused me. I'd avoided Tori's texts as long as possible but had finally filled her in on what had happened late Saturday. Jenna had tried to stop by, but I pretended not to be home.

By the time Monday morning rolled around I couldn't wait to get back to work, if not for any other reason than it gave me the opportunity to crawl out of the dark hole I'd buried myself in since Friday night.

While I'd been stewing and fretting and feeling sorry for myself, Jenna had been persistent and texted me on Sunday, suggesting we meet at the hospital during her dinner break, on my way home from work. It stood to reason that she wanted to know about my date. Or non-date, as it'd turned out.

As soon as I was finished at the library, I headed to the deli down the street and picked up freshly made soup and sandwiches, as neither of us was enamored with hospital cuisine.

Jenna arranged her dinnertime to coincide with my schedule. When I walked out of the building I was met with a blast of torrential rain. Seattle's typical fall weather had started early this year. The downpour and the gray, dreary skies matched my mood. This was exactly the kind of evening when I enjoyed snuggling up with a good book in my favorite chair in front of the fireplace.

Burying my face in a book was the way I dealt with stress. If I could escape in a novel, then I could forget, or at least pretend to forget, what was going on in my head and my heart. When Peter and I decided to divorce, I reread all of Jane Austen's published works in record time. I knew almost from the start of our marriage that we weren't right for each other. To our credit, we'd made a good-faith effort to make it work for Tori's sake, to the point that we were both miserable. Peter was the one who had the courage to admit we weren't ever going to be happy together. While it was painful to admit, I had agreed.

Admitting defeat has never come easy for me. I'm one of those people who would have stuck it out to the bitter end. And our marriage would have turned ugly if Peter hadn't taken the initiative to end it. We parted while we were still able to be friends.

I had tried to escape into a novel on Sunday, but it hadn't worked. My mind refused to stay on the page. My thoughts repeatedly returned to Logan. After that one date, I was forced to admit that whatever he or I had hoped for in a relationship wasn't meant to be. Without question we were different, as different as any two people could be.

The disappointment came when I realized how much I liked him. He wasn't afraid to share his opinions, and I admired his ability to see things in a way that made me think. I enjoyed the sound of his laughter, too. It came from his belly without restraint. It wasn't loud or obnoxious. Hearing him laugh never failed to make me smile or laugh along with him.

The soup special at the deli was minestrone, which sounded perfect, and I'd bought two bowls, along with turkey sandwiches on thick white cottage bread. The bread, made fresh daily, was my favorite. For the most part I avoided white bread, but not this time. Bread was comfort food at its finest.

I arrived at the hospital cafeteria about five minutes before Jenna, and had our meal set up and ready when she came in. She slipped into the chair across from me and didn't even bother to look at what I'd brought for dinner. "So?" she said, assuming I knew the question, which of course, I did.

"So," I repeated slowly, reaching for my sandwich. Holding

it in both hands, I shrugged. "It's not going to work with Logan and me."

"Red light?"

My first thought was to agree, but a small part of me held out hope, which was uncharacteristic of me. I had all the evidence I needed that it wasn't in the cards. That didn't keep me from thinking about him or looking for him, waiting and hoping to see him walk into the library with that sexy swagger of his.

"Yellow," I murmured, after taking the first bite of my sandwich.

"I take it things didn't go well on Friday?"

"Not good at all."

Jenna's eyebrows shot up. "How can he still be a yellow, then?"

Unsure of how best to explain my feelings, I gave another shrug. In as few words as possible, I gave her the lowlights of the evening. She listened intently, and when I finished, she glared at me.

"What?" I demanded, knowing that look far too well.

"Logan tried to make it right, that's what," she reminded me. "Why wouldn't you give him a second chance?"

"I was upset." Clearly, Jenna had never had an entire sports bar full of construction workers laughing at her. My pride had been bruised. I was reacting to embarrassment and emotion, which can be a hellish combination with me.

"He *did* try to apologize, right?"

"Yes, and . . . well, it appears he is just as willing to see the last of me, too."

"Oh?" Her question was filled with doubt.

She wanted proof, and so I provided it. "Logan has come into the library every Monday for weeks. He didn't show today." Saying the words aloud made my heart ache. Despite everything I'd told myself over the weekend about nipping this little romance in the bud, I was devastated not to see him. The entire afternoon it felt as if I was dragging my heart against the floor the way a toddler carries around their favorite blanket.

"Logan will return," Jenna said with confidence.

"And you know this how?" True, she was my best friend and best friends build each other up, but it was total speculation on Jenna's part.

"Well, I've never met Logan," she admitted, "but from what you've shared about him, I think he's giving you time to cool your heels. Mark my words, he'll be back."

"Doubtful." I shouldn't be encouraged by speculation, but I was. Far more than I was willing to let Jenna know.

"Time will tell," Jenna said, digging into her soup.

Eager to change the subject, I asked, "How was your weekend?"

A twinkle showed in her eyes. It was my turn to give her the arched-brow look.

"I spent a good part of Saturday with my mother."

"And?" There had to be more.

"And Rowan Lancaster just happened to be at Parkview at the same time."

"Interesting?" I made it into a question, anticipating she would fill in the blanks.

"Rowan and I had coffee while we waited for Triple A."

"Triple A?"

"It's part of the story that I'll explain later. Don't distract me."

"Okay," I said, and avoided rolling my eyes.

"Rowan and I talked almost nonstop for nearly an hour. He was full of questions about me. *Me*," she reiterated. "I can't remember the last time a man actually took the time to listen and to ask me questions about myself. He asked about Paul and Allie, and his interest was genuine. I can't tell you how many men I've dated who never asked one word about my children, as if they preferred to think of them as invisible," she continued. "No one I've dated before seemed to understand that my kids, whether living at home or not, are an important part of my life."

I understood what she was saying, and we'd discussed that before. One of the biggest complaints we'd both had when we dated was how men would talk about themselves, without much interest in our lives or in our families. Rowan wanting to learn more about her life had made a huge difference in how Jenna viewed him.

"He spoke very little about himself, which only made me want to know him better."

"There's a light in your eyes," I said, smiling. "I suspect Rowan's the one who put it there."

"The problem is . . . he's a surgeon."

"Yellow light." Jenna routinely avoided dating anyone in the medical field, especially doctors.

"And he works at this hospital."

"Yellow light again." I could argue they worked in different departments, but I didn't think Jenna was interested in my opinion.

"He's a little mysterious," she added. "He doesn't talk about himself much."

"Another yellow light."

"But I like him. Rowan has been wonderful with my mother. Caring, gentle, patient. And kind."

"Green light."

"It's getting greener all the time."

"Did he ask you out again?" If she felt this strongly about him, then he should have read the signs and made his move. It confused me that he hadn't.

Jenna's mouth tightened. "No, he didn't. While we were talking, a business associate of Rowan's broke into our conversation to introduce himself. Rich Gardner is the CEO and director for Parkview. I'm pretty sure he's interested in me. He gave me his business card along with his personal phone number."

Now I was intrigued.

"He's good-looking, suave, and polished. It felt like he was hitting on me, which is crazy, seeing that I was having coffee with Rowan. Unfortunately, the tow truck arrived, and Rowan had to leave."

"You haven't seen or talked to him since?"

"No. I have the feeling Rowan fully expected me to pick up on the less-than-subtle hint from Rich and to go out with him."

"Well, would you?"

Jenna didn't pause for more than a second. "Nope. I've dated far too many men just like him."

So Dr. Rowan Lancaster was in my best friend's sights. The last time I'd seen that light in her eyes was when she'd first started dating Kyle.

"But as it happened, I did hear from Rich."

"You gave him your number?"

"No. He found it in the paperwork for Mom and reached out to me later that same afternoon. He invited me to attend some business affair."

"And?"

"I declined, which seemed to come as a shock to him. I don't think many women turn him down. By most anyone's standards, he's a catch. For me, not so much."

"You realize that will only make him try harder."

"Probably, but my answer will be the same."

I silently applauded Jenna. She knew what she wanted in a man, and she wasn't willing to compromise.

"You're holding out for Rowan, then?"

"I am," she admitted. "If for no other reason than I want to know more about him." The look was back. Jenna wasn't one to give her heart easily, and it pleased me that she saw something others hadn't in the mysterious Rowan Lancaster.

"I'm happy for you." At least one of us had enjoyed the weekend.

"I know nothing turned out the way you wanted with Logan, and I'm sorry. I know how disappointed you are."

"I'll get over it soon enough," I said, downplaying my

disappointment. "No biggie. It's funny about your situation, you know?"

Jenna reached for her sandwich. "What's funny?" she asked, looking up.

"Life. You're alone for the first time since Allie was born. Over all the years you were raising your children, you met dozens of single men and not even one caught your eye. You've dated far more than I have over the years. Yet you finally found someone who interests you and he works right here at this hospital. Talk about irony."

"I know. It is strange, isn't it? I have no clue if Rowan feels anything toward me, so I'm not going to put much stock in it."

"You're joking, right?" I asked, laughing. "Come on, Jenna. Clearly Dr. Lancaster has gone out of his way to spend time with you. Do you think that he gives every patient as much time and care as your mother? Of *course* he's interested. My guess is he's looking for some clue from you that you feel the same way. Do you need me to tell him for you?"

"Maureen Zelinski! Don't you dare. This isn't junior high."

I did my best to hide a smile. I should be the last person on earth giving Jenna advice on how to handle a relationship. I was a babe in the woods when it came to men. I didn't know what I was doing; what happened with Logan was a good indicator of that fact.

By Tuesday, I felt better. I was less distracted and eager to get back to myself and my routine. I felt a strange dichotomy of relief and disappointment when Logan didn't make a showing again. If I was honest with myself, I wasn't expecting that he would, and I comforted myself with the fact that it was probably for the best. I slept better Tuesday night than I had since the Friday-night fiasco.

On Wednesday I had my weekly lunch with my daughter. I called Tori early in the morning to suggest we break our pattern and try a different restaurant.

"But I like Maddy's Café," she protested.

"We're in a rut," I insisted, feeling a small twinge of guilt for the white lie. The truth was, I was afraid I'd catch a glimpse of Logan at the construction project across the street, and I had no desire for him to see me, either.

"Mom, please. It's convenient for both of us. If we don't go there, where would you want to eat?"

I hadn't thought that far ahead. The idea had been half-concocted, and I didn't have another place in mind. "I was going to leave it up to you to make a suggestion."

"Fine, I choose Maddy's. And, Mom, you're not fooling me. I know why you don't want to meet at our regular place."

This was a losing battle. I should have known Tori would see through my flimsy excuse. "Okay, fine, you win."

This wasn't what I wanted. I couldn't prevail in every battle, especially when I was matching wits with my daughter.

As usual, Tori had a table and was already seated by the time I arrived. And wouldn't you know it, she got one by the window again, directly across from the construction site.

She greeted me sympathetically. "I'm sorry things didn't work out for you Friday night."

I wasn't comfortable rehashing the details with Tori, especially now, when it demanded all my reserve fortitude not to glance across the street.

I looked up and sighed. "Can we not talk about this?"

"Okay, but just so you know, I am hoping that you *do* see Logan."

"Tori, please."

"The fact you wanted a different meeting spot tells me you aren't nearly as sure about not seeing him again as you say. Can you honestly tell me that you don't want anything more to do with him?"

"He and I are done. Now drop it, Tori. I'm serious."

"So am I. Don't close yourself off because of one unpleasant evening. He said he was sorry."

Jenna had told me the same thing, but seeing that Logan had apparently taken me at my word and hadn't reached out told me it was best to put him behind me and move on.

"I believe I'll have the spinach salad this time," I said, staring intently at the menu.

"Mom," Tori said and groaned. "I can't believe how stubborn you're being."

"Maybe I should try the veggie panini instead? I never have. Have you?"

"What you should try, Mom," Tori said, glaring across the table at me, "is giving Logan another chance."

I glanced up and sighed. "He doesn't want to see me."

"How can you be so sure?"

I didn't want to go into a long explanation. "I know, trust me."

"How do you know?" she challenged.

"Because . . . he hasn't stopped off at the library this week."

I didn't mean to look across the street. I really didn't, but it was as if there was an invisible connection. Sure enough, Logan was there, eating lunch with his work crew. Just as I looked out the window, he looked across the street and our eyes met. We stared at each other for several uncomfortable seconds. The contact was broken when the server came to the table to take our order. As I turned my attention to the menu, a deep sense of sadness flooded my heart.

How I wished things would have gone differently for us.

Chapter 14

Jenna

My arms were loaded down with bags from my favorite discount store as I pushed open the front door with my shoulder and half stumbled into the house. It made me recall my father telling me that a heavy load was a lazy load. I should have made two trips from the car, but I was excited. For the first time in as long as I could remember, I'd gone on a mini–spending spree. I'd bought myself a new set of dishes. Lovely ones, and expensive, with a bright floral pattern, a set of four, with dinner and salad plates, bowls, and cups and saucers. They were exactly what I needed to brighten up my meals, the majority of which I ate alone. My old set was one I'd used for the last twenty years—practical and plain. I'd never thought much about it before. And then Allie had moved out, and I decided I wanted a change.

Life with an empty nest was far different than I'd anticipated. When Allie first left for college, I'd celebrated with Maureen. It did feel good to have the entire house to myself, but what I hadn't expected was the silence. The home I loved had become an echo chamber. I'd even started to turn on the television just so there'd be noise.

When I'd left the house, my mission was to buy new tableware. After I found the dishes, I happened to see thick, luxurious towels on sale. The minute I felt their softness, I was sold. I bought two sets. One in bright red and the other in royal blue. All at once I found a need for color in my life. As it was, my current towels were nearly threadbare. I hadn't thought much about their poor condition until I felt the beautiful towels.

I worked hard to keep a balanced budget and to help the kids as much as I could with college expenses. My father had set aside trust funds for all his grandchildren; otherwise, I would've never been able to afford to send Paul and Allie to college.

I quickly sorted through my purchases, washed the dishes, and put them in the cupboard. As I threw the towels into the washing machine, I heard the front door burst open.

"Mom!" I heard Allie shout. "Where are you?"

"In the kitchen. Allie, what's wrong? What on earth are you doing here in the middle of the day?"

"Oh Mom. I am so embarrassed," she blurted out between sobs, running into my arms.

"Honey, what happened?" I asked, immediately alarmed.

My question was followed by more sobs, sniffles, and finally snorting sounds as Allie struggled to breathe. She looked wretched and appeared as though she had showered but let her hair dry naturally, which was strange for her. Anyone who knew Allie knew she was all about perfect hair and the products that went with it. I recalled the summer she went with a church group to help the homeless in Portland, Oregon. It was a two-day trip and she packed two suitcases. One entire suitcase was filled with her hair products. We'd had a long discussion about her insensitivity to the needs of others.

She tried to speak and couldn't. All she seemed capable of doing was shaking her head.

"I can't help you if you don't talk to me," I said gently.

"I'm . . . I . . . am trying." Allie gasped a couple of times, trying to control her crying. "I don't know . . . if I can live in the dorm any longer. I want to move home."

Whatever had happened was serious, I could tell. "Take a deep, slow breath," I said, keeping her in my arms. I couldn't imagine what had happened to cause this reaction. My guess was that it had to do with Wyatt. She'd been full of talk about him since the night of the frat party. He was smart, handsome, and perfect in every way, according to Allie, but if my daughter's dating history was any indication, I expected this relationship to fizzle out quickly. And if Allie's hysterics were any indication, it had happened sooner than I'd expected.

I gently patted her back as she cried all over my shoulder. "Does this have anything to do with Wyatt?"

"No," she cried. "He . . . didn't . . . do anything. Thank God he wasn't there to see my humiliation." Slowly, she was gaining control of her emotions, although none too soon.

"Okay, okay," I said, doing my best to be as reassuring as possible. "Start from the beginning and tell me everything."

Sniffles were followed by one loud sob as I led her to the family room off the kitchen, where we sat down. "No one . . . told me."

"Told you what?" I asked in the same even, unemotional tone.

"The notice about the . . . drill."

This wasn't making a whole lot of sense. I wondered if *drill* was another word for test. It'd been a lot of years since I was last in college. Terms can change. "Drill? Are you talking about a test you took?"

"No," she cried, reacting like I was being dense on purpose. "A *fire* drill!"

This conversation was getting more difficult to follow by the minute. My daughter was declaring that she was moving back home because no one told her about a fire drill? This was going a bit overboard.

"I'm sure there was a notice," I said, hoping that would help her to be more reasonable.

"There was . . . on the community bulletin board . . . but I . . . didn't see it . . . and later . . . I was gone . . . when . . . we . . . were . . . reminded." Each word was pronounced between hiccupping sobs.

A box of tissues was close by, and I retrieved one for her. Allie grabbed hold of it and blew her nose. My daughter had always been something of a drama queen. The teen years hadn't been easy ones for her. Living in a dorm and away from home for the first time seemed to magnify problems, making them appear larger than they were.

"Okay, so you missed the fire drill. Were you with Wyatt?"

"No . . . and I didn't miss the drill."

Now I was totally confused. It was clear this wasn't going to be a short conversation. "If you didn't miss the drill, then why are you so upset?"

"Because I was in . . . I was . . . in the shower."

Oh no, I could see where this was going.

"I had one leg shaved." She sucked in a deep breath to calm herself and continued talking. "And conditioner was in my . . . hair."

"Oh Allie." I briefly closed my eyes and cupped my hand over my mouth.

"It gets worse, Mom."

"Oh sweetie." This seemed bad enough.

"I . . . had to get out of the building quickly, otherwise I would've had to pay a two-hundred-dollar fine . . . and . . . and I didn't have my robe."

The robe had been a gift from my mother before Allie left for college. Mom wanted to make sure her granddaughter had the proper covering when wandering between her dorm room and the showers.

"It was in the dryer."

Oh dear. "What did you do?"

Allie closed her eyes as if trying to erase the incident from her mind. "I . . . I had to use my towel. I wrapped it around me and hurried outside. Mom, it was humiliating."

I couldn't even imagine. "Honey, I know you're embarrassed."

"It was awful. Everyone looked at me and pointed in my direction."

"I'm so sorry."

"How can I face anyone after this? I want to move back home." Allie's eyes pleaded with me, amid the sniffles.

"Let's talk about this," I said, getting up and putting the teakettle on the stove. Tea was the go-to for important conversations with my kids, too. I hoped I'd be able to talk Allie down from overreacting, seeing that I'd already withdrawn trust funds for her room and board for the semester, which was no small change.

"You always say that when you have no intention of agreeing."

"Do I?" I asked, taking my new cups and saucers out of the cupboard. I paused for a moment to admire the pattern, liking it even more than I had originally.

Once the water boiled, I poured it on the teabags in the teapot that had once belonged to my grandmother. I reserved it for special occasions. The tea brewed as I pulled out a serving tray and put the cups and saucers on it with cream and sugar; then I poured the tea and carried it into the room.

Allie looked at the tray and then at me. "When did you get new dishes?"

"Today."

"Why? There's nothing wrong with the old ones."

I found it silly that she would focus on my new dishes. "I was in the mood for a change. Aren't they pretty?"

"I guess."

"You don't like them?"

"They're all right . . . It just threw me. We've had the same dishes ever since I can remember."

Because she was already overemotional, I ignored the comment and handed her the cup and saucer.

"Before you say anything, Mom, I can't go back. I can't. Everyone will make fun of me."

"By tomorrow your fire-drill incident will be old news. This is what life is like, Allie. We make mistakes, embarrassing things happen, we learn from them, and move forward."

"That's easy for you to say," she argued. "Besides, what am I supposed to learn from this? Not to take any more showers?"

"No, but you might make it a habit to read the community bulletin board more often."

Her frown was huge. "You don't want me to move home, do you?"

"You know I've already paid your room and board for the entire semester. This is money your grandfather put aside for you, and to waste it would be wrong, as I can't get a refund at this point. I'm sorry this happened to you, Allie. You do have a choice, though: You can let this break you, or you can let it make you."

Allie rolled her eyes. "Mom, that's so cliché."

I could see the beginnings of a smile that she struggled to hide. Setting down my teacup, I reached over and gave her a gentle hug.

"You feel better now?" I asked.

She nodded and sipped her tea. "Did you buy anything else?" she asked.

"New towels."

That didn't seem to bother her nearly as much as the dishes had.

"I need towels, too. Did you get some for me?"

"No, they were for my bathroom," I said.

"Oh," Allie said, surprised.

The struggle to provide for my children as a single mother had come to an end. Not completely, of course. I still wore Walmart underwear while Allie had the latest in designer jeans. It was time to splurge a little on myself. New dishes and towels weren't going to break the bank. I was about to say as much when the phone rang.

The hospital's number showed up on my phone, and I hesitated to answer it, not wanting to put in overtime hours.

"Aren't you going to answer that?" Allie asked.

"Of course." I reached for the phone, and my heart immediately sped up when I realized it was Rowan.

"It's . . . me, Rowan. I was thinking . . . I know you said you weren't interested earlier, but in case you've had a change of heart, I was wondering if you might like to take a drive with me to look at the fall colors." His words were stiff, emotionless, as if he was expecting me to turn him down.

While Rowan was most likely trying to protect his heart, mine, on the other hand, was doing silly jumping jacks. I struggled to hide my eagerness before responding. This was what I'd wanted, what I'd been hoping would happen.

"I'd understand if you'd rather not."

"Actually, that sounds lovely. When were you thinking?"

Right away his voice softened with relief. "I looked at the schedule and noticed you are off tomorrow."

"Yes." Three days on, three days off.

"I am as well. May I pick you up around ten?"

"Sure. That would work perfectly. Would you like me to pack a lunch for us?"

He hesitated, as if he hadn't thought that far ahead. "No, we'll find someplace to eat. Don't go to any trouble."

"Okay."

There didn't seem to be anything more to say, and so we ended the conversation.

"Who was that?" Allie asked.

"Rowan Lancaster. Dr. Lancaster. He is the surgeon who repaired your grandma's hip."

"You're dating a *surgeon*?"

You would've thought I'd announced that I'd taken up jumping out of helicopters to fight forest fires.

"How long has this been going on?"

"Nothing is going on," I said. "This is the first time he's asked me out."

"Does Paul know?"

"There's nothing for him to know. Dr. Lancaster has been wonderful with your grandmother. I've gotten to know him a little and admire him. Don't make a big case out of this."

Allie's frown tightened her face. "It's like I hardly know you anymore."

"Don't be ridiculous," I said, brushing aside her words.

"You've always steered clear of doctors."

I couldn't argue with her. "Things change."

"I guess so," she said with a sarcastic edge.

"How'd you get to the house?" I used this question to

change the subject. Normally she would've taken the bus, but in her emotional state that didn't seem likely.

"Wyatt dropped me off."

That was what I'd assumed, although she didn't mention it until I asked. "Then it's time to get back for your classes. Come on, I'll drive you."

"Mom," she cried.

I could see the panic setting in as her eyes rounded, as if I was asking her to do the impossible.

"How am I supposed to face everyone? I'm the laughingstock of the entire dorm."

"Like I said, this incident will be old news soon enough. We all have embarrassing moments at one time or another. It won't be long before you'll look back at what happened and laugh."

"I will never laugh about this. Never."

"Oh Allie." I did feel sorry for her. "Chin up, kiddo, you'll get through this."

"I can't go back. Not yet," she pleaded.

"What *I* can't do," I replied, "is let my daughter move back home because she's too embarrassed to return to her dorm room."

"Can we go to lunch before you take me back?" She was finally conceding.

"Sure thing. What are you hungry for?"

"Chinese."

"China West?" It was our favorite. The almond chicken was big enough for us to share and each take home leftovers.

"Can I order the dumplings?"

"Only if you share."

After Allie had dried and fussed with her hair and makeup, we drove to our favorite Chinese restaurant. We were seated and had ordered when out of the blue the questions started again.

"You like this surgeon, don't you?"

Rather than go into a detailed response, it was easier to simply nod.

"You got all flustered when he called. That's not like you."

I raised the small teacup to my mouth and took a sip, feeling out of my element. "I'd hoped he was going to ask me out and was disappointed that it took so long."

"Why do you think he finally got up the nerve to call?"

"I'm not sure." If I was to guess, however, I'd say it was because Rowan had learned that I'd turned down a date with the CEO from Parkview.

Chapter 15

Jenna

After our lunch, I dropped Allie off at her dorm. I suspected she intended to skip classes for the rest of the day; I didn't blame her if she did. Seeing that I was already out and about, I decided to stop off and see if my mother needed anything.

When I pulled into the parking lot at Parkview, I noticed the slot for the director was taken, which meant Rich Gardner was currently at the facility. After I refused his first invitation, he'd contacted me a second time. Once again, I had a handy excuse; I was scheduled to work. I wished now that I'd been more adamant and let him know I wasn't interested.

As I walked down the hallway to Mom's room I could hear her laughing. She had a visitor. It didn't take me long to recognize Rowan's voice. This was a surprise, and a pleasant one. He'd been on my mind ever since his call earlier in the day.

"And then, oh my! You wouldn't believe my Jenna. At age

ten she decided she wanted to go live with the Amish. She had her suitcase packed and was ready to head out until her father told her the Amish wouldn't allow her to listen to her Walkman. Only then did she have a change of heart."

Rowan laughed.

I rolled my eyes. I could hear that Mom was telling tales on me. Unwilling to let her continue, I made my way into the room. Rowan had his legs crossed in a relaxed pose, sitting in the reclining chair next to Mom's bed. Seeing him smiling and relaxed did funny things to my stomach. Every time I'd been with him he'd seemed proper and reserved. To see him at ease and enjoying himself was a rare treat.

"Mom," I said, placing my hand firmly on my hip. "Just exactly what are you doing?"

"Oh hi, Jenna." She wore a huge smile. I could see water had pooled in the corners of her eyes from laughter.

"What's so funny?" I asked, looking from one to the other.

"Your mother was telling me about you as a child," Rowan told me, his eyes full of mirth.

"I bet she was."

"So it's true what your mother told me. You tricked your brother into thinking he was attending a costume party in high school when it was a birthday party for his best friend."

Containing a smile was difficult. "Tommy looked pretty cute in that wedding dress and veil," I countered.

Rowan chuckled and shook his head, as if he found it hard to believe I would pull such a nasty stunt.

"He deserved it."

"Now, Jenna," Mom interjected.

"Mom," I said, defending myself. "Tommy found my journal and took it to school and let several boys read it." If Allie was mortified by her little incident earlier that day, I could easily top it with what had happened to me. My brother was a sneak and a thief. He deserved every catcall he got while wearing that wedding dress. It took him several days to recover, and he never stole my journal again.

"Jenna was embarrassed to have her secret thoughts revealed, but it had a happy ending," Mom added.

"Happy ending when I paid Tommy back, you mean."

"No, dear, if I remember correctly, you had written in your journal how much you liked Tommy's friend John Livingston."

I groaned, vividly remembering how horrified I'd been that John had read the secret desires of my teenage-tender heart. "Don't remind me."

"But don't you remember what happened after that?" Mom asked.

Nothing good had come of the embarrassment that I could recall.

"Jenna, John asked you to the next school dance the following September. Surely you haven't forgotten that."

It was almost a year after the diary incident, and I'm certain the only reason he did was because he knew I was a sure bet. He'd already asked three other girls who had all turned him down. Then, and only then, had he approached me. His biggest mistake was telling me that I wasn't the first girl he'd asked, or the second, or even the third choice. At times, boys could be so lame. The sad thing was this: Those boys grew up to be men with little improvement in their social skills.

"Either way, it's a fun story," Rowan said.

Looking at his watch, he uncrossed his legs and stood. "I need to get back to the hospital."

"Nice to see you, Rowan," Mom said.

"I'm glad you're making a good recovery, Carol, and I'll see you tomorrow at ten, Jenna," he said.

His gaze held mine and all I could do was nod, letting him know I was eager to see him.

"Later, then," he said, as he made his departure from the room.

Mom didn't wait more than two seconds before she sat up farther in bed. "You're dating Rowan?" Delight lifted her voice a full octave higher than normal. "Oh Jenna, he is the most wonderful doctor. Now, don't you let that man slip through your fingers."

"Mom, please. He asked me out for a car ride to see the fall colors. It isn't a marriage proposal."

"I know, I know," she agreed. "But everyone has to start somewhere."

"Yes, Mother," I said, hiding my amusement.

It did my heart good to find Mom doing so well. I'd been keeping my brother apprised of her recovery, and he was planning a trip to see her sometime later in the month.

Although Mom was making the best of the situation, I knew she hated being away from home. Progress was slow, but she was adjusting to her limitations, although it wasn't easy. Since transferring to the rehab facility, she'd worked hard with both the physical therapist and occupational therapist. If her recovery continued at this rate, it wouldn't be long before she'd be able to move back home.

I took the chair recently vacated by Rowan. There was a second one in the room, but I chose that one.

As soon as I was comfortable, Mom asked, "I've been worried about Mr. Bones. Are you sure he's getting fed? He's picky, you know. He only likes one brand of cat food. I don't remember how much was left in the bag. Check for me, would you?"

"Sure, Mom, no problem." I should've known she would be worrying about that ungrateful cat. That my mother would concern herself over this silly feline tickled me. Here she was in a rehab facility following a complicated hip surgery, learning to walk all over again, and her biggest fear was that the feral cat she had befriended wasn't getting his preferred cat food.

She must have read something in my face, because a worried look came over her. "Thank you. I do fret about him. I found him shortly after we lost your father. Having Mr. Bones around gave me someone to look after and care for, and I needed that. I should have named him Comfort Cat, because he's become such a comfort to me."

I'd never thought of that cranky cat as helping my mother through the grief process. My attitude toward him did an instantaneous turnaround. If Mr. Bones meant that much to my mother, then I'd feed him a filet mignon if he wanted one.

Mom got teary-eyed after mentioning my father. While

she'd done her best to adjust without him, she still missed him every second of every day.

Wanting to find a way to calm her, I opened my purse and brought out a tube of my favorite lotion. I'd noticed the skin of her arms and legs had become dry. "How about if I rub lotion on your legs and arms while I'm here?"

Mom nodded appreciatively. "That would be lovely."

I started with her arms, smoothing the scented lotion into her skin. As I massaged, I relayed my conversation with Allie and what had happened earlier in the day. Mom found the story as entertaining as I had and promised not to repeat a word of the incident to anyone, especially Allie.

I switched to Mom's other arm and we chatted away. We were laughing and enjoying each other when Rich Gardner casually strolled into the room.

"Jenna," he said. "It's good to see you."

I noticed that he all but ignored my mother.

"Hello," I said, without a lot of warmth. "Mom and I are having a good visit."

"Can I get you anything?" he asked. "No, but thanks." I squeezed a fresh blot of cream into my hand, attempting to let him know we were in the middle of something.

"Would you be available for dinner tomorrow?"

Mom's eyes flared briefly as she glanced over at me.

"I already have plans." I didn't know how much more direct I could get.

He shrugged as if it was nothing. "Another time, perhaps."

"Perhaps," I said, even though I didn't mean it. I had no intention of dating him. He gave me weird vibes. Not that I thought he was dangerous or had an ulterior motive. My second impression of him hadn't improved.

Mom waited until Rich had left the room. "Mr. Gardner has asked you out before this?"

"I'm not interested," I said. Recapping the tube of lotion, I set it back inside my purse.

"Oh my, but he's handsome. If things don't work out with Rowan, you might consider Mr. Gardner."

"Mom!"

"Just saying," Mom said, with that twinkle in her eyes.

Rowan picked me up promptly at ten o'clock the following morning. He looked wonderful in jeans and a dark corduroy jacket. He'd sent me a text earlier in the morning, asking if I was up for a short hike. I was, and had dressed appropriately.

He led me to his car and opened the door. I noticed he had an entire set of new tires. The leather interior was plush and comfortable. Once he was inside the vehicle himself, he turned to look my way.

"I did a bit of research on the best location to view fall colors and decided we should drive up to Gold Creek Lake. There's a mile-long trail there that will give us a good view."

"Sounds great."

"It's an hour drive, give or take a few minutes," he said as he started the engine.

"Perfect."

"I didn't think we'd be comfortable sitting in the car for several hours. The hike offers us a chance to stretch our legs.

The information I read said the trail is less than a mile and goes all the way around the lake."

"I believe we have a plan," I said, leaning back into my seat.

With that settled, Rowan headed to I-5 and then cut over to I-90, heading toward Snoqualmie Pass. The music on the radio was easy listening. I tapped my foot to the familiar songs, enjoying myself.

"Tell me more about yourself," I said. "When we had coffee, you let me do all the talking."

He grinned, as if that had been his plan from the start. "What do you want to know?"

I shrugged. "Let's start with your childhood."

"Okay. I have a mom and dad, both alive and retired, living in Florida now."

"Where did they live before?"

"Charleston, West Virginia. My father was a surgeon, too, and my mother a nurse."

This seemed to be a familiar story. I wanted to ask if his ex was a nurse but decided against it.

"Siblings?"

"One. A sister, two years younger."

"She's a nurse?"

"No, an accountant." He glanced over at me and grinned. "Surprised you, didn't it?"

It did, but just as I was about to say something, we passed the community of North Bend. Directly ahead of us was an entire forest of trees in brilliant shades of red, brown, and yellow. It was as if God had taken a brush and painted the landscape in bold colors. The beauty of it took my breath away. For several moments I was incapable of speech.

"Oh my," I whispered in awe, once I caught my breath.

"It is beautiful," Rowan said, but his gaze lingered on me rather than the landscape. "I've always loved autumn," he said. "In West Virginia, it's all this and more."

"More?"

"One day I'll show you and you can judge for yourself."

He spoke as if we had a future. With anyone else I would have heard warning bells. I didn't appreciate a man who took me for granted or made assumptions. With Rowan, I felt none of that. When I paused to analyze my feelings, I realized I wouldn't mind having a future with him. It was far too early in the relationship to make any predictions. At this point, though, I was interested, more so than I had been in anyone for a very long while.

As we continued to drive, the colors appeared to get brighter and more intense. Rowan found the exit to Gold Creek and steered into the parking lot by the lake. We left the car and, after stretching our legs a bit, started out on the short hike. The weather was in the low fifties, with slight winds that made it feel more like the low forties. I was glad I'd bundled up.

After I stumbled on a twig, Rowan took my hand and we started walking at an easy pace. Unlike my mother, who would have been able to identify every tree, I was sadly at a loss. It didn't matter, as I was more interested in the company than a horticultural study.

We walked in silence, because the majesty of what we

were seeing had that kind of impact on us. It was like walking into an old European church—we were that much in awe.

"A season," I said in almost a whisper, breaking the silence. "It's more than a change in the weather."

"What do you mean?"

"I was just thinking about this beautiful season of autumn, and how there are other seasons, too, like different seasons in our lives. Like this season I'm in right now: It's a new one for me, with my youngest in college. I'm living alone now for the first time. Before I married Kyle, I lived at home, then in a dorm, and later shared an apartment. I've always had someone with me."

"Do you mind being alone?"

"I . . . I don't know. I haven't quite figured it out yet. I have a nook where I sit in my bedroom that looks out over Elliott Bay, and I love to spend time there and look at the water and think."

"Happy thoughts, I hope?"

"Some are, for sure. But sometimes, I'll admit, I sit and do nothing but worry. Other times, I read. In the spring, the sun comes in that window and all I'll do is linger there with my eyes closed and soak in the sunshine."

"Seasons," Rowan reflected thoughtfully. "You're right. We all have seasons, don't we?"

"We do." We had reached the edges of the lake. It was serene and still, picture-perfect.

"Jenna?" Rowan whispered, making my name a question.

I glanced up at him, waiting, wondering.

"I would very much like to kiss you."

Smiling, I said, "I'd very much like it if you did."

Leaning down toward me, Rowan gently pressed his lips to mine in a tender kiss as though he half expected me to change my mind. I raised my arms and circled his neck, letting him know that this was what I wanted, too. Immediately, he deepened the kiss. What began as a gentle touch of lips quickly grew into an explosive exploration. We kissed once, twice, with each kiss growing in intensity. By the time we broke apart, I wasn't entirely certain I could remember my name.

Chapter 16

Maureen

I hadn't spoken to Logan since the disastrous first date at the sports bar. I knew he continued to work at the same construction project, because I'd seen him when I'd met Tori for lunch. To the best of my knowledge, he hadn't stopped by the library. If he had, then he'd taken steps to avoid me. It shouldn't bother me. I was perfectly content with my life exactly the way it was. I'd let that mantra run through my mind every time I felt a regret, which I hated to admit was often.

Once a month I was required to work late on Thursday night. The late shifts were on a rotation basis and it was my turn. I didn't mind. Those who came into the library in the evenings were a different breed of reader. Many were students, whom I enjoyed helping.

I was busy assisting an eighth-grader in finding what he needed to complete his homework assignment when I sensed something wasn't right. I had a sixth sense about such things.

Last Thursday evening, I'd heard that someone had purposely pulled the fire alarm. It had been a nightmare for the staff to get everyone out of the building, only to learn it had all been a hoax.

A restlessness swept over me. After all the years there, I knew the entire library intimately, and I had the ability to sense when something was amiss. The vibe of the room, the tone of whispers. I couldn't put my finger on exactly what it was that alerted me this time, but I could feel it.

Returning to my desk, I instantly knew what it was, or, rather, *who* it was. Logan was in my section, leaning his backside against the closest bookshelf with his arms crossed over his chest.

My mouth went as dry as the Mojave Desert. My heart felt like it was about to pound straight out of my chest and hop across the floor. My steps slowed as I approached him.

For the longest moment, neither one of us spoke.

Logan finally broke the ice. "I'm returning one of the books."

"Which book?" I asked, although I was well aware of the last two books I'd recommended.

"This one. Worst book I've ever read." It didn't surprise me when he handed over the espionage title.

"You finished it?"

"Yes," he admitted, splaying his fingers through his thick head of hair. "Wasted several nights reading it."

"Books are as unique as those who read them. You weren't obligated to finish it, especially if you didn't enjoy it."

"First off, I couldn't suspend my disbelief in this crazy,

convoluted plot. I knew how it would end before I finished the second chapter."

I didn't tell him, but the same thing had happened to me; I'd figured it out by the fifth chapter. "I don't understand why you continued to read a book that didn't hold your interest."

"You liked it enough to suggest it, so I wanted to give it a chance."

"What does my recommendation have to do with anything?" I asked. I shifted my eyes away from him, unable to look at him. He looked good, and it was hard for me not to stare. Instead of his construction coveralls, he wore jeans and a button-up shirt, and casual leather shoes rather than his steel-toed boots. It felt like I hadn't seen him in an eternity. I hadn't been willing to admit how much I'd missed our talks, especially around the books we'd both read.

"If you enjoyed it," he continued, "then I felt certain the book had to have at least one redeeming aspect."

"It's been one of our most popular titles all summer long. It's a *New York Times* bestseller."

"Big deal."

"That *is* a big deal," I argued. "When the title was first released, the waiting list for the book was well over a hundred patrons."

"That's supposed to impress me?"

"It should. It tells you other readers were eager to—"

"I don't care about other readers," he said, cutting me off. "I want to know what *you* think."

I'd purposely selected that title to get his opinion, though he didn't know my intentions. The book *was* popular. There'd been a lot of hype about it even before it was published. The library had been given an uncorrected proof before the publication date and I'd had a chance to read it, one of the first in the library to do so. I hadn't wanted to admit that I'd been disappointed with the story. Like Logan, I caught on to the plot twist quickly.

"I'm waiting," Logan taunted. "What's wrong? Cat got your tongue?"

"Arguing over books is inappropriate, especially in the library."

"Fine. Then let's continue our discussion later."

"What . . . What do you mean?" He seemed to have taken my words literally.

"It means exactly what I said. We should continue our talk somewhere else after the library closes."

"But . . ."

Ignoring me, Logan walked over to one of the stuffed chairs and plopped down, reaching for his phone. He was typing a text message when I walked over and stood in front of him.

"You didn't let me finish," I insisted, using my stern librarian voice.

He looked up and sighed. "Fine. Finish whatever it is you wanted to say."

My mouth kept opening and closing as I struggled in a desperate search for the right words. I was convinced I resembled a puppet with a broken string. "I don't think meeting to talk is a good idea," I managed to say before I lost my breath.

"Of course you don't, because if we had an honest discussion, you'd end up agreeing with me. That book is a waste of time and money. I'm disappointed that you would recommend it when you clearly thought it was as overrated as I did."

That wasn't what I'd meant at all, and Logan knew it. "I . . . can't meet you."

"Why not?"

I was relieved I had a sound excuse. "I'm working late tonight, and if I don't catch the nine-thirty bus, I'll need to wait until ten-twenty." It went without saying that waiting for the bus that late at night wasn't a good idea.

"I'll drive you home, then."

"Ah . . ."

"Okay. I'll forget the whole bad book recommendation on one condition. You'll need to admit that I'm right, here and now, and that you were wrong."

"Admit you're right?" I flared and shook my head. "I don't think so."

He grinned, knowing I had walked into his trap. "Then you'll meet me once the library closes and we'll hash this out once and for all."

"Ah . . ." I couldn't seem to get any other words to break free of my tongue.

"That's what I thought." He returned his attention to his phone.

"What's that supposed to mean?"

"You refuse to admit I'm right, and at the same time, you refuse to defend your position."

As much as I wanted to simply walk away and end this entire discussion, I couldn't make myself do it. "All right. You win. Where do you want to meet?" If he suggested the sports bar again, there was no way I'd agree.

"The Bird Feeder."

"The *what*?" It sounded like some place in a city park.

"The bar in the Beverly Hotel. It's one street over. From what I hear, they serve the best margaritas in town."

"The Bird Feeder serves margaritas?"

"You got a problem with that?"

I blinked, wondering how I'd gotten myself into this. "No . . . I suppose not."

"Good." He looked down at his phone once again.

I walked away and busied myself while Logan continued to be absorbed in his phone.

The library didn't close for another forty-five minutes. I'd expected him to leave and to meet me at the Bird Feeder once I'd locked up for the night. That he'd wait for me was somewhat of a surprise until I realized that he expected me to bail. I wouldn't stand him up, because I was a woman of my word.

Once the library closed, we headed downtown. The night was clear and dark, and the wind off Puget Sound chilled me. I wrapped my coat more securely around me.

"Have you been to this place before?" I asked, wanting to know if this was another regular hangout for his friends.

"Nope."

That was interesting. He'd chosen neutral ground. I should be pleased, and I was, although I didn't want him to know it.

"How do you know this isn't a loud place where we can't hear each other?" I asked.

"I don't. The reviews didn't mention anything about the noise level."

It sounded like he'd gone online to find a place I would consider acceptable. Apparently, he'd learned his lesson after what had happened at the sports bar. Tonight had been a setup, and I'd fallen for his scheme. In fact, I'd made it easy for him, declaring it was improper for us to be arguing inside the library. I didn't know why I'd even said such a thing. It wasn't uncommon for us to debate over books before; we did it all the time, and always within the walls of the library.

The bar was cozy and inviting, with several quiet conversation areas. I knew Logan preferred bar seating, but when I started toward it, he pressed his hand against the small of my back.

"Two empty chairs over in the corner," he said, steering me in that direction.

Once we were seated, the server approached with two paper coasters. "What may I get you?" she asked in a friendly voice, eager to please.

Logan looked to me to order first. "I'll try one of your margaritas," I said. Seeing that I was living dangerously, I might as well have a drink.

When the server looked at Logan, he asked for a brand of beer I didn't recognize. Settling back in the overstuffed chair, Logan crossed his leg over his knee. "So," he said, "how have you been?"

I blinked. This was an odd question, considering the

circumstances. I wasn't sure what to tell him or what game he was playing.

"It shouldn't be a hard question, Marian."

I looked down at my hands, which were clenched together in my lap. "I'm okay. What about you?"

He shrugged. "I sort of missed you. Missed our conversations mostly, but I also missed seeing you."

I paused, uncertain. Was Logan *flirting* with me? I decided to play along, the best I could.

"You *sort of* missed me?"

"Nope, not sort of. I missed you for real."

Attention from men was foreign to me, and I didn't know how to react to it. It was easier for me to learn French than to understand a man's intentions.

The server returned with our drinks. She set down my margarita and Logan's beer. I gasped when I saw my drink.

"Something wrong?" Logan asked.

"I can't drink that," I complained.

"Why not?"

"It's huge. I've seen smaller birdbaths." Now I understood where the bar got its name.

Logan chuckled. "Don't worry about it, I'm driving."

It took both my hands to lift the monstrosity. The first taste was delicious. Oh my, I could see I was headed for trouble. The salt on the edge of the glass intensified the lime and the sweetness of the tequila; I licked my lips, wanting to taste as much of the saltiness as I could.

"Good?" Logan asked.

"Too good."

"Enjoy," he insisted, saluting me with his glass of beer.

I took a second drink, deeper this time. "We were going to discuss the book, remember?"

He shrugged. "You agree with me about that book. Admit it."

I cupped my hand over my mouth and nodded.

"That's what I thought. Now, that wasn't so hard, was it?"

He was right. It wasn't hard at all.

"So, did you miss *me*?" He was completely at ease, leaning back in the chair, his calf resting on his knee as he held his beer in his hand.

"A little." The alcohol was already loosening my tongue. Not a good sign.

"Only a little?"

I took another sip and was amazed to realize the birdbath was half empty. "I'm not good at this relationship stuff. My marriage didn't last long."

"I'm sure my ex is happier without me, too, if it makes you feel any better."

We'd never had this kind of personal conversation before, and I had a lot of questions. "Have you been divorced long?"

"Ten years."

I was getting braver by the minute, asking things I'd wanted to know for a long while. "Have you dated much?"

"Rarely, but I'd like to date you."

The blush was back in my cheeks, and at record speed. He'd thrown me completely off balance.

"Why?" Tori would probably want to shoot me for asking, but I needed to know.

He took a long, slow drink of beer, thinking carefully before responding. "You won't like my answer," he said.

"Why won't I?"

His eyes held mine for a long moment. "You'll think I'm a chauvinist."

"Well, are you?"

He shrugged. "I don't think so. I just feel like you need and want someone in your life. But you're uptight and defensive around men. It's like you're challenging anyone from the opposite sex to show any interest in you."

The room was starting to wobble. I waved my hand at him. "That's the most ridiculous thing anyone has ever said to me. Man or woman. I can assure you I don't need a man."

"You need a man who understands and appreciates you for the woman you are."

I stared at him, not knowing what to say.

"The problem is, you won't give a guy a chance."

Again, I was at a loss for a comeback. Although it was painful, I had to admit that he might be right.

"I don't think anyone's had the courage to tell you this before."

"Maybe," I agreed, and quickly took it back, waving my hand in his direction. "Wait a minute. Not 'maybe.' That was the alcohol speaking. If you ask Jenna, she'll tell you that I'm probably one of the most fun people you'll ever meet."

"Jenna?"

"My best friend. We've known each other since our college days."

Logan grinned, and I couldn't hold back my own smile.

"So, how about giving me another chance, Marian?"

My index finger made a sweeping move from one arm of the chair, arching up and over to the opposite one. "Okay, with one rule: no more sports bars."

"Done."

I sighed, still uncertain we had anything in common. "Do you like sports?"

"Does a bear—"

I cut him off. "I get the picture."

"You want to attend a game with me?" he asked.

"Okay. But wait. Before I agree, what sport is it?"

"How about a Seahawks game? I have season tickets."

"The football team?"

"Have you even been to a game?"

I shook my head.

"Ever see a televised game?"

I shook my head again.

"That's okay, there's a first time for everything. There's a home game this Sunday."

I cupped my mouth with my hand. It was hard to believe that not only had I agreed to have a drink with Logan this evening, but I was about to attend my very first football game.

"Give it a try," Logan urged. "You might like it."

I blinked several times, because he suddenly looked like he had two faces. "Okay," I said. "It sounds like fun."

Unfortunately, I didn't know if that was the alcohol speaking or me.

Chapter 17

Allie

"Come on inside," Allie said, using her code to open the door to enter the house. "My mom's away for the day on some hot date."

Mackensie followed her in and paused to look around. Allie was proud of her home and watched as her friend scanned the interior. Her mother had a knack for design, and for making things comfortable and inviting. She had a good eye for color, too. The walls were a warm gray with pearl trim.

Allie's friendship with Mackensie had grown over the last couple weeks. Mackensie had been supportive and gentle with Allie following the embarrassment that had happened the day before, defending her when Allie had been unmercifully teased by her dormmates.

Mackensie nodded approvingly. "I like your house."

Allie shrugged, pleased that her friend showed appreciation

but not wanting Mackensie to know how much it meant to her that she did.

"It's home, or it used to be." After her last visit, Allie had her doubts. She moved into the kitchen and opened the refrigerator. "You hungry?"

Mackensie was right behind her. "Not really." Then she quickly changed her mind and asked, "What have you got?"

Allie sadly shook her head. "Not much. Mom used to keep the fridge filled with snacks, fruit, veggies, and cheese—that sort of thing—but it looks empty now. OMG, even the milk has expired," she said, removing the carton from the shelf before dumping the contents in the sink. She tossed it into the recycling bin under the sink.

"How about popcorn and a movie?" Allie asked.

"Sure."

They slouched down on the sofa and rested their feet against the edge of the coffee table while they sorted through the available titles. When Allie came across *Casablanca,* she rolled her eyes.

"My mother has this thing about Paris," Allie explained. "She and her best friend are planning a trip there next spring."

"What does *Casablanca* have to do with Paris?"

"I don't have a clue." As far as Allie was concerned, her mother's obsession with the city was weird. "She's been taking French classes online to hone her skills, even though she had six years of French, between high school and college."

Allie let Mackensie make the film choice while she searched the cupboard for microwave popcorn.

This had been the second full day she'd skipped classes.

Allie's mom had convinced her to head back to school. She said the embarrassment would all blow over, but first thing that day on her way out to an early-morning class, one of the girls on her floor had made a snarky comment about seeing Allie half naked. Humiliated, she'd returned to her dorm room and went back to bed, burying her head under a pillow.

Mackensie sought her out shortly after getting a text from Allie, and the two decided to escape for the rest of the day. Allie wanted to get as far away from campus as possible. She wasn't sure how they'd decided to come to the house. Knowing that her mother was likely to be gone for the day made it feel like a good choice.

"My mother's changed since I left for college," Allie said, frowning as she took down two bowls from the new dishes her mother had recently purchased.

Mackensie twisted around so she could look over her shoulder. "Changed? How?"

It sounded silly to say it out loud. "She bought new dishes."

"So?"

"Four place settings," Allie said with a sigh. "That's one day's worth of dishes for her. Two meals if I'm home and only one if both my brother and I are here. It's like, I don't know . . . like minimalistic."

Mackensie nodded. "I know what you mean. It's the same with my mother. She told me she couldn't afford for me to fly home for both Thanksgiving and Christmas and that I had to choose one or the other," she said. "Mom's punishing me for leaving California and coming to school in Seattle."

"You can have Thanksgiving with us," Allie offered. In fact, she'd like it if Mackensie joined them. They could go Black Friday shopping together and spend their school break together.

"Wait, sorry," Allie amended sarcastically. "I don't know if we'll have enough dishes if you eat dinner with us."

"Don't worry about it, I'll be fine."

Allie immediately felt bad. "That was a joke. We always go to my grandma's house for Thanksgiving and she has this beautiful china set my grandfather got when he was in Japan while in the Army. There's always plenty of room for guests."

"I thought you said your grandmother broke her hip."

"She did, but that won't keep her out of the kitchen on Thanksgiving. Besides, my mom will be cooking right alongside her. She'll make sure my grandma doesn't overdo it."

"You sure it'll be okay?" Mackensie asked.

"Of course. I'll clear it with Mom first, but she won't mind, and neither will my grandma. The more, the merrier."

The popcorn had finished popping and Allie removed the bag from the microwave and quickly divided it between the two bowls. Rejoining Mackensie on the sofa, she reached for the remote.

"*Adventures in Babysitting*?" Allie asked once the movie started. "I loved that movie."

"Me, too," Mackensie said, crunching on the popcorn. "It's an old one . . . It was filmed before we were even born. I found it on Netflix when I was thirteen and laughed so hard I peed my pants."

"My mom and I watched it when I had the flu. I think I

was in the sixth grade when I saw it the first time, and I loved it."

For the next hour and a half they were involved in the movie. Once it was over, Allie placed their dirty dishes in the dishwasher. She doubted her mother would even know she'd stopped by. Whoever this doctor was who'd asked her out was someone important. Following his phone call, her mother had walked around with her head in the clouds. It didn't bother Allie that her mother had a date. Over the years, as Allie was growing up, her mom had gone out with plenty of guys. There was something special about this one. Something different.

"I was thinking," Mackensie said, tapping her index finger against her lips. "You said your mother has changed since you moved out."

"She has," Allie said emphatically, and reinforced it with a nod.

"But so have you!"

It was true, although Allie hadn't given it much thought. She was an adult now, with voting privileges, living on her own . . . well, if living in a dorm with other students counted as living on her own. She no longer had to account for her every move—where she was, who was with her, the "be in by midnight" type of restrictions that she had while living at home. These days, Allie went to parties her mother knew nothing about. She'd tried marijuana, made out with Wyatt, and played beer pong and guzzled shots with the guys— things her mother would faint over if she ever found out.

"You know what you need?" Mackensie said, getting

excited. She bounced onto her knees on the sofa and waved her arms excitedly.

"What?"

"A tattoo."

"I can't believe you said that," Allie said, shaking her head. It went without saying that her mother would throw a hissy fit if she found out Allie was even *thinking* of getting a tattoo.

"Why not? You're your own person now, an adult. Your body is your own and you can do anything you want with your body."

Allie hesitated. "I don't know. My mother nearly went into convulsions when I got my belly button pierced." Knowing her mom would never approve, Allie had asked a friend to do the piercing for her. After her mom had found out, she gave Allie the lecture of her life that went on for what seemed like hours about possible infections, about being irresponsible and doing something so underhanded.

"Come on," Mackensie pleaded. "If you get one, I will, too."

"You will?"

"Sure, why not? Haven't you ever thought about it before? I mean, everyone our age has a tattoo these days."

In all honesty, Allie had thought about it more than once. A couple of her friends had tattoos and she loved them. Sydney had one on her calf of a blooming red rose that was stunning. Erica had a cross tattooed on the inside of her wrist that was simple and beautiful. Both were tastefully done.

"What do you say?" Mackensie coaxed.

"I'll think about it," Allie said, weighing her options.

"Don't! If you think too much, you'll talk yourself out of it."

"I heard it's painful." Pain made her squeamish.

Mackensie shrugged as if it wasn't a big deal. "It depends on where you have it done. It hurts, sure, but not that much. It's the end results that count. You won't be sorry. Come on, Allie, don't be a wuss."

Allie chewed on her lower lip as she considered having a stranger poke her with a sharp needle.

"Maybe your mom would freak out, but what about your dad?" Mackensie said, encouraging her. "I bet he'd stick up for you."

"My dad," Allie repeated, and rolled her eyes. "My dad was nothing more than a sperm donor."

Mackensie's smile faded. "Yeah, mine, too."

"I guess we both lost out in the daddy department."

"Guess so," Mackensie agreed. She brightened, in an obvious effort to change the subject. "If you do get a tattoo, what will it be?"

Allie mentally reviewed a couple ideas and quickly settled on one. "An arrow."

"Why an arrow?"

"Because I'm going in a new direction."

"Perfect."

"It is, isn't it?"

"So, are you gonna do it?"

Allie didn't hesitate. Yes, she would get that arrow, but on her midriff, where her mother wasn't likely to see it. "Yes, I'll do it, but you're coming with me."

"No time like the present," Mackensie said, looking happy and satisfied.

Ten minutes later they were out the door in search of the tattoo parlor Mackensie had heard about that was close to the campus.

Chapter 18

Maureen

I did some research on the Seahawks and football, although most of the statistics went over my head. I'd been curious about the team but never enough to watch a game. Fridays were known as Blue Fridays, and it seemed the entire town dressed in blue-and-green jerseys. I knew that was connected to the football team but had never cared enough to participate.

Football was like a foreign language to me; the rules made no sense. From what I could gather, one team was given the ball and had four attempts to move it ten yards. The other team would try to stop them. How difficult could that be? The rest of what I read was convoluted and difficult to understand. I decided I'd figure it out once I was at the game, and as Logan was obviously a fan, he could explain what I didn't grasp on my own.

By late morning on Sunday I'd torn my closet apart, looking for something appropriate to wear. My wardrobe consisted primarily of career outfits: skirts, jackets, dress pants, and dresses. Casual for me was a nice pair of pants and a sweater. This was a date of sorts . . . okay, a real date. Nearly all my other dates—and there were shockingly few in the last few years, as Tori had been eager to remind me—were for dinners or some other social event. Football wasn't a social event, I didn't think, or was it? I hadn't a clue what to expect or what the proper attire was for a football game.

I'd talked to Tori about Logan inviting me to the game and she was excited. Unfortunately, I hadn't thought to get her opinion about appropriate wear. She was spending the day with her in-laws, and it would be awkward to call or text her.

At the last minute, with time ticking, I chose a simple skirt and knee-high boots along with a red turtleneck sweater. Simple but classy.

The game didn't start until 5:20 p.m., but Logan insisted he would be by to pick me up at two o'clock. Almost three and a half hours before the game seemed excessive to me, but he insisted.

My doorbell rang at exactly two. Logan must have been standing outside my front door, waiting for that precise moment. I was ready, eager and elated. I did my best to hide my excitement, almost afraid of these unfamiliar emotions. This happiness, this anticipation—it all felt foreign to me. My life was regimented and orderly, with little fluctuation in my day-to-day routine.

When I opened the door, Logan stood there, dressed in what I had to assume was a football jersey. He had a green-and-blue machine-knitted scarf wrapped around his neck. His eyes widened, and his mouth sagged opened when he caught sight of me.

"Is something wrong?" I asked, sensing his uncertainty.

"I did mention we were headed to a football game, right?"

"Yes. Is what I have on inappropriate?" I glanced down at my boots. I loved these boots, and the sweater was one of my favorites.

He rubbed his hand down the side of his face as though unsure what to say. "You might be more comfortable in jeans."

"Jeans?" I questioned, a bit dismayed. "Okay, if you say so."

"You do own a pair of jeans, don't you?"

"Sure. Give me a couple minutes and I'll change."

I found myself feeling like I was going to be totally out of my element again, like I'd been at the sports bar. You can't squeeze a square peg into a round hole, the saying goes. Except I kept trying. I liked Logan. We were different, but that excited me more than it discouraged me. He was genuine, the real thing; I especially liked that he was comfortable in his own skin, and that he forced me to see his perspective in ways I never had before.

As I headed toward my room, Logan called out, "If you have anything green or blue, put that on."

"Okay," I said, and called to him, "Make yourself at home."

I quickly found the newest pair of jeans I owned. They'd been a birthday gift from Tori. Skinny jeans. I knew where they got their name, as I had to work to get them over my thighs and hips. Once I had them on, I had to hop up and down to get them to button. The only green item in my closet was a T-shirt Jenna had given me as a St. Patrick's Day joke. It was the best I could do. It clung to my front a little more than I was comfortable with, but I didn't have any other option. The only blue blouse I had was made of silk and wouldn't go well with tight-fitting jeans.

When I returned I found Logan standing in front of the fireplace, looking at photographs on the mantel. The first one was of Tori's high school graduation. The second was of her wedding. Another photo was of my parents, who had moved to Arizona once they'd retired. The last picture was of my brother, Joe, and his family. He lived in Nevada now.

"Is this better?" I asked Logan, holding my arms out, palms up.

He turned away from the photos and froze when he saw me.

"I apologize for the Saint Patrick's Day shirt; it was the only green one I had."

"You look"—he started, seeming to struggle to find the right word—"great."

"I do?"

He nodded enthusiastically. Apparently my too-tight jeans and top were a hit. This was encouraging. As soon as he helped me into my coat I locked up the house and we left. Logan drove one of those big pickup trucks that was so high off the ground that I felt like I needed a stepstool to get inside the cab. I'd had trouble climbing into it when he'd taken me home after our drinks at the Bird Feeder; at the time, I'd been wearing another pencil skirt, which had made it impossible. Logan had taken ahold of me by the waist and hoisted me into the seat. That was the second time I'd needed a boost from him; the first being at the sports bar.

"Need help?" he asked.

"Not this time," I returned cheerfully. It wasn't pretty, but I managed to climb into the truck and felt downright proud of myself. It was hard not to pat myself on the shoulder.

"You ready for some football?" he singsonged.

"As ready as I'll ever be."

I soon discovered that just getting to the stadium was an experience all its own.

"Where did all these cars come from?" I asked. The traffic was horrendous. There wasn't a parking spot within a mile of CenturyLink Field. Swarms of football fans headed toward the stadium, crowding the streets and sidewalks. Music could be heard everywhere, and parking lots were filled with vehicles. Barbecues were set up behind them, and people had the tailgates down on their trucks or their hatchbacks open on cars, using the back area as places to serve food and drinks. I'd never seen anything like it. Logan explained the word *tailgating* to me. The atmosphere was festive, and people were laughing and in good spirits.

Logan parked in a lot that charged an atrocious amount of money. It cost more to leave the car for a single football game than I spent on a bus pass for an entire month. As far as I was concerned, this was highway robbery. Logan didn't seem to mind, though, so I kept my opinions to myself.

Once we were parked, Logan paid the fee. I glared at the

woman who collected it, thinking she should be ashamed of herself. The stadium was about five blocks away. Logan took my hand as we joined the throng that was headed to the game. He held on to my hand naturally, like it was a normal thing. I didn't mind; I enjoyed being linked to him.

"You mentioned you have season tickets," I said, thinking he must really enjoy football if he was willing to spend the time and expense to attend all the home games.

"I got them as part of the divorce settlement. I had to give up my dog for these tickets."

"You gave up your dog?"

"Not much of a sacrifice, seeing that it was a toy poodle and something of a drama queen."

"The dog or your ex?"

"Both."

I laughed. I couldn't imagine Logan with a toy poodle. Maybe a collie or a German shepherd. He was a big-dog kind of guy. It made me wonder about his ex-wife and what had happened to their marriage.

Once we were at the stadium entrance, it took us a significant amount of time to make it through security. Logan had prepared me in advance, letting me know I could bring only a tiny purse into the stadium. Our seats were on the club level. Logan boasted that he'd had tickets for several years before he was able to buy into the club level, whatever that meant.

"While we are waiting for the game to start, you can get your hair painted blue and green if you want," Logan mentioned.

"Excuse me?" He had to be joking.

"It's all part of the fun."

I laughed when I realized he was serious. "I think I'll pass. Maybe another time."

His grin was boyish in his enthusiasm. "I hope there will be other times like this, Maureen. Lots of other times."

His eyes held mine long enough for my stomach to flutter at the sincerity and warmth in his eyes. "I hope so, too," I admitted shyly.

I had begun to see why we needed to leave so early for the game. Fighting the traffic, finding a place to park, walking to the stadium, and making our way to his seats had taken a good amount of time. While Logan appeared to be proud of his seats, I wasn't impressed with the lack of comfort. I shifted a couple times, looking to adjust to the hardness of the plastic. At the price they charged for these tickets, you'd think the seats would at least be fur-lined.

"You hungry?" Logan asked. "How about a hot dog?"

"Sure, that would be great."

"I'll be right back."

Logan was gone for a long time. I kept busy watching the action on the field. It appeared that some of the players were anxious for the game to start, because they were on the field tossing, catching, and kicking the football. After twenty minutes, I checked my watch and was beginning to wonder if he'd gotten lost. That was a ridiculous thought, seeing that he'd had these same seats for several years. When he returned, his arms were laden with a cardboard box full of food, along with a large plastic bag.

I took the cardboard container with our hot dogs and drinks while he reclaimed his seat.

"What's all that?" I said, referring to the bag.

He opened it and handed me a football jersey with a large number 12 on the back. "This is for you. I had to guess on the size. If it doesn't fit, I'll exchange it later."

"You didn't need to do this, Logan." The gesture blew me away.

"I wanted to, seeing that we'll be attending other games together."

"Hopefully," I added. I hadn't made it through the first one yet.

He had several items in that plastic bag. A plastic cushion for the seat, along with a knitted Seahawks scarf that matched the one he wore, and a pair of earrings. At the very bottom of the bag was a pair of warm gloves.

"Logan, this is way too much."

He shrugged. "If you're going to be a 12th man . . . uh, woman . . . you need to dress the part. Besides, I wanted to do this for you—make you one of the team."

This was a side of Logan I hadn't seen until now, this generous, happy side. If this was what watching football did for a man, I was all for it.

Once I'd slipped on the jersey and wrapped the scarf around my neck, Logan handed me the hot dog. It was perfect, loaded with mustard and relish. I couldn't remember the last time I'd eaten one. It came with a bag of potato chips and a soda. Because I'd been so nervous, I hadn't eaten much all day. Rarely had anything tasted better.

Logan watched me with a funny look. I was afraid I must've attacked the food like a half-starved hyena, and I paused, thinking I'd embarrassed myself.

"I'm sorry; I guess I was hungrier than I realized," I said, when he refused to break eye contact.

His smile was as big as I'd ever seen it. Lifting his hand, he used his index finger to wipe a smidge of mustard from the corner of my mouth.

"Nothing to apologize for, Marian. Everything is perfect." He took the first bite of his own hot dog, wolfing it down with the same enthusiasm I'd shown.

Logan explained that because today's game was on prime time, the newscasters' booth was located on the edge of the field. Logan was familiar with the names of the players and fed me tidbits of information as I read over the program.

As the Seahawks were introduced, fireworks and hoopla began, unlike anything I'd experienced outside of the Fourth of July. The fans cheered wildly, their enthusiasm boisterous and loud. The game hadn't even started, and already the crowd was in a frenzy. I could only imagine what it would be like later.

By kickoff, I was grateful for the extra layer of warmth. The wind off Puget Sound was chilling. It gave me a good excuse to stay close to Logan. My shoulder butted up against his as I soaked up his warmth.

It didn't take me long to discover the difficulty the players experienced in advancing the football ten yards. In fact, on the first attempt, the Seahawks went backward, or, as Logan said, they lost yardage. A lot of what was happening on the field confused me. Logan did his best to explain it, as well as why the game was frequently stopped by penalties. Before long, I was clapping and cheering with the rest of the fans in the massive stadium.

The game flew by. In the fourth quarter with less than a minute to go, the Seahawks were down by three points.

"We need a field goal to tie, or a touchdown to win," Logan explained.

The Hawks, as I heard people calling them, had the ball on the forty-yard line, and with only mere seconds left in the game, the main guy—the quarterback—threw a long pass to a receiver racing toward the goalposts. The entire stadium jumped to their feet, and there was a collective gasp when the player leaped into the air and made the catch, landing in what Logan called the end zone.

The crowd went wild. If I thought the stadium was noisy before, it was ten times louder now. Like everyone else, I was on my feet, clapping, screaming with happiness, and jumping up and down. Although I didn't understand a lot of the rules, I didn't need to know much to recognize a last-second win.

Logan grabbed me around my middle and lifted me off the ground for a huge hug. I tossed my arms around his neck and squeezed for all I was worth. It was amazing and wonderful. The moment was perfect.

Before I could fully understand what had happened, we were kissing. And I mean kissing like there was no tomorrow. I'd been kissed before, but never with the raw hunger and excitement of that moment with Logan. At first I was too stunned to pull away, but it didn't take long for me to become fully engaged. My fingers wove into his hair and I slanted my head to one side and returned the kiss with the same enthusiasm, opening to him. I don't know how long we clung to each other, caught up in the kiss. We stopped when we realized people were looking to get past us in the row to leave the stadium.

Logan reluctantly broke it off and, taking my hand, led us toward the swarm of elated fans heading to the exit.

"Did you see that catch?" he said, still caught up in the excitement of the last-minute score.

"I did. I can't believe a football player could leap as high as a ballet dancer, but I've been proved wrong."

"Wait. Did you just compare a dancer in tights to a football player? You're kidding, right?" Logan snorted, as if I'd said something hilarious.

"I'm not joking; after all, football players wear tights."

"Okay, okay, you're right, but that's a stretch—no pun intended. I have to say that I don't think any of the Seahawks players would enjoy being compared to a dancer twirling around on toes in the middle of a stage, though."

"Anyone in the ballet is as good of an athlete as any one of your precious Seahawks."

"You win, you win," he said, laughing. "The last thing I want to do is get into another argument with you, especially after that kiss."

I should have known he'd bring up the kiss. "It was nice," I readily agreed.

"The kiss or the game?"

"Both. I had a wonderful time."

We walked hand in hand to where Logan had parked his truck. The streets were already clogged with traffic, cars making their way to the freeway on-ramps or to the ferry terminal, heading home to the Kitsap Peninsula.

"You work tomorrow?"

"I work every Monday."

"Can I see you after work?"

"For?" I wasn't willing to meet up at the sports bar, if that was what he had in mind.

"For whatever you want," he told me.

I hesitated, but for only a few seconds. "Okay," I said, and realized I was already looking forward to Monday.

Chapter 19

Jenna

Sunday after work I tried calling Allie but got no answer. I left her a message, but she didn't return the call. So I sent her a text. It was a simple question for her, nothing big. But I became concerned because it wasn't like my daughter to ignore me. I tried another text.

Were you at the house recently?

The second time was a charm. She answered.

Why? Am I not allowed in my own house?

Of course, you are. I found an empty popcorn bag in the garbage and didn't know where it came from.

Yeah, I was there. Big deal.

Allie, where is this attitude coming from?

You're the one making an issue out of me stopping by.

I read through our exchange a second time and decided a call might be a better idea. This time she picked up.

"What?" Allie asked flippantly.

"Tell me what's wrong," I said, remaining calm. Allie could be prickly, and almost always there was an unrelated issue behind the attitude.

"Nothing's wrong," she insisted.

I knew my daughter and her foibles. "You did something you regret, and you don't want to tell me," I guessed. That was what it usually turned out to be.

"I didn't do anything," she snapped.

Taking the phone away from my ear, I looked at it, as if it might reveal what was going on with Allie.

"Can Mackensie spend Thanksgiving with us at Grandma's?" she asked, changing the subject. "Her mom said she had to choose which holiday to fly home, and she chose Christmas."

This was a favorite tactic of Allie's, to sidetrack me with a question or concern to take the focus off her and direct it elsewhere.

"Of course she's welcome," I said, then tried to redirect Allie. "You know that sooner or later I'll find out what's bugging you. I'd rather hear it from you firsthand."

I could hear Allie breathing hard, as if considering her options. "I talked to Paul and he's cool with it," she blurted out. "I'm an adult. I can do what I want with my own body."

This didn't sound good. A chill went down my spine, a sure sign I wasn't going to like what she had to say. "Allie, what did you do?"

"Okay, fine, you're right, you'll see it sooner or later. I got a tattoo."

"You did *what*?" I blurted out, unable to hide my shock.

"It's no big deal," Allie cried, her words ringing with anger. "Almost everyone in school has one, and before you get all bent out of shape, I had a professional do it."

That she used a professional was one thing for which to be grateful. I closed my eyes and silently prayed for wisdom.

"Aren't you going to read me the riot act?"

"I should," I said, doing my best to remain cool and levelheaded. "Oh, Allie, how could you? A tattoo is forever." Right away my head went to places I'd rather not think about. Unsanitized needles. Infection issues. And that was the tip of the iceberg. My daughter had gotten a tattoo. Little good it would do now to say any more. The deed was done. A lecture from me wasn't going to help.

"It was my decision and I'm not sorry. I've got to go," Allie said, eager to get off the phone.

"Me, too. I've got to check in with your grandma."

"Is Grams doing okay?" Allie asked, her voice softening with love and concern.

I knew Allie had stopped by Parkview two or three times and how much those visits had buoyed my mom's spirits.

"Grams is doing fine."

I expected her to disconnect, but Allie quickly added, "Sorry about earlier."

"Okay. Don't ever worry about coming by the house. It's always going to be your home."

"I know."

"Talk later," I said. I was just about to end the call when she interrupted me again.

"Mom?"

"Yes?"

"Did you have fun on your date?"

"I did." In the last forty-eight hours my mind and my heart had dwelled on little else. I'd enjoyed every minute of my time with Rowan. The weather was perfect, the fall colors inspiring, our short mile walk around the lake invigorating. And the kisses we shared, well, those had blown my mind.

"I'm glad you had a good time. Bye, Mom."

"Bye, Allie." I disconnected and then stood frozen, not knowing what to think.

I immediately went to my window on the bay and sat with my back against the side wall, my knees tucked under my chin as I looked out over Elliot Bay. The skyscrapers of the Seattle skyline blurred my vision as I wrapped my arms around myself. I'd done my best to hide my distress about her tattoo. Bending forward, I pressed my forehead against my knees. It could be worse, I mused, looking for the silver lining in all this, although at the moment all that came into view were dark clouds and even darker thoughts.

*

I hadn't heard from Rowan since he'd dropped me off late Friday afternoon, but I hadn't worried, as he'd mentioned he was back on duty Saturday and Sunday. That didn't explain the next two days after that, however, and I feared I'd read more into our time than I should have. I comforted myself with the thought that if he gave every patient the attention he'd given my mother, then it stood to reason why he had such little free time to connect with me.

I'd spent time with my mother on Sunday afternoon and she was progressing well, but I still was surprised to get a call on Wednesday from Parkview telling me that Mom had passed all the necessary requirements to return home. This was unexpected, as we'd figured she'd need at least another week, but they explained that she had shown such determination and had fully cooperated with her therapists. They were confident she would continue with her exercise regimen upon returning home. Mom was ecstatic. By the time I arrived at the facility, she was nearly bouncing off the walls, eager to leave.

"I didn't think you'd ever get here," she said. If there'd been a chandelier, she would've been swinging from it.

"I came as soon as I got the call," I said, smiling. Her happiness was contagious. Although she'd passed all the physical requirements, I was still a bit concerned about leaving her alone at home. As soon as Parkview called, I'd packed a few items, intending to spend a couple nights with her at the house to make sure she was settled in.

Upright and using her walker, Mom glowed. "Look, Jenna!" she said, standing on her own, "No hands!"

"Mom, be careful," I chastised, but I couldn't keep from grinning. My mom had probably warned me to be cautious when I'd first learned to ride a bicycle.

Since she'd been at the facility, Mom had accumulated more stuff than I'd realized. I had to make several trips to and from the car, hauling out her things. The PT assistant waited for me to return so she could review the list of home exercises and medical instructions. The physical therapy sessions would continue, and I'd already talked to Mrs. Torres, who had agreed to take Mom to and from her PT appointments on the days I was working.

"I can't wait to see Mr. Bones," Mom said as we packed her last items.

The thankless cat had shown zero appreciation for the attention and care I'd given him. I certainly didn't do it for him; I did it for Mom, who had worried endlessly about her scrawny, beloved friend.

Getting her in the car demanded some patience. It wasn't easy for her to move and twist around, but she didn't complain. I deeply admired my mother and was happy that the worst of this ordeal was over. Once she was home, everything was sure to improve. I knew people tended to heal faster in a familiar environment.

When I parked the car in front of the house, she let out a small cry of delight. "You put pumpkins on the porch."

"They're from your garden. The cornstalks are from the local farmers' market." I'd made a festive harvest arrangement as a small homecoming present for her.

Mom clapped her hands. "It's perfect, just perfect."

The day was overcast and threatening rain, as it often did in October in the Pacific Northwest. From the way my mother viewed the world at this moment, however, it might as well have been the middle of summer and sunny skies. She chatted excitedly, eager to get outside and work in her yard and garden as soon as she could.

"Oh look," she said. "The oak leaves have turned. Your father loved that tree, yet he complained every fall when he had to rake up the leaves."

I'd loved that tree, too. One of my favorite childhood memories was with my brother, Tom, burrowing deep under the piles of leaves Dad had raked. Gathering them in our arms, we'd toss the piles into the sky, letting them cascade down on us and making a huge mess of his orderly piles. Dad would grumble at first, then join us in our game. Afterward, he'd make us rake everything up. Never once did we complain.

Mom wasn't in the house more than a few minutes when Mrs. Torres arrived with a hot dish in her hands.

"I made you dinner," she said, carrying the ceramic baking dish into the kitchen and setting it on the counter. "Didn't seem right for you to worry about cooking your first night home."

We both thanked her.

"You're a good neighbor and an even better friend," Mom said, tearing up at the kindness of her closest friend.

While they visited, I warmed up the chicken-and-rice casserole in the oven. It seemed like it was months ago that Mom had her surgery, instead of a few weeks. I remembered how Maureen and I had been talking about our trip to Paris when the call came in on that day.

Mrs. Torres left after turning down our offer to join us for dinner. She wanted to get home in time to watch her favorite television show, *Judge Judy*, which came on every evening.

"Love that no-nonsense judge," she proclaimed. "We need more like her. What this world lacks is good old-fashioned common sense."

Mom was exhausted, and at the same time jubilant. "Check on Mr. Bones, would you?"

"Don't worry—he knows when it's dinnertime."

She smiled, leaned her head back against her chair, and closed her eyes. "It feels so good to be home," Mom quietly observed, but then opened her eyes. "I should be helping you."

"You are helping by sitting right where you are," I assured her. "I'm going upstairs to unpack, but I'll be right back."

It'd been a long time since I'd slept in my old room. It had changed from my high school days. Gone were the posters from the boy bands that I'd swooned over as a young teen. The room had been repainted and the bedspread and curtains were new as well. It still felt very much like my room, despite the differences. I unpacked and was setting my toothbrush by the sink when the doorbell chimed.

"I'll get it," I called, racing downstairs, as I feared Mom would try to answer it.

Opening the door, I had a ready smile that grew wider

when I saw Rowan standing on the front porch. My breath caught with surprise and pleasure. I smiled like I'd won the lottery.

"Rowan," I exclaimed, unable to hide my delight.

"Rowan?" Mom said, perking up.

"I hope I'm not intruding," he said, as I stepped aside to let him into the house.

The threat of rain had turned into a reality by now, and drizzle leaked onto the porch. The sky might be gray, but there was sunshine in my heart. Oh, that sounded like something Allie would say, but for me, it was true.

"Of course you aren't intruding," Mom told him, welcoming him into her home.

"It's good to see you, too, Jenna," he said, grinning in my direction.

I noticed he had trouble tearing his gaze away from me, and me from him.

"This is a nice surprise to see you here," he said. It was as if he'd forgotten my mother was in the room.

"Jenna insisted on staying with me for a few days, but I'm sure I'm perfectly fine on my own," Mom said. "She worries when she doesn't need to."

My mother seemed oblivious to the way Rowan and I couldn't stop looking at each other.

"How is it you happened to stop by, Rowan?" Mom asked.

Rowan gave my mother his attention. "I heard you'd been released, Carol, and decided to stop by to see how you're adjusting to being at home." He sat in the stuffed chair closest to my mother, turning sideways so it was easier for her to see him without twisting.

"I'm fit as a fiddle," she said, smiling.

The timer for the oven dinged, indicating that the casserole had finished baking.

"Dr. Lancaster, won't you stay for dinner?" Mom said, eager to have him join us. "There's more than enough. It will take Jenna and me a full week to finish this casserole."

Rowan looked to me, seeking my approval.

"Please do," I said enthusiastically, hoping to encourage him. "I was about to make a green salad." A salad would entice him to stay? It was hard not to roll my eyes. Instead I made a slow exit into the kitchen, afraid I'd say something else ridiculous.

"In that case, I will stay," Rowan said. "It isn't often I have the chance to enjoy a home-cooked meal."

I hadn't thought about that before. He was a single man fully engaged in his career, and I had to wonder how many of Rowan's meals came from the hospital cafeteria. I cringed at the thought.

I couldn't talk, though, as I was going through a rather nasty breakup with Burger King and Taco Time. Since Allie had moved into the dorm, I found it easier to stop off and grab a fast-food meal. It felt like too much effort to cook for one. As a result, the last time I weighed myself, I saw that I'd gained five pounds. Right then I knew I needed to get a handle on this and make healthier choices.

While Mom and Rowan visited, I finished the salad, setting it and the casserole on the dining room table. It was a simple dinner, but you'd think it was a feast, the way my heart sang to be sharing it with Rowan.

When everything was ready, I called them into the dining room. Mom came in her walker, carefully maneuvering herself into her chair. She did well, and I was pleased at her progress.

Once the three of us were seated, Mom looked to Rowan. "Would you say the blessing for us?" she asked.

For a moment, Rowan looked uneasy. He recovered quickly and bowed his head, murmuring a humble prayer of thanksgiving.

"That was lovely," Mom said approvingly.

I handed Rowan the salad bowl, and when he took it I winked at him. He smiled, and I smiled back.

The conversation over the meal flowed effortlessly. In a joyful mood, Mom did most of the talking. Rowan and I added bits and pieces to keep the discussion going whenever there was a lull. By the end of dinner, I could see that she was tired, and that it was time for her to get a good night's sleep in her own bed.

Rowan helped her into the bedroom, although she protested the entire way, insisting she didn't need help. I had to agree, she probably didn't; but I felt better seeing her safely there. He left the room, and I helped Mom undress, put on her nightgown, and stayed with her as she brushed her teeth, washed her face, and put on her night cream.

"I think I'll read a bit," she said as I kissed her cheek good night.

When I returned to the kitchen, I found Rowan had rolled

up his shirtsleeves and was washing the plates and setting them inside the dishwasher.

"Would you like an apron?" I asked, teasing him.

"No, thanks."

"You'd look handsome in one, in case you change your mind," I teased.

He grinned and looked away, as if the two of us alone was a problem and he needed a distraction. "I wasn't sure what to do with the leftovers," he said, glancing toward the casserole dish on the table.

"Don't worry. I'll take care of that."

We silently worked together for several minutes before Rowan spoke. "I meant to call you," he said.

"You're busy," I said, dismissing his excuse. "I understand."

"That's not it."

The response puzzled me.

He unrolled his shirtsleeves and his attention was on the task. "Do you remember the night of your mom's surgery me mentioning that I'd recognized you from the Christmas party?"

I wasn't sure how that connected with the here and now. "I remember."

His gaze bounced away from mine, almost as if he was unsure he should continue. "You were laughing with a few of the other nurses, and the sound of your laughter caught my attention. When I saw you, it was as if the entire room lit up with sunshine. I couldn't stop staring at you. If someone hadn't bumped into me, I may have been standing there looking at you for the rest of the evening."

Dish towel in hand, I was rooted to the spot. I had no idea I'd had this impact on him.

"Jenna, I have one failed marriage and a lot of baggage. Because of that, I decided not to ask you out. But for the life of me, I couldn't forget you."

This was all new to me.

"Being as subtle as possible, I found out everything I could about you. More than anything, I wanted to get to know you, but I didn't make the effort. You're beautiful and loving and warm, and the truth is I wasn't sure how you'd react. My life is consumed by work. I've dedicated my life to my career, and you . . . quite frankly, you frightened me."

"I frightened you?" *Me?* I was probably the least threatening person he would ever know.

"It's embarrassing to admit. When Gardner approached you that day I had the flat tire, I thought my chances were over. I couldn't imagine you wanting to date me when he clearly was interested in you."

I wanted to explain that I'd met and dated too many men like Rich Gardner and that I wasn't the least bit tempted, but I didn't get the chance, because Rowan continued.

"When I learned it was your mother I would be operating on, I felt like it was fate. This was my one chance and I didn't want to blow it. Last Friday, just being with you was . . . I don't know how to explain it. It was the best day I've had in years. When we kissed, it was everything I knew it would be and more."

"It was for me, too," I whispered, hardly able to find my voice.

We started to walk toward each other when his phone buzzed. Groaning, Rowan reached for it, read the text, and sighed. "I've got to get back to the hospital. Have I said more than I should?"

"No." I rushed to assure him. "Not at all."

"I haven't frightened you off?"

I laughed softly. "Nope."

His shoulders relaxed. "That's good to know, Sunshine."

"Sunshine?"

He nodded. "That's the way I've thought of you ever since I saw you that first time."

Reluctantly, he started toward the door, then hesitated. He turned back, gathered me in his arms, and hugged me. "I need to go."

"I know. Get going. We'll talk more later."

"Promise?"

"Promise."

His hold on me tightened briefly. "I don't dare kiss you; otherwise, I won't be able to leave." His lips gently brushed against the top of my head. "Hugging you will have to hold me over."

It would need to do the same for me.

Chapter 20

Jenna

I'd planned to stay with Mom a couple nights and could see that she was beginning to rely on me a bit too much. With Dad gone, it was easy for her to look to me for companionship. Because she needed an excuse to keep me with her, she asked me to do the very things she needed to be doing herself. I was glad when Tom called and offered to come up to stay with her for a few days. It was good for both Mom and my brother, as well as a break for me.

And the timing couldn't have been better.

"So if I'm right, you have today off." Rowan had called me from his car after he left the hospital. "How about dinner?"

He could have invited me to fillet a salmon on the Seattle docks and I would have agreed. Our conversation earlier in the week had been cut short when he was called into the hospital for an emergency surgery. The things he'd said had played in my mind ever since. I was eager to pick up the conversation where we'd left off. That he had been interested in me as far back as last December had come as a shock, but his confession thrilled me. I was seeing a strong green light with this man.

"I'd like to cook for you," Rowan continued, "and one day I will. I would tonight, if I wasn't so tired."

"You cook?" *Could this man get any more perfect?*

"A little here and there. I enjoy it, although I don't get a chance to do it often. It hardly seems worth the effort to go to all that trouble for one person."

I'd been going through the same dilemma myself. Since leaving Mom's house, I'd started eating salads twice a day without dressing. Those extra pounds were stubbornly clinging to my hips. It would have been easier to remove them with a hammer and chisel.

"I hear you."

"What do you like?" he asked. "Italian? American? Mexican? A good steak?"

"You choose. I'm not a picky eater."

"Will do. I'll pick you up at six-thirty."

"Perfect."

Before Rowan showed up, I called to check on Mom and my brother. I didn't mention Rowan and I were having dinner together for fear she'd read more into it than warranted. I learned Tom was helping her cook dinner. When we finished talking, Mom handed the phone over to my brother.

"How's it going?" I asked.

"Great. Mom seems to be moving around well, doing

more for herself." I was relieved that my brother wasn't as much of a pushover as I was.

That was welcome news.

"Her bridge friends stopped by for a visit early this afternoon."

Although Tom didn't mention it, I knew seeing her friends had done my mother a world of good.

"I'm grateful you were able to get away to help," I said. Having my brother step up had been a relief.

"It all worked out. A little mother-son time is good for us both."

I agreed. Mom had perked up as soon as she heard Tom would be spending a few days with her. It worked well, as his wife was away on a business trip and he had several personal days that had built up at his firm that he needed to use or lose. His children were older than Paul and Allie and were each living on their own now.

"I'll be back with Louanne and the kids for Mom's birthday," Tom said.

I knew having all the family around for Mom's seventy-fifth birthday would mean the world to her.

Rowan picked me up at six-thirty just as he said he would. He paused once inside the house. His eyes rounded with appreciation and his jaw sagged open.

"Wow," he whispered in admiration.

Before he arrived, I'd been running around the house like my hair was on fire, searching out the perfect dress, carelessly tossing outfits onto my bed until the mattress was covered from one end to the other. Rowan's gentle, warm look made every minute of that frantic search worthwhile.

"I don't think I can wait a minute longer to kiss you."

I wasn't willing to wait, either. When he reached for me I went willingly into his embrace, wrapping my arms around his neck. I stood on the tips of my toes and succumbed to him, breathing him in. Although Rowan claimed he hadn't been in a relationship for a long time, his kissing skills were fine-tuned. Within seconds I was lost. After several extended kisses, he released me.

It took another few moments for me to find my footing. We held on to each other loosely, and I could see that he was as affected by the exchange as I'd been.

"That's quite the greeting," I said, smiling up at him.

"You have no idea how long I've been waiting to do that."

Rowan drove into the downtown area of Seattle. He'd chosen a family-run Mediterranean restaurant called Shawarma Kebab. It was small, with only a few tables covered with red-checkered tablecloths, surrounded by mismatched chairs. The aroma of lamb, cumin, and turmeric filled the room. We were seated by a friendly server, who handed us menus.

"This is one of my favorites," Rowan explained. "The food is wonderful." The server returned for our drink order and brought an appetizer of spicy olives and cheese with pita bread, which we hadn't ordered. "Doctor, my mother insists you have this," the server said. "It's on the house."

Rowan instantly shook his head. "Thank your mother for me, but we can't accept this without paying for it."

The young man adamantly shook his head. "You saved our mama's life. Please, Doctor, let us do this small thing for you."

Rowan looked uncomfortable. I knew he didn't want to insult the family and at the same time he felt awkward accepting even this small gift. He looked to me as if seeking my advice.

"Thank your mother for us," I said softly.

Smiling, the server bowed slightly and left us.

"This happens every time I'm here," Rowan said, looking guilty. "On my last visit I insisted I pay full price for my meal and they agreed for next time." His arm stretched across the table and he took hold of my hand, lacing our fingers together. "Obviously when they saw that I had a beautiful woman with me, they couldn't resist sending out another gift of food."

His compliment made me blush.

While Rowan ordered the wine, I studied the menu. I could see it was going to be a difficult choice. Everything sounded amazing, although many of the dishes were foreign to me.

"The fish with the tomatoes and capers is one of my favorites," Rowan offered, when it was plain I was having a hard time deciding.

I enjoyed fish, and eagerly accepted his recommendation with one small question. "What's Lebanese rice?"

"As I remember, it's rice with vermicelli and pine nuts."

He read through the wine list, asking several questions. After he'd ordered, the waiter opened the bottle and poured us each a glass. He smiled at me from across the table.

The young man stood ready to take our food order.

"I'll have the fish dish you mentioned," I told Rowan, who gave the waiter the full name of the dish. He then made his own selection.

Rowan couldn't have made a better choice for me. It consisted of white fish cooked in a spicy tomato broth, the rice, and a side salad with olives and feta cheese.

The wine was the perfect complement to our dinner. Rowan had lamb and we both cleaned our plates. Leaning back in the chair, I placed my hands over my stomach.

"I don't think I could eat another bite. What a wonderful dinner." In my mind I couldn't imagine a more perfect evening. So often my dates looked to impress me with a meal at a high-end steak house. I was pleased Rowan hadn't. This small, out-of-the-way cozy restaurant had been perfect. The entire family seemed involved in one way or another. The parents worked in the kitchen while their adult children waited tables. Our meal set the tone for the evening. It was intimate and congenial.

It was close to nine by the time we arrived back at the house.

"Would you like to come in for coffee?" I asked. Neither one of us was eager for the evening to end.

"I'd like that."

When I unlocked the door, Rowan followed me into the kitchen. My coffeemaker was the one-cup-at-a-time kind. I stood in front of the counter, waiting for the hot liquid to brew. Rowan stood behind me, his presence warming me. He wrapped his arms around my middle and nuzzled my neck. Shivers ran down my spine, and I leaned my head to one side to grant him easier access to my neck and shoulder.

Closing my eyes, I surrendered to the sensations as his lips grazed the sensitive skin at the curve of my shoulder. I sighed with pleasure.

"It's times like these that make me regret the long hours I put in at the hospital," he said.

From our earlier dinner conversation, I knew he'd been in surgery early that morning and had worked more than thirteen straight hours. These hours weren't unusual for him.

The first cup finished brewing and I reached for the second.

Rowan's hold on me relaxed when I handed him the mug. "I never expected this to happen," he said. He stepped away from me and blew into the side of the coffee to cool it down.

"What do you mean?"

"You and me," he said as he studied his coffee. "I never dreamed it was possible that you could be interested in me."

"Why would you think that?"

"I failed. My marriage was a disaster and I'm not a man who accepts defeat easily. I accepted that I wasn't good husband material. When I first saw you I was tempted, so tempted, but my fear of failure held me back. I don't want to make the same mistakes again, especially if you and I have a chance at . . ." He paused, as though unsure he should continue, afraid of getting ahead of himself. "I sincerely hope you feel the same as me about this."

I didn't hesitate. "I do."

At my response, his features relaxed. "I realize this sounds like lyrics for a song, but if we move forward I want to be sure I'm the right man for you."

The coffee machine made a loud gurgling sound as it finished brewing the second cup. We moved into the next room and sat close to the fireplace.

"If you don't mind, I'd like to know what went wrong in your marriage."

Ending our evening discussing Kyle was a romance killer. I had to wonder what it was that he needed to know. Rowan had spoken little of his own marriage. All I knew was that his wife and daughter lived in California. He'd mentioned them only once, in response to a direct question.

"If answering is too painful or if you'd rather not, I understand, Sunshine."

His pet name for me melted my heart. Holding my coffee cup close to my chest, I told him about Kyle's affairs. As much as I wanted to blame everything on my ex-husband, I realized I had my own failings as a wife.

"After Paul and Allie were born, I continued working. All my reserve energy went toward mothering them. Kyle resented that. He needed a wife who fawned over him, who did whatever he needed to boost his ego. That wasn't me. My kids came first."

If Rowan was worried that I harbored any ill will toward my ex then he shouldn't, because I didn't. The one thing that still bothered me about Kyle, however, was the lack of attention and love when it came to our children. Paul and Allie had needed their father, and Kyle had basically ignored them. I never spoke negatively about Kyle . . . at least not in front of the children. It wasn't necessary. They were wise enough to know the kind of man their father was from an early age.

"Anything else you'd care to know?" I asked, ready to ask a few questions of my own.

"No. Thank you for telling me this much. I'm sure this wasn't easy."

Before I had a chance to form my own question, Rowan took the coffee mug out of my hand and set it down next to his own. His eyes held mine prisoner as he leaned toward me. Without hesitation, I came forward to meet his kiss. The evening had been wonderful in every way, above and beyond anything I'd expected. Twisting around, I wrapped my arm around Rowan's neck and yielded to him. His kisses were magic, better than any I could remember.

We were both heavily involved in kissing when in the back recesses of my mind I heard the slight echo of a *click-click*. It sounded like someone had just opened and closed the front door.

"Mom!" My daughter's voice rang out in horror as she stepped inside the door and saw us sitting in the family area.

Allie eyes went round and her mouth hung open. All she seemed capable of doing was standing and staring at me and Rowan.

"Sorry," she blurted out. "I . . . I didn't know you had company." Her cheeks filled with color.

"Allie, this is Rowan, Dr. Lancaster. He's your grandmother's surgeon."

"Oh." She appeared incapable of any words more than a single syllable.

"Is everything all right?" I asked. It wasn't like Allie to stop by without calling me first to make sure I was home. Her hands were full, holding two big laundry bags.

"I thought I'd come here to do my laundry . . . All the machines in the dorm were busy. Should I leave?" She glanced at Rowan as if to apologize.

All at once I noticed she had someone with her. I suspected this was Wyatt. He was young and had a head of wild, auburn hair that seemed to stand straight on end. He stared down at the floor, appearing as uncomfortable and unsure of what to do as Allie was.

"I assume you must be Wyatt?" I asked, hoping a change of subject would dispel the shock we'd all had.

He raised his hand in greeting and tucked the tips of his fingers into his back jeans pocket, still wearing an awkward and uneasy look.

"I thought you were staying at Grams'." Allie appeared to regain her wits.

"I was . . ."

"I didn't know you had company, otherwise . . ."

"It's fine, honey. No problem. You didn't interrupt anything."

My daughter's eyes narrowed with a frown. "It didn't look that way when I came in the front door. From my vantage point it seemed he had his tongue all the way down your throat."

"Allison Marie!"

"Sorry, Mom. I'm calling a spade a spade, that's all."

By now I was convinced my face was bright enough to be

used as a fog light. I was about to ask that she apologize to Rowan when Allie dragged her two bags of dirty clothes toward the laundry room.

"I believe that's my cue to leave," Rowan said.

He slid off the sofa and carried his mug into the kitchen. After reaching for his coat, Rowan started for the front door.

I followed him. "I am so sorry," I whispered, giving him a light kiss.

He grinned and kissed the tip of my nose. "I'll see you tomorrow, Sunshine."

Chapter 21

Maureen

Much to my surprise, I'd actually enjoyed the Seahawks game. And, oh my, the kiss Logan and I shared after their last-second win would stay with me forever. I didn't put much stock into it. I didn't dare. I was convinced it was the exhilaration, the excitement, and the happiness of the moment that had caused Logan to kiss me. Still, I didn't care what had led to it. I'd liked that kiss.

A lot.

On Monday, right after the Sunday Seahawks game, Logan had stopped at the library to tell me he was unable to keep the dinner date we'd agreed to the night before, as he'd been asked to oversee an out-of-town project in Moses Lake, over in eastern Washington. He'd have to head out that afternoon, and he'd be away a week—possibly two. To disguise my disappointment, I'd loaded him up with books that I felt he'd enjoy reading while he was away. No one had ever accused me of being a compulsive talker, but suddenly, I couldn't keep my mouth closed. The words spilled out of me like I couldn't speak fast enough. Jenna had experienced this same thing earlier, and now it was my turn. If Logan noticed anything abnormal, he didn't mention it. Before leaving the library, he casually mentioned that he'd give me a call once he got back in town.

I rationalized that the separation was probably a good thing, as Logan was growing on me; the time apart would give me the perspective I needed to clear my head.

Logan rattled me. He had from the beginning. He wasn't like anyone I knew. I'd never thought about plumbers as being super-intelligent, knowledgeable, or even well informed. To be truthful, I hadn't thought of construction workers much at all. Logan was changing my outlook. He read three newspapers a day. He kept up on current affairs as if he was considering running for Congress. Every time we were together, I learned something more about him. Somewhere along the way, I realized I'd stereotyped him because he was a plumber and I'd totally underestimated him. Until we'd met, I hadn't realized I'd carried this prejudice.

That man loved his Seahawks. He knew the names of every player on the team and the positions they played. And their competitors. Basketball was another sport he enjoyed, and hockey. These games were as foreign to me as football was.

Something that came as no surprise was how much he enjoyed his Friday-night habit of bellying up to the bar after work for a draft beer with his crew. I'd seen him with his peers only once, but I'd been there long enough to see that he was familiar with the crowd, and that he was well liked.

The days dragged by with Logan out of town. Jenna and I caught up with each other on Sunday, and we finally were able to watch *Casablanca* from beginning to end and to continue finalizing our plans for Paris. On Tuesday after work, we met up to shop for groceries. Jenna was shopping for her mother and refilling her own kitchen cupboards that Allie had raided when she'd stopped by the house to do her laundry. It was good to get some extra time with Jenna, as she'd been so involved with caring for her mom.

"Have you heard from Logan since he's been away?" Jenna asked as she examined a head of lettuce before adding it to her cart.

I added bananas to my own cart. "He sent me a text message to let me know they held him over past the first week."

I wasn't a fan of text messages. His text had been brief, telling me the day he'd be returning. Brief and to the point. I must have read it a dozen times, searching for some hidden meaning.

"Did you answer him?" Jenna added parsley to a plastic bag and tossed it into her cart.

"No . . . I didn't think it required an answer."

Jenna paused and stared at me. It was one of those looks that appeared to question my emotional IQ. "Did it ever occur to you that he might have been telling you that he missed you?"

"The thought *had* crossed my mind." It had. I was searching for a hidden message in that brief text. After some thought, I'd convinced myself it simply wasn't there.

"Come on, Maureen." Jenna threw her arms in the air. "Get with the program."

This was my problem in a nutshell. I was out of my element when it came to men and relationships. Way out—as in outer space, as far as the Earth was to Mars. I didn't have the ability to read between the lines. If Logan was telling me he missed me, it would have helped tremendously if he'd said it straight out.

Why was it that people had to play games with their words? I wasn't any good at that, either. Well, other than Scrabble. I played a killer game of Scrabble. Maybe I'd ask Logan over and we'd go head-to-head over a Scrabble board. That was more my level. That I could do and do well.

"Text him now," Jenna insisted.

"Now?"

That look on her face was back. I swear one of Jenna's looks could melt kryptonite. She wasn't going to let me get away without texting Logan.

Exasperated with me, she abandoned her cart and held out her hand. "Give me your phone."

Clenching my purse tighter against my side, I shook my head. "No way am I letting you text Logan." Then again, maybe she would know exactly the right thing to type. I hesitated, reconsidering. "What are you going to say? Are you going to tell him you hijacked my phone? Or are you going to pretend to be me?"

She weighed my words. "I'm going to pretend I'm you."

Horrified at what Jenna might say, I kept my phone in my hand. "I'll text him myself, thank you very much."

This was worse than when we were in college. I'd always been the nerd. Jenna had insisted that boys were afraid of me and that it was the reason I rarely got asked out. I hung around mostly with Jenna, which did wonders for my social life. Jenna was always fun to be around; if I wasn't with her, then I would escape into the library. I would have buried my face in a book all through college and been a recluse if not for my best friend. I could see myself, even to this day, living in a cabin in the woods, surrounded by dozens of books, content to never leave. Yup, I was grateful that she was my friend, if for nothing more than to bring me out of my cocoon.

"Do it now," she insisted again.

"Okay, okay," I said. It was crazy how nervous this was making me. Staring down at the screen, I didn't know where to start or what to say. Jenna must have seen the problem, because she offered a suggestion.

"Tell him you're looking forward to his return."

I hesitated.

"You *are* anxious for him to get back, aren't you?"

I didn't want to admit it, but under her penetrating glare, I gave in and nodded.

"That's what I thought."

I typed in the text and stared down at the words, then took a deep breath and hit the send arrow. I returned my phone to my purse and was about to close it when my phone dinged. I jerked it back out to read the message.

"Is it from Logan?" Jenna demanded.

I nodded, holding my breath as I read the message. A warm, happy feeling came over me. I had trouble concealing a smile. I wasn't even sure he'd respond and was overwhelmed that a reply had come so quickly. Maybe Jenna was right—in that one text, Logan *had* been trying to engage me and to tell me that he missed me.

"What'd he say?" Ever curious, Jenna tried to read over my shoulder.

"He wants to know what I'm reading," I said. Holding back my delight from his return text was impossible, and before I knew it, I was grinning like a Cheshire cat.

"He wants to know *what*?"

"What book I'm reading," I repeated. One of the best parts of our relationship was how Logan and I communicated through the books we read. We didn't often agree, but as we came to know more about each other I discovered that our opinions had aligned more often than not.

"Well, aren't you going to answer him?"

"I'm shopping. Nothing bugs me more than people who have their eyes or ears glued to their phones while walking down the street or while shopping. It's ridiculous, and I refuse to become one of them."

"You do plan on answering him when you get back home, I hope?" she asked, thinking she'd have to prod me along some more. I didn't need her to shout out instructions at me like a sideline coach. Well, maybe I did.

"Yes, when I can think straight."

"Promise?"

"Yes, I promise. I like this guy," I confessed to Jenna.

"Green light?"

I nodded with a smile. "Yup, green light."

She looked smug and pleased, so I turned my cart away and headed to the dairy section for two-percent milk and fat-free sour cream.

Once I was home and had put away my groceries, I sat down with my phone. Staring at it again as if it would give me verbal instructions, I heaved a sigh and replied to Logan's text, listing the most recently read book on my nightstand as well as the latest bestsellers that had arrived in the library. It wasn't more than a minute after I sent off my reply that my phone rang.

It was Logan calling me.

"Hello?" I said tentatively.

"My fingers are too fat to text," he said, as if apologizing for the call.

"I'm not any good at texting myself," I assured him. "How are you?"

"Bored. The money's good over here because of the overtime, but I'd rather be back in Seattle."

"I'd rather you were, too." *Did I just say that?* I felt myself blush and was about to make an excuse to get off the phone before I made another gaffe.

"So, you miss me," Logan said, jumping on my comment.

He sounded pleased, and I pictured him pumping his fists in the air like the player who had scored that last-minute touchdown.

"A little." I let him have his moment of glory. Besides, it was the truth. I did miss him.

"Good. I miss you, too. Hey, did you notice the Seahawks won their away game this weekend?"

Yes, I'd heard. "Against the Patriots."

"You watched the game?" He sounded more than a little stunned.

"No, I was busy, but I read about it on Monday. I feel like I have a vested interest now that I have a '12th Woman' jersey."

A soft silence followed.

"I'll be back—"

"When will you—"

We both spoke at once.

"Go ahead," Logan instructed.

"No, please, you first. You said you'd be back sometime this week?"

"Depending on traffic over the pass, I should return sometime Thursday. The shop wants me on the construction site by the library Friday morning."

"That doesn't give you much downtime."

"No complaints here. I'm grateful for the work. Working construction has its ups and downs. For most of my career I've spent at least a month out of work every year, generally in the winter. Sort of enjoy that time off. I look forward to doing projects around the house."

Logan was the only union worker I knew.

"Well, have a safe drive home."

"I will."

Neither one of us had a lot more to say. I'm not much of a conversationalist, especially over the phone, and it didn't appear he was, either. We ended the call.

It was dinnertime, but I wasn't that hungry. Talking to Logan left me feeling antsy. I wasn't sure why. I felt an urge to do laundry and scrub my bathtub. Despite what my daughter insisted, I wasn't a neat freak, but I did like a clean home. This wasn't my typical cleaning day, though. Whatever it was that drove me to unload my hamper and pick up a scrub brush fell solely at Logan's feet.

Somewhere between polishing the chrome on the tub and finishing the last load of laundry, I had an idea. It was bold, and unlike me. I remembered the Seahawks game and the short conversation Logan and I had about the ballet. We had argued about who was more physically fit: professional football players or professional ballet dancers.

Just that morning, I'd received an email about the New York City Ballet coming to Seattle and that tickets were on sale. They were expensive. I didn't care. I intended to treat myself, and at the same time, to prove a point to Logan. I would get a second ticket for him to show him that ballet dancers were as athletic as any one of those muscular Seahawks players.

It was the perfect way to prove my point. Logan wouldn't be able to watch their graceful, lithe bodies circle the stage without being forced to appreciate the discipline, skill, and talent required for such a demanding career. I'd put them up against football players any day of the week.

If I remembered our conversation correctly, Logan had never attended a ballet. I had never attended a football game, either, until Logan invited me. I'd learned a great deal and had enjoyed the game. Attending the ballet would be as educational to him as the Seahawks game had been for me.

Sitting down at my computer, I went online and purchased two tickets. If Logan was unable to attend, I'd give the second ticket to either Jenna or my daughter. Tori had been attending the ballet with me since she was five years old. I'd taken her to the holiday performance of *The Nutcracker* and she'd loved it. Now it was tradition; we made a point of going every Christmas.

I wanted Logan to experience it. Excitedly, I decided to send him a text message.

I have a surprise for you once you return.

It didn't take long for him to respond.

What would that be?

You'll have to wait. You're going to like it.

Maureen, are you asking me out on a date?

I am.

I like surprises.

Good. Do you own a tie?

A tie? Maybe.

A nice sweater will do. No work boots.

Where are you taking me?

You'll find out soon enough.

I hadn't felt this much anticipation in a long time. Logan was about to get a lesson in culture that he wouldn't soon forget.

Chapter 22

Jenna

It was the end of my twelve-hour shift and I was tired and eager to get home to soak away the day in a tub of overly hot water. I hadn't talked to Rowan in a couple days. He was busy; I was busy, too. We wanted to keep our relationship away from the hospital staff and the inevitable gossip as much as possible.

With my purse slung over my shoulder, I was heading toward the hospital exit when I heard someone call my name.

"Jenna. Jenna Boltz."

I turned to find Rowan's nurse, Katie. She speed-walked the last few feet to reach me and arrived breathless. Her face was pale, and she looked like she was about to burst into tears.

"Thank God I caught you," she said, placing her hand over her heart as though to calm it.

"What's wrong?" The panic in her voice startled me.

"It's Dr. Lancaster . . . I don't know what to do."

"What's happened?" My heart started to race. A dozen alarming scenarios went through my mind.

"He needs . . . he needs someone. Can you come?"

"Of course. What's happened?"

"Hurry."

Katie's response confused and worried me even more. Doubts rushed at me like pesky mosquitoes. Fears, too. Had he been hurt? Had there been an accident? She didn't respond to my questions as I followed her.

"Please tell me what's going on, Katie," I pleaded a second time.

"Dr. Lancaster was operating on the severely broken leg of a nine-year-old boy who unexpectedly went into cardiac arrest." She paused, tears filling her eyes. "He did everything humanly possible to save him, but it was too late. Oh Jenna. He lost it, right in the operating room. Somehow he composed himself before he went to tell the family. He's terribly upset—he needs you."

"Oh no." My heart ached for the parents and for Rowan. "Where is he?"

She exhaled. "I'm not sure . . . I didn't see him after he spoke with the parents, but I think he might be in his office."

She led the way through the narrow hallway to the physicians' row of offices. Rowan's door was closed. I could hear what sounded like books slamming against the wall. My eyes widened, and I looked to Katie for assurance that my being there was the right thing.

Dealing with death, especially that of a child, was never

easy. Each medical professional learns to handle the loss of a patient in his or her own way. Working in the intensive care unit, I'd grown more accustomed to it than others. Obviously, I didn't like to lose a patient. None of us did. But death happened, and it was a reality in our line of work. With some patients, death would come like a thief, quick and unexpected. With others, it would come as a friend, especially to those with lingering illnesses who had long since accepted and welcomed the end of their suffering. Yet others struggled to hold on, fighting it to the end, refusing to let go. Over the years, dealing with death had become a natural part of my duties as an ICU nurse: If there was no chance of recovery, I saw it as part of my job to help my patients and their families make the transition from life to death.

"Has he experienced this before?" I asked Katie.

She shook her head. "No. I've never seen him lose a patient. The boy apparently had a heart defect that no one was aware of. I didn't know what to do to help Dr. Lancaster afterward, until I thought of you."

I wanted to ask why she had sought me out. I'd assumed none of the staff was aware Rowan and I were seeing each other. We hadn't been as stealthy as we'd thought, or Katie was intuitive.

Tears gathered in her eyes. "Dr. Lancaster likes you. He trusts you, and I thought . . . I hoped you might be able to help him through this. Please," she whispered, pleading with me, her eyes bright with tears.

Uncertain of what I could do to help, I knocked on his office door. Unwilling to wait for an answer, I opened it and tentatively stepped inside. Every textbook from the shelf was on the floor; the framed degrees on his wall were askew.

Rowan stood in the middle of the room, his shoulders heaving with exertion. When he saw me, he glared with a fierce frown. "Now isn't a good time, Jenna."

"So it seems," I said calmly, and pointedly looked at the mess of large textbooks littering the floor.

"What are you doing here?" he demanded, shoving his fingers through his hair with such force it was a wonder he didn't uproot a handful.

"I came to see you," I explained.

"Another time. Please."

"In a minute," I said, tiptoeing through the books until I reached him.

He glared at me, his eyes full of agony. I ignored the lack of welcome. Not knowing how else to comfort him, I moved closer and placed my hands around his middle and hugged him. For several uncomfortable seconds he remained frozen, his arms hanging lifelessly at his sides with his fists clenched. I might as well have been holding on to a mannequin. He was stiff and angry, furious with God and mad at the world.

About the time I was ready to give up and grant him the privacy he wanted, a deep shudder went through him, raking his body from head to toe. With a loud groan, his arms came around me. He held me so tightly against him that for a moment I was unable to breathe. I must have made a small protesting sound, because his hold immediately loosened.

He inhaled sharply and buried his face in my shoulder. It felt as if he never intended to let me go.

After what seemed like several minutes, he finally spoke. "He shouldn't have died."

I pressed my hand to the back of his head, offering what comfort I could. "You aren't the one who gets to decide who lives and dies."

"His parents are devastated," he said, choking out the words.

Rowan had been the one to tell them they would need to bury their son. That was by far the hardest job any surgeon faced. Drawing in a deep breath, Rowan released me and held me at arm's length as he looked deep into my eyes, seeking answers. I had none to give him. No reassurance. No words of wisdom. Nothing.

"How'd you find out?"

Katie remained on the outside of the open door, looking uncertain. When I didn't answer, he answered for me.

"Katie?"

The young nurse, who'd been waiting in the hallway, entered the trashed office. "I hope you don't mind, Dr. Lancaster. I . . . I didn't know what else to do. I thought Jenna might be able to help."

He frowned at her disapprovingly. "We'll discuss this later."

"Please don't be upset with me." Her lower lip trembled.

"It's fine, Katie," I said, answering for him. "I'm grateful you came for me." I could see that she'd be crushed if he admonished her. My eyes searched out Rowan's, silently pleading with him not to fault his staunchest advocate.

"We'll talk tomorrow," Rowan told the nurse.

Katie's eyes lowered, and she left.

Reaching for his hand, I held it in both of my own. "I think we could both use a cup of coffee."

"I'm more in the mood for a shot of whiskey."

"I don't think the cafeteria carries that," I said. Bending down, I picked up a bulky textbook and placed it back on the shelf.

Bending over, he picked up several volumes and returned them to their proper place. Working together silently, it didn't take us long to clear the floor and put the office in order again.

When we finished, he turned away so that I could no longer see his face. "You can go, Jenna."

I stiffened before I realized why he wanted me gone. No man wanted to be thought of as weak, and I'd seen Rowan at a low point. "But I thought we'd go for coffee."

"I appreciate what you're doing, but it'd be best if . . ."

Prompted by instinct, I acted impulsively and stepped in front of him. I knew if Rowan saw my face, he wouldn't want me to leave. At the same time, I sensed it was his anguish speaking, asking me to leave. I knew nothing I did would take away the pain of losing that child and having to tell the boy's family. Yet I felt I had to do something, something more than a hug and helping him put the textbooks back on the shelves.

I grabbed hold of him and jerked him toward me. Then I planted my hands on either side of his face and locked my lips on his.

I kissed him.

I kissed Rowan as if it was the end of the world and this was my last act on earth.

He was startled, and at first resisted. I wouldn't allow it, dominating him, giving him everything I could in that kiss. When we finally broke apart, a shocked silence followed. I was about to release him when he brought me back into his arms, took hold of my face, angled his mouth to mine, and kissed me in return. His kiss was by far gentler than mine had been, his lips roving leisurely over mine, encouraging me to respond, and I did, in ways I never had with any other man. My hands slid up and over his shoulders; my fingers wove into the short hairs at the base of his neck. We kissed with the intensity that life and death bring.

By the time we separated, we were both breathless, our shoulders heaving as we tried to breathe normally again.

Neither of us spoke. We stared at each other, and I was convinced we didn't know what to say.

Finally, I managed to stammer out, "I . . . probably should be going."

Looking as confused as I felt, he nodded. I went to move away when he caught my hand and entwined our fingers. "No," he whispered, clearing his throat.

"No?"

"No," he repeated. "Stay a while longer, Jenna. You mentioned coffee."

"You want coffee now?" I'd been the one to suggest it, but only as a means of distracting him.

"No, I want you."

His words rattled me, and I took a small step back, my

hand automatically going to my heart and staying there. It was a protective action. Everything was happening too fast, like the speed of light. To this point, I'd dated cautiously, carefully. Everything had changed with Rowan and I had yet to catch my mind up to my heart, to think this through.

"Does that shock you?" he asked, reading my hesitation. "It shouldn't."

"I . . . I don't know. I need time."

He smiled softly and then nodded. "I'm not going anywhere."

"I'm leaving now." Taking small steps, I continued to back out the door. That was when I realized the door to his office had remained wide open. Anyone walking by would have been able to see inside, to see us kiss—our lips and bodies locked as if there was no tomorrow. This was the very thing we'd tried to avoid.

The hospital gossipmongers were going to have a field day, passing this information around. It was sure to move faster than any virus.

Once I was out of his office, I hurried to the parking garage as if to outdistance the questions filling my head. I was grateful Rowan didn't try to stop me. As soon as I was in my car, I fumbled inside my purse for my phone to call Maureen. If ever I needed a friend, it was now. When I was confused and unsure, Maureen was my go-to person. She'd talked me off more cliffs than anyone.

"*Bonjour*," she greeted me cheerfully when she answered, reminding me of our Paris plans.

"Rowan wants me," I blurted out, not stopping to return her greeting in French or otherwise.

"Green light!" she cried triumphantly. "What's wrong? You don't sound happy."

"I am . . . I think."

"He's a green light, and if you're honest with yourself, Jenna—how many of those have you had of late?"

The montage of men I'd dated since my divorce had all proven to be disappointments. It took longer to recognize some than others. In the end, I was left with one letdown after another.

I felt close to the precipice, closer than I'd been in all the years since Kyle, ready to fall in love and yet . . . afraid, so very afraid. I'd been here before and knew the dangers. I was convinced there was something I didn't see, didn't know, that would hit me in the face and knock me out cold.

"Jenna, talk to me," Maureen said, cutting into my thoughts.

In that moment, I knew what had caused me to flee from Rowan as if the hounds of hell were in pursuit. "I'm afraid, Maureen."

"Of being loved and wanted?"

"No." It wasn't that. "No, of being disappointed yet again. He's too good, too perfect. He calls me Sunshine, and when he kisses me, I forget everything, including my name."

"Jenna, stop. You're beginning to sound like me."

"There's a phrase my dad used to say. Something about waiting for the other shoe to drop, which never made any sense to me, but it does now." Although I wasn't quite sure what any of this had to do with shoes dropping.

"Take a deep breath," Maureen advised.

I did as she suggested and held it as long as I could before releasing it. If this was supposed to offer me confidence, it failed.

"Now what?" I asked.

"Take one day at a time. Go slow. Adjust your expectations and give yourself permission to fall in love."

My dearest friend sounded sensible and wise. I started the car and the engine came to life. I backed out of my assigned parking spot.

"Can you do that?" Maureen asked.

"I'll give it my best." I tried to sound confident, but I was wary. Life had taught me to move forward cautiously. I wouldn't give my heart away again. I'd done it before and been disappointed too many times.

Chapter 23

Jenna

Mom was doing so well. I left work early on Halloween to help her pass out treats to the neighborhood kids. She'd been home for only three weeks, and, thankfully, her independent spirit was kicking in again. The entire incident with her hip and the subsequent surgery and recovery process had helped her to move past the lingering grief she'd had since losing my dad. She was back to her old self, spending time with her bridge friends and with Mrs. Torres, and spoiling her cat.

Her seventy-fifth birthday was coming up, and after everything she'd endured, Tom and I decided to throw her a birthday party.

"What do you think, Mom?" I asked, after presenting her with the idea.

"A party sounds great. That way, I can thank all the people who were so wonderful before and after my accident."

That was my mother. The party's intent was to honor her,

yet she wanted to use it as a chance to thank those who had helped her through the accident and her recovery.

"I'll see if Paul can get home for the weekend," I said, adding my son's name to the top of the invitation list. Mom was a wonderful grandmother. Since they'd left for college, she took time each week to connect with each grandchild, with either a phone call or little notes of encouragement she'd drop in the mail with Starbucks gift cards.

"Seeing Paul would be lovely. I enjoyed Allie's visits while I was at Parkview. She brought that friend of hers, too."

"Wyatt?"

"No, it was a girl. I think her name was Mallory. No," she said, correcting herself. "It's Mackensie."

Allie and Mackensie were as thick as thieves these days. I was grateful my daughter had found a good friend. Back in the day, it'd been the same with Maureen and me. Our friendship had lasted through the years. That didn't mean it would be this way with Allie and Mackensie. Friends, like much else in life, sometimes come in seasons.

Things were looking better with Allie these days. She seemed to be settling into college life after those bumpy first weeks, which made me happy.

I was hearing less and less from Paul, though, and I missed our talks. I suspected that he worked far too many hours, and I worried that he wouldn't be able to keep up with his studies. He'd been warned by his adviser about the intensity of the engineering courses.

My mom continued to chat away as the doorbell rang with another trick-or-treater. I handed out the candy and then returned to better listen to Mom as she continued to chat. With no one in the house to talk to on a regular basis, when she got the opportunity, she thoroughly enjoyed the chance to share.

"Paul has been good to me, too," she continued. "Did you know he called me at least three times a week to check on me? I know he wanted to come visit, and he would have, if not for his job and his studies." Mom's eyes glowed with pride. "He's an exceptional young man, you know. Young adults these days aren't nearly as responsible as my generation."

I was glad to hear that Paul had set aside time to call his grandmother, even though he didn't seem to have as much time for me.

"Oh, and be sure to invite Rowan," Mom said, cutting into my musings about Paul.

Rowan. My mind wandered off at his name. Because he'd been away at a medical conference, I hadn't seen him in nearly two weeks.

I heard he'd attended the services for the young boy who'd died on the operating table. In retrospect, I wished I'd gone with him. I would have, had he asked me, but he hadn't. I didn't hear anything about the service until it had come and gone.

As I'd suspected, the gossip about us had spread faster than a California brushfire. I'd walk down the hall and hear the whispers. As soon as I came into view there would be silence until I passed, then the voices would pick up again. A couple of the nurses in my unit had asked me this past week if Rowan and I were dating.

"He's hot," Penny had expressed to me with an envious look. She'd cornered me in the cafeteria during my dinner break and I had no escape.

"We've gone out a couple times," I'd answered, uncomfortable talking about our relationship with anyone besides Maureen.

"This is a first for him, you know . . . dating someone from the hospital."

"I wouldn't know," I said, eager to change the subject. I pushed aside my half-eaten Subway sandwich, stood, and excused myself.

"Jenna," my mother said. "You look like you're a million miles away."

I shook my head, hoping to scatter the questions buzzing around in it. "What were you saying?" I asked.

"We're making up the guest list for my birthday party."

"Right." The doorbell chimed, and I quickly distributed candy to another host of neighborhood children. While I was up, I grabbed a notebook and pen and returned to Mom's side.

"Be sure and put Dolores on the list."

I wrote down Mrs. Torres's name.

Mom went on to list the names of several of the staff from Parkview who'd helped in her recovery. I was still writing down their names when the doorbell alerted me to more trick-or-treaters.

I answered the call to duty, praising the little boy who'd dressed up like Colonel Sanders holding a KFC bucket half filled with assorted sweets. People were incredibly clever with their children's costumes. The most creative I got with Paul was a Superman costume, when he wore his swimsuit over a pair of his sister's tights and a red cape.

When I returned to the pen and pad, Mom had thought of several other names. "The physical therapist. Oh dear, I don't remember her full name now. You'll need to ask Rich Gardner for it. Be sure to put his name on the list, too. He's such a kind man."

I might have misjudged Rich Gardner, but I didn't think so.

"Did you write down his name, Jenna?"

"I got it. Anyone else? What about your friends from church?"

"That would be lovely," she said. "I wanted to ask them but wasn't sure how many we should invite. I'd like to have the party at the house, mind you, and not rent out the convention center."

I smiled. "Okay, I'll get the invitations ready." I'd order the cake and see about a few decorations as well, knowing it would be easier for me than Tom, as he lived out of state. It pleased me to be able to honor my mother on this special birthday.

"Be sure to mention that I don't want or need any gifts." Mom was adamant. "At my age, I have everything I need."

"Will do." I tucked the notebook with the names of the invitees back into my purse. Thirty minutes passed without the doorbell ringing. I turned off the porch light and left for home soon afterward.

*

The text message from Rowan asked me to meet him in the hospital cafeteria for my dinner break. Why not? Keeping our relationship under the radar at the hospital was a lost cause. Seeing us together wasn't going to surprise anyone. Since Rowan had been away our communication had been limited to a few text messages. It was good to know he was back. I'd missed him far more than I thought I would or should.

The first person I saw when I entered the cafeteria was Rowan. He sat at one of the tables with his phone, glaring at the screen. He didn't notice me at first and rubbed his hand down his face, as though confounded. When he glanced up and saw me, the tightness around his mouth and jaw relaxed and he smiled. Seeing him certainly did my heart a world of good.

For one irrationally long moment we stared at each other, neither one of us able to look away. My heart raced like I was in the last mile of the Boston Marathon.

"Jenna," he said softly. He looked exhausted.

"When did you get back?" I asked, setting my tray down on the table across from him and taking a seat.

"Late last night."

His texts had been brief and harried and written between lectures and often late at night.

"I would have phoned . . ."

Stretching my arm across the table, I took hold of his hand. "It's all right, I understand."

"I'm glad. I thought about you. Missed you."

His words pleased me. "I thought about you, too."

His phone hummed, indicating he had a text. He glanced down, read the message, and frowned.

"Is everything okay? You look upset." My question hung in the air like an overinflated balloon, as if he were debating how best to answer.

"It's nothing," he said. "My daughter is asking me to buy her a new car, which is ridiculous, seeing that she has a perfectly good one now."

"Kids," I said, grateful it wasn't anything as traumatic as another death. "Did I mention Allie got a tattoo a while back?"

"A tattoo of what?"

"An arrow. She claims she's headed in a new direction, whatever that means."

Rowan grinned, something he didn't do nearly as often as he should. A simple upward movement of his mouth worked wonders with his appearance. I'd always viewed his features as sharp, angular. Everything about him softened when he smiled. His eyes brightened, and there was a vulnerability, an openness, in him that I'd viewed at rare times.

Reaching for my hand, he squeezed my fingers. "How about a play? *Come from Away* is playing at the Fifth Avenue Theater. I understand it's a marvelous production. Could I interest you in an evening at the theater?"

"I'd like that."

Rowan quickly checked online for tickets, then we agreed to the day and time. "I'll look forward to this Saturday."

"Me, too."

My phone dinged, indicating a text message. It was from Allie.

I'm bringing Wyatt over to the house. Thought u should know, seeing how you freaked out the last time I brought a friend home.

I didn't freak out.

Whatever.

I wasn't going to argue, especially over the phone with text messages.

Thanks for giving me a heads-up.

Later

Rowan and I enjoyed our break. It was hard to return to work, and I knew it was for him, too.

The lights were on at the house when I arrived home, which meant Allie was still there. As soon as I opened the garage door and parked the car, Allie appeared in the doorway to the house, her arms akimbo. She glared at me with narrowed, intense eyes. Her face was full of accusation.

"Hello to you, too," I said as I climbed out of the car. The look she wore was familiar.

She moved aside when I approached the doorway. Stacks of clean laundry were neatly folded atop the dryer. The clothes didn't belong to my daughter. They were men's jeans and shirts. It didn't take long to put two and two together.

"You're doing Wyatt's laundry?"

"Yes. He gives me rides. It's the least I can do."

I set my purse down. "Is something wrong?" I said, trying to quickly address whatever was bothering her, rather than let it brew.

"Yes. I'm upset," she said, raising her voice a half-octave. "I gave Wyatt a tour of the house."

This was said as if I should be keenly aware of some outrageous deed on my part, although I couldn't imagine what it was that had produced such ire.

"And?"

"And, I went into my room," she said, her outrage growing with every word. "MY. ROOM," she repeated, enunciating each word slowly and harshly.

"And the problem is?"

"Mom!" she cried, tears cresting in her eyes, ready to fall down her cheeks. "Your clothes are in my closet."

So that's what this was all about. "Allie, my summer clothes are in your closet."

"But that's *my* room."

"I know, but you aren't using your room right now, and your closet was practically empty." Allie had carted nearly everything she owned to her dorm room. My closet had been bursting with four full seasons of clothes. It had made perfect sense to me to use that empty space in her closet, so I could store my spring and summer outfits away from the fall and winter clothes I was currently wearing.

Allie was having none of it. "You can't put your things there. That's an invasion of my privacy."

Now didn't seem to be the time to reason with her. "In other words," I said, remaining calm, "you want me to move whatever is mine back to my room."

"Yes," she cried, as if that was understood.

"Even though you're not living at home and will be in Japan for six months starting with the spring quarter?"

"Yes." The girl had a look that would cut through rock. "Don't you see how wrong this is?"

Frankly, I didn't. However, arguing wasn't going to help. Seeing how upset this made her, I decided to wait until she was in a calmer frame of mind and readdress the subject then. Okay, I'd admit I should have discussed using part of Allie's closet for my things. In retrospect, I probably should have stored my clothes in Paul's room, not Allie's.

"Furthermore"—she wasn't finished yet—"does Paul know what you've done to *his* room?"

It'd been a year since Paul had last lived at home for any extended period. This last summer he'd been home for a grand total of five days. He'd worked forty-plus hours a week at the restaurant. Almost everything remained exactly as he'd left it. His rock-band posters remained on the walls. His sports trophies were on the shelf, along with a variety of other awards. My son didn't need his bedroom to become a memorial.

"Do you mean the easel and painting I'm working on in there?" I hadn't signed up for the art classes the way I'd wanted to. Growing impatient, I'd decided to paint and was working on a field of wildflowers.

"Exactly. How could you, Mom? It's . . . It's like you don't want Paul or me in your life any longer."

"Don't be ridiculous."

"I'm not. That's just the way I feel."

Allie was feeling rejected and insecure.

"This is your home and will be for as long as I live here," I assured her. "And if I move, then that house will be yours, too. You will always be welcome, no matter where I live."

Allie sniffled.

"And I'll always be your mom. Nothing will ever change that."

"You got new dishes and towels, and you're using our rooms. It's a lot to take in, you know?"

"I know," I said softly, and held my arms open for a hug. My daughter came to me and we hugged each other close.

A horn sounded from the driveway.

"That's Wyatt," she said, and broke away from me. "He went to get us a pizza. I've got to go."

"Okay," I said, releasing her. I watched as she loaded up the clean clothes into a laundry basket and headed out the door to Wyatt's car.

The house was still and silent after she left. After twelve hours on my feet and the emotional confrontation with Allie, I needed nothing more than time to myself. Returning to my room, I ran the bath water and while I waited for the tub to fill, I curled up on the padded bench that looked out over Puget Sound. After taking in several deep breaths, I let the view calm me.

My window on the bay.

Chapter 24

Maureen

I checked the address that Logan had given me on my car's navigation. He'd invited me to dinner at his house in West Seattle, and now, as I pulled into his neighborhood, I had a major attack of butterflies. My hands went to my stomach, hoping to hold my nerves at bay. This invitation was important. I hoped it would give me a window into his world, as I knew only a little about him. He recently mentioned that he had a son and daughter, both living in this area with their families.

The plans were all in place for us to attend *Swan Lake*, performed by the New York City Ballet. I couldn't wait. I hadn't told Logan exactly what I'd had in mind, only that it was a surprise. All he knew was that he had to wear business casual. I knew he was apprehensive, but I wasn't overly worried. I'd been in unfamiliar territory myself at the football game, and I did just fine.

Logan's home looked like it'd been built in the early 1960s. It had two dormers jutting out from the roofline, and steps led up to the front porch between two brick columns. The lawn was carefully maintained and there were purple cabbage plants in planters decorating either side of the small porch. That he'd kept the house and yard up so well showed pride of ownership.

I'd never had a man cook me dinner, and the invitation had made me anxious, which was why I'd needed some bolstering from Jenna and Tori before the date. They'd enthusiastically encouraged me to go. Unsure of the protocol, I brought a bouquet of autumn flowers with me.

Straightening myself, I squared my shoulders and walked up the concrete walkway to the house.

After I rang the doorbell, I stepped back and waited. When the door opened, a young woman answered with an apron tied around her waist. I blinked, afraid I'd arrived at a stranger's house.

Before I could apologize, the woman recognized my confusion and broke into a huge smile. "You must be Maureen."

Too stunned to speak, I nodded. I was expecting Logan to answer, not someone I didn't know.

"I'm Misty." She held open the screen door for me. "Dad's on the back patio getting your steaks ready to grill. He asked me to watch for you and let him know when you arrived. Come inside. This is my chance to drill you with questions before I let Dad know you're here."

The comment would have alarmed me if not for her huge

welcoming smile. He hadn't said anything about his daughter joining us. Coming into the house, I was greeted by a warm fire in the brick fireplace. The mantel had framed photographs spread across the top of it.

"You don't say much, do you?" Misty cheerfully noted.

"Sorry." I didn't know what to say, thrusting out the bouquet of yellow and brown chrysanthemums tied with an orange ribbon to Misty. The arrangement looked manly enough for Logan to enjoy them.

"Dad has talked about you so often that I feel like I already know you. But I actually don't, so this is the perfect time to ask you a few questions." She smiled again. "I hope you don't mind."

"I'm glad to meet you, Misty . . . and sure, ask away." I silently wondered what it was that I was agreeing to.

"My real name is Melissa, but I got tagged with Misty as a kid."

"I go by Maureen, but your dad sometimes calls me Marian." It'd irritated me in the beginning, but not so much now that I was familiar with his sense of humor, and it was with fondness that he used it these days.

I slipped off my coat, which she took and hung in the hall closet. I followed Misty into the kitchen and watched while she put the flowers in a vase. "Dad was nervous about this dinner and asked me to help. I hope you like brussels sprouts. I roasted some of those to go along with the steak and baked potatoes Dad's preparing."

"I do like them. You didn't need to go to all that trouble."

"It wasn't any trouble. Besides, I was anxious to meet you."

She opened the oven to check the potatoes. "They're perfect," she said, and turned it off.

Looking out the kitchen window, I saw Logan diligently standing in front of the barbecue.

"Come sit down. Dad will be in any minute now."

We parked ourselves in the living room on the chairs next to the fireplace. I could see the family resemblance. Misty had the same tilt of her mouth as her dad had. Over the last weekend I'd paid a lot of attention to Logan's lips. I enjoyed his kisses.

"I have a brother, Matt. We're both married, two kids each. We all live within blocks of each other. You're the first woman Dad has invited to the house since my mother left him. Just so you know, he's never mentioned any other woman to us besides you. I do have one big question, though."

I took a big gulp in anticipation of the question but nodded, indicating she should ask away.

"Do you mind telling me what happened that Friday night a few weeks back? He was pretty upset and said he'd made a big mistake with you."

I didn't want to rehash that night at the sports bar. "It's a long story to squeeze into a few short minutes."

"I guess that means you'd rather not discuss it?"

"You'd mentioned we only have a short while before your dad finishes with the steaks."

"Right." Misty tilted her head to one side. "You're not at all like what I imagined."

I suspected I might be a disappointment to her. "How did your dad describe me?" It might not have been a good idea to ask, but I couldn't help being curious.

"He didn't tell me much about your looks. Dad's not hung up on appearances. You're petite, which surprises me. And pretty. He likes you, and that's saying something when it comes to my dad. He's been alone for a long time now. My brother and I were convinced that he intended to stay that way. Do you mind sharing with me how you met my dad?"

"At the library. I'm a librarian." That was an easy question to answer.

"Dad didn't tell me that."

I would have assumed Logan would have explained at least that much to his daughter. "He came in on his lunch break one Monday and asked me to suggest a good book. That's how we began talking. In the beginning, he came in once a week, almost always on a Monday, and he'd have a few comments about what he'd read from the book I'd recommended. After a while, he began to show up more frequently throughout the week, and then he asked me out and I . . . went."

"Cool," she said. "Dad has always been a reader."

"I am, too."

"That makes sense seeing that you're a librarian. He told me you were levelheaded and that you had strong feelings about certain subjects."

That was an accurate description of me. I heard the sliding door off the kitchen open.

"Misty?" Logan called.

"In here."

Logan appeared and paused when he saw me. A big smile lit up his eyes, making them sparkle. "Hey." He turned his attention to his daughter. "You should have let me know Maureen was here."

"No way," Misty said cheerfully. "And miss the opportunity to interrogate her?"

An instant look of concern marred his face. "Thanks for the help," he told his daughter. "I'll take it from here."

Misty shared a knowing smile with me. "I believe I've been told that my company is no longer needed, and not in the friendliest of terms," she said in a stage whisper. She was grinning, and I could see she hadn't taken offense. She disappeared into the other room and returned with her coat.

"Have fun, you two. Great getting to know you, Maureen. Here's my number in case you ever want to chat. I'll connect with you later, Dad."

"Glad we had a chance to meet, Misty."

"Bye, sweetheart." Logan walked her to the front door and kissed her cheek before she left, thanking her for her help.

Once the door was closed, he turned to me. "It's good to see you. I apologize if Misty made you uncomfortable."

"Really, it's fine. She loves you and is curious about me. That's only natural."

And it was fine. I liked meeting one of his children, and I'd been enjoying getting to know him better. This past Sunday, Logan had come to the house to watch the Seahawks away game. I'd popped popcorn, set out a bowl of nuts, and made a plate of cheese, crackers, and sliced meats, as well as a veggie tray. He'd brought beer. We'd sat close together on my sofa and he'd looped his arm around my shoulders, resting his ankles on my coffee table as we watched the game together. Unfortunately, the Seahawks had lost. I discovered that Logan was a "Monday-morning quarterback," a term I hadn't heard before but which he explained to me. He analyzed the game, the plays, and the mistakes, disgruntled by their performance and the loss.

"What did my daughter have to say?"

"Not much."

He laughed. "I know my daughter. Did she grill you with questions?"

"A few. She said I was the first woman you'd invited to the house since your divorce. I took it as a compliment. I take it as one now."

"Did she say anything else that might come back and bite me?"

"No . . . only that she and your son had assumed you'd given up on dating."

"I had," he said, "until I met you." He disappeared into the kitchen, as if this was more than he'd wanted to admit.

I followed behind him. The table was set, something I hadn't noticed earlier. Two grilled steaks were sitting on a platter in the middle. He opened the oven and, using a pot holder, brought out the aluminum foil–wrapped baked potatoes and the brussels sprouts.

"Anything I can do?"

"There's a salad in the refrigerator. Dressing is in the door."

I opened the fridge and brought out the salad bowl and the dressing and set those on the table beside the steaks. Once everything was out, we sat down.

On an earlier phone call, Logan had asked me how I liked my steak. It was cooked to perfection. "This is delicious," I assured him after my first bite. There was more food here than I could possibly eat. After all the trouble Logan had gone to to make this meal special, I'd do my best to enjoy as much as my stomach could handle.

"I can grill a great steak and a mean rack of ribs, but this is a forewarning: That's the extent of my repertoire."

"That suits me just fine."

He attacked his dinner, enjoying his food. "I was afraid I'd mess up everything else, which is why I asked Misty for help."

I took another bite.

"It was a mistake to ask her. I should have known she'd turn it into a reason to cross-examine you."

"Stop. I truly enjoyed meeting her." In fact, I had been thinking that it was time I introduced him to Tori and her husband. Logan and I were getting more serious, and it all seemed to be happening at a fast clip. I could understand why Jenna had felt the need to slow things down with Rowan. I probably should have done the same but couldn't bring myself to do it.

"Misty's going to be bugging me now, wanting to know every tiny detail of what's happened between you and me. I like to keep some things to myself, you know?"

I understood. Tori knew that I'd gone out with Logan a few times, but that was all. I hadn't mentioned that he'd come to the house last Sunday for the game.

"Dinner was wonderful, Logan," I said, after I'd eaten all I could.

"Thanks."

"What prompted you to invite me?" I asked. It was a dangerous question, seeing that our relationship remained undefined. We were both on foreign soil, unfamiliar with how this would play out.

He picked up his plate and carried it to the sink and set it inside. His back was to me, as if he didn't want me to read his expression.

"I wanted to let you know how much you mean to me, and this was the only way I could think of doing that."

Sucking in a small breath, I tried to calm my heart down, certain it was about to pound straight out of my chest.

"While I was working in Moses Lake, I couldn't believe how much I missed you," he continued. "It's not like I see or speak to you every day while I'm here, but at the game . . . at the Seahawks game when we kissed that first time . . ."

"Yes?" I prompted in a whisper, which was all my vocal cords would allow. He still had his back to me, as though speaking to the window above the sink.

"Maureen, that kiss was great. Special . . . I don't know how else to describe it. I felt this connection with you, this excitement and happiness that I haven't experienced in so long that I hardly knew how to react."

The kiss also had a powerful impact on me. We'd kissed again last Sunday before he'd left my house, but nothing would ever match that first kiss we'd shared at the football game.

"It was hard for me, too, while you were working out of town." Admitting this didn't come easy. I felt like I was opening myself up and exposing places in my heart that I'd kept under wraps for years.

He turned around, his gaze holding mine prisoner. "This dinner tonight." He hesitated, as if he was unsure he should say more.

"Yes?"

"It's my way of telling you that I'm glad to have met you, that you're important to me. The truth is, I don't know where this relationship is going. The last time I was on a date, I was in my early twenties. Things sure have changed."

"They have," I agreed.

"I guess what I'm trying to say is that wherever this is taking us, I'm along for the ride."

Logan wasn't a smooth-talking man with a lot of romantic words. This was probably about as romantic as he got. It was enough for me.

More than enough.

Chapter 25

Jenna

Rowan and I had been spending a lot of time together, making up for when he'd been away. Following the play, we next decided to take an afternoon to wander through Pike Place Market. We'd stopped at the fish market and watched the vendor toss a hefty king salmon ten feet across a display of seafood bedded on crushed ice, much to the delight of the crowd that had gathered around the booth. Although it was early November, the tourists continued to flock to the market.

Our plan was to purchase our dinner and cook it ourselves at my home, rather than eat out. We picked up a fresh Dungeness crab, along with a nice wine, corn on the cob, some lemons, bay leaves, and a crab-boil spice mix, as well as ingredients for a salad, a variety of fresh vegetables: small bell peppers, jícama, radishes, green onions, lettuce, and cherry tomatoes.

Afterward, we stood in line for a latte at the original

Starbucks directly across the street from the market. The day had been cloudy with breaks of sunshine, a picture-perfect early November afternoon. I wrapped a wool scarf around my neck and was grateful I had on a warm sweater under my raincoat. Mom had knit me that red scarf for Christmas one year, and it was one of my favorites.

I enjoyed Rowan's company. He was beginning to open up to me, becoming freer about the details of his life. Getting him to talk about himself was a slow process, like peeling layers off an artichoke, looking to find the best part in the center. Eventually, he'd trust me enough to reveal his heart. I was patient.

This afternoon had been wonderful. We'd laughed and joked. I found him to be good company, entertaining me with his dry wit. I linked my arm around his elbow and couldn't remember a day when I'd been happier.

Quite simply, Rowan was the epitome of what I'd been looking for in a man and a relationship. He was the green light I'd been waiting to find all these years. Since my divorce, I'd stayed away from men in the medical profession, and I realized now how foolish I'd been.

After our lattes, we drove to my home. I knew I'd be most comfortable cooking in my own kitchen. Rowan opened the wine bottle and poured us each a glass while I unpacked the crab and the other foodstuffs.

He tied an apron around his waist and searched until he found a cutting board and a big bowl for our salad. Rowan worked on assembling the salad while I put a large stockpot filled with water on the stove to boil the crab.

Rowan continued to work with his back to me. "I can't

remember a day I've enjoyed more," he said, chopping up the jícama.

"I can't, either." I reached for my glass of sauvignon blanc and took the first sip. It was chilled perfectly and delicious. "You know a lot about wine, don't you?" I'd been impressed with the questions he'd asked the proprietor in the wine shop.

"A little. I enjoy wine."

I did, too, and every so often had a glass before bed to help me sleep. Mostly I drank red wine, but after listening to Rowan discuss the different varietals of white wine, I was willing to venture out and sample more of the whites, especially the ones Rowan had recommended. The bottle he'd bought was a Washington State wine from Yakima Valley, where my parents were raised. My first sip told me it was an excellent wine.

A ding rang on my phone, and I saw that it was Allie.

You home?

I dried my hands on a dish towel, excused myself, and answered.

Yup. Need anything?
I'm coming by for my black boots. Mackensie is bringing me.
Stop on by. I have company.
The same guy you were making out with earlier?

I rolled my eyes and answered.

Yup.

Setting aside my phone, I looked at Rowan. "Allie is stopping by with a friend later."

Rowan nodded and continued to work on chopping the vegetables for the salad.

He'd rarely mentioned anything about his own daughter. Well, other than recently, when he'd told me about her asking for a new vehicle. I didn't remember him saying anything about a resolution.

"Did everything turn out all right with your daughter's request for a new car?"

He shrugged. "There wasn't much to discuss. She has a perfectly good vehicle. End of story."

"What is it with kids?" I asked rhetorically.

"Allie giving you problems?" He turned to face me.

I shrugged, unsure of how to answer. "Yes and no. She freaked out recently over me putting a few of my clothes in her closet. It was thoughtless of me, I suppose. Allie never hesitates to let me know what's on her mind. I wish that was the same case with my son."

"What's going on with Paul?" Rowan asked.

It impressed me that he remembered my son's name. In retrospect, I realized I'd talked a great deal about my two children and knew next to nothing about his daughter.

Rowan looked expectantly toward me, and I saw that he was waiting for me to answer his question about Paul.

"That's just it. I don't know what's going on with him. I rarely hear from Paul. It used to be that he called at least once or twice a week. Now it seems I'm lucky if I hear from him once or twice a month. We've always had a good relationship. Something is going on with him, but I don't know what."

Now that I'd started talking about Paul, more concerns bobbed to the surface. "I feel like he's hiding from me." Keeping secrets wasn't like my son, which led me to believe that whatever it was could be serious. When we talked about his classes, his responses were vague. A couple times he'd abruptly changed the subject. I was afraid he was working too many hours and his grades had slipped. He'd always maintained a high grade point average, so I didn't feel the need to complain or to demand that he quit and concentrate on his studies.

Rowan asked the logical question. "Have you asked him about it?"

I shook my head. "I haven't, but I know I should. I've been close to my children their entire lives. Paul has always been mature for his age. After Kyle and I split, he became the man of the house. He took out the garbage, changed the burned-out lightbulbs, and when something needed to be repaired, he worked with my dad to see that it was done. And he always looked out for his little sister. They are tight."

"Could there be a girl in his life?" Rowan asked. "That might explain the lack of contact. She could be taking up all his free time."

That was a logical guess. "If so, he hasn't mentioned her. Most of our conversations lately have centered on his job. He works in a restaurant and seems to enjoy it. I'm worried that it's interfering with his studies, but he's assured me it hasn't."

"He sounds like he's a levelheaded young man."

"He is. Paul's the kind of kid who will be a success in whatever he decides to do in life. He has a strong work ethic and stellar character."

"It could be that he doesn't want to burden you because of your mother's situation."

Rowan was likely right.

"For a while I thought I was imagining things."

"I'd never second-guess a mother's intuition," Rowan said, smiling.

My heart swelled with gratitude at his understanding. "I can always tell when something is wrong with Paul or Allie, or if they are trying to hide something from me. They used to joke that I could read their minds, which isn't far from the truth. That's just how close the three of us became over the years."

"You say that Allie and Paul are close."

"They are."

"Then Allie might know what's up. You could ask her. She wouldn't need to break her brother's confidence, but she might be able to reassure you."

Talking to Allie wasn't something I'd considered. Knowing my daughter, she'd be unable to keep a secret from me, especially if she was worried about her big brother. Now that I thought about it, the fact that she hadn't discussed anything having to do with Paul should probably reassure me that everything was okay.

The front door banged opened and Allie blew into the house. That's the only way I could describe it. When my daughter was on a mission, there was no stopping her.

"Hi, Mom," she said as she raced up the stairwell.

"Hey, Allie . . ."

My words were met with a rush of wind as my daughter flew past me. No more than a few seconds later she came back down the staircase, her knee-high boots in hand.

Rowan joined me and placed his arm around my shoulders as we stood side by side at the bottom of the stairs.

"You remember Rowan, don't you?" I said, unwilling to have her rush out the door without greeting Rowan.

Allie smiled. "Sure. Good to see you again."

"You, too."

"Where are you off to in such a rush?" I asked; I could almost see her groan at the delay. "Be—"

"To a party. Don't worry," she said, cutting me off. "I know the rules."

"Good girl." I leaned forward to kiss her cheek when her friend came rushing through the front door.

"Allie, can I borrow—Dad?" She froze when she saw me and Rowan standing together.

"Mackensie?" Rowan said, in apparent shock. I knew he hadn't seen his daughter in person for years. He dropped his arm from around me, stunned that she was in front of him. "What are *you* doing here?" Rowan shook his head as though unable to believe what he was seeing. "Why aren't you in California?"

"I'm attending school here now. If you cared the least bit about me, you'd know that." Her words were like snake venom as she struck out at Rowan. Her shoulders were straight and stiff, and her eyes hardened with every word.

"When did you transfer?" he demanded.

"Wait," I said, taken aback, unsure what was happening. I raised my hands to my head and looked to Rowan. "This is your daughter? Mackensie, Allie's friend, is your daughter?" I was more confused than ever.

"Yes. I had no idea she was living here."

"No idea?" I repeated it back, to be certain I'd heard him clearly. "You told me she was at school in California."

His jaw tightened. "The last I heard, she was."

The last he heard. He didn't know where his own daughter was living?

Allie seemed as perplexed as me. "I don't understand, either." Allie turned to Mackensie. "I thought you said your dad was nothing more than a sperm donor."

Rowan stiffened at the comment.

So did I. In our discussions about family, Rowan had talked little about his divorce and even less about his daughter. I hadn't realized how little until now.

"You didn't know Mackensie had transferred to the University of Washington?" I asked, wanting to be sure I had the details right.

"Mom. He doesn't know anything about Mackensie because he's like dad. He doesn't care about her, or anyone else."

A lead weight dropped in my stomach, and for a moment I found it impossible to breathe.

"Rowan?" I asked, my voice sounding nothing like my normal self.

In response, he continued to stare at his daughter.

"All those text messages you sent were from right here in Seattle?"

Mackensie shrugged.

"Not once did you let me know you were in town. Not once." His words were hard, laced with hurt and pain.

"Why should I?" she demanded. "You don't care about me. You never have."

"You know that's not true," Rowan said.

Mackensie grabbed ahold of the sleeve of Allie's jacket. "Let's go. We've got a party to get to."

The girls rushed out the door, closing it behind them.

I remained rooted to the spot, unable to move, hardly able to breathe. Rowan had abandoned his daughter the same way Kyle had conveniently forgotten he had two children.

"Jenna." He said my name softly. "Let me explain."

A sad, sick feeling stole over me. "What can you possibly say that would explain this?" I asked. More than once Allie had mentioned that Mackensie and she had a lot in common, beginning with the fact that they had both grown up without a father.

"I love my daughter," Rowan insisted. "Her mother—"

"So you're blaming her mother?"

"Yes," he insisted.

I imagined that was the same excuse Kyle used when his significant others had learned he had two children from a previous marriage. It was my fault. I'd taken his children away from him, prevented him from having any kind of relationship. One of his wives, I forget which one, had told me so. She didn't know about Paul or Allie until after they had married. Kyle had conveniently forgotten to mention his children. The blame had all fallen on me.

And now Rowan was making the same claim. His ex was at fault. She'd kept his daughter away from him. I was too smart to believe that.

I refused to look at him. "I think you should go."

"If you'd let me explain," he said in a consoling tone, as if being reasonable and gentle was going to win me over.

Shaking my head, I refused. "I've heard everything I need to hear. No wonder you never wanted to talk about the past. You'd put your daughter in your past, right along with the end of your marriage."

"I've always supported my daughter."

"That doesn't impress me, Rowan." Kyle had done the same thing: He'd paid child support, but he gave nothing more of himself to his children. That Rowan had done the same with his daughter was unacceptable to me.

"Please go."

For a minute, I thought he would argue with me, or at least put up some sort of defense. He must have recognized that it wouldn't do any good to try to talk to me. I didn't want to hear anything he had to say. I could be reasonable and forgive a lot of things, but an absentee father wasn't one of them.

Chapter 26

Allie

Allie was concerned. Mackensie had been acting strangely ever since they'd left the house following the confrontation with her father. The party they'd both been looking forward to all week had turned out to be a bust.

After putting in money for their share of the alcohol, the first thing Mackensie did was head into the kitchen for a shot of whiskey, abandoning Allie. She'd been drinking steadily ever since they arrived, with Allie keeping an eye out for her from afar.

"I think we should go," Allie said, finding her friend sitting in the cold on the top step of the back porch. Music blared from inside the house, giving Allie a headache. She normally enjoyed hard rock, but it was being played at decibels that threatened to shatter her eardrums.

Mackensie had her eyes closed. "I think I'm going to be sick."

Sure enough, not a minute later, Mackensie leaped to her feet, leaned over the side of the railing, and heaved up everything inside her stomach that wasn't permanently attached. When she'd finished, she pressed her hand over her mouth and groaned.

"Can I get you anything?" Allie asked, worried for her friend.

Mackensie shook her head. "I want to leave."

That was the best news Allie had heard all evening.

Seeing that her friend was in no condition to drive, Allie got the car keys and led Mackensie through the party and out the front door. Noticing Mackensie's paleness, no one tried to waylay them.

This was a switch. Mackensie was the more sensible one of the two, or she had been until that night. Allie suspected the change had to do with accidentally bumping into her dad. Allie'd had no idea Dr. Lancaster was her father, or that Mackensie's father lived in Seattle. Mackensie went by her mother's maiden name of Nelson, so she made no connection whatsoever that Dr. Lancaster could even possibly be Mackensie's dad.

Once inside the car on the passenger side, Mackensie leaned her head back and closed her eyes. "Did you see the shocked look on my dad's face when he saw me?" she asked, like it was a joke.

Allie wasn't amused. The only shocked look she'd noticed had come from her mother. It would take a long time to forget the pain that had flashed in her mother's eyes when she'd learned Rowan had abandoned Mackensie the same way Allie's father had done with her and her brother.

Upset by what had happened, Allie had been eager to get away. In the hours since, she'd had time to think about everything but was still confused and frustrated by what had happened. She'd been good friends with Mackensie almost from the first day of classes. They did almost everything together. Mackensie had made it sound like no one in her family cared about her. But for some reason, Allie wasn't so sure. There was something about the way Mackensie had looked at her dad when she saw him, and the way Dr. Lancaster had responded to her, though she couldn't put her finger on it.

"Are you taking me back to the dorm?" Mackensie asked, groaning.

"Are you going to be sick again?" It didn't seem possible that she'd have anything left in her stomach to lose.

"No. I want to curl up in a tight ball and go to sleep."

"I'm driving as fast as I can." Allie had had two beers herself, which she had intentionally spaced out over the night, as she didn't want to risk getting pulled over and ticketed. The university police often patrolled the roads around the school, especially when they got news of a party and its location.

Once she arrived at their dorm, Allie had a hard time getting Mackensie up the stairs to her room and into her bed. Mackensie groaned, fell onto the mattress, threw the covers over her head, and passed out, clothes and all. Allie waited a few moments to be sure Mackensie was sound asleep and safe before returning to her own room.

It turned out to be a restless night for Allie. Every time she closed her eyes, her mother's stricken look filled her mind.

This doctor was different from the other men her mother had dated. Allie had seen Dr. Lancaster and her mother together only twice, but it was obvious that her mother cared about Rowan. This must have been far more than a shock or a surprise to her mom. She'd read the hurt on her mother's face, all too well.

Hurt. Pain. Disappointment. Discouragement.

Up early the next morning, Allie made a quick trip for coffee and delivered it to her friend. She had kept Mackensie's keys to check in on her. After knocking loudly against the door, Allie let herself into her friend's room. Mackensie was still asleep. Her roomie must have gone home for the weekend, as her bed was still unmade.

"Please, be quiet," Mackensie said, holding her head in her hands. She sat up, leaning against one elbow, and kept her eyes closed. "You sound like a herd of panicked antelope charging through the room."

"Sorry," Allie whispered. "But I come bearing a gift from the gods."

"You brought me coffee," Mackensie said eagerly, and then winced as she reached for the coffee, bracing her back against her pillow and the wall. She took a sip of the hot coffee and then sighed, as if tasting ambrosia.

Allie sat on the bottom half of the mattress and held on to her coffee with both hands. "Why'd you transfer out of Santa Monica?" she asked. "It couldn't have been for the weather in Seattle."

It was raining, typical weather at this time of the year. Water drizzled against the outside window, highlighting the question of Mackensie's move from sunny California to western Washington.

Mackensie took another swallow of her coffee. "I don't know. I felt like it."

"No real reason, then?"

"Why would you ask?"

"I don't know." Allie was unsure how far to press her point, but, following her gut, she said what was on her mind. "I was thinking it might be because of your dad living here."

For a long, uncomfortable moment, Mackensie didn't answer.

"You knew he lived and worked here, didn't you?"

"Yeah. So what?"

"But you never let him know you'd transferred schools or that you were in the area."

"Big deal," she said sarcastically, twirling her index finger in a circle. "You want a prize now?"

"No, but I'd like to understand why."

Mackensie sighed heavily, apparently irritated by the whole interrogation. "Why do you care?"

Allie raised her knees, placed her arms around them, and rested her chin on her bent knees. "My mom likes him."

"Great. She can have him. I don't want anything to do with him, and neither does my mother."

Something wasn't right. Deep down, Allie was convinced Mackensie wasn't revealing everything about her relationship with her father. Allie knew that Mackensie texted him regularly, demanding stuff. The last request had been way over the top, claiming she needed a new car. Mackensie had laughed when she'd sent it. She'd wanted a new BMW and he'd refused. When he refused, Mackensie had been furious.

Allie had casually commented that if she had done that to her father, he would have blocked her number. A couple other times, Mackensie had brazenly shared the exchanges between her and her father. Allie silently noted that Mackensie's father had always seemed to answer in a calm and wise way, when it would have been easy for him to retaliate with the kind of sarcasm she saw in Mackensie's texts to him. The only reason that Allie could see that Mackensie was angry with her dad was because he wouldn't let her manipulate him.

Allie recalled a time when she was about eight years old, running errands with her grandmother. She'd recently had a birthday and gotten all kinds of presents, including two dolls. Allie had seen a doll at the store that day, and she'd begged her grandmother to buy her that doll. No matter how hard Allie tried, how much she fussed, her grandmother had refused, reminding Allie of the new dolls she'd been given as gifts.

Allie was stuck on that doll, and her grandmother's refusal had hurt. She'd been convinced her grandmother didn't love her, so she pouted all the way home. Later, her grandmother had placed Allie in her lap and pressed Allie's small head against her heart. She told Allie something she'd never forgotten. "Oh Allie, my Allie. I know you're disappointed I didn't buy you that doll. You have two brand-new dolls to play with at home."

"But I wanted *that* doll," Allie replied, with tears in her eyes.

"I know, and I wanted to buy it for you."

"Why wouldn't you, then, Grams?"

Her grandmother had kissed the top of her head. "Sometimes it's much harder to say no than to say yes, sweet Allie."

Harder to say no than yes. That was what Mackensie's father had done. He'd told her no, knowing she had no need for that new car. It didn't mean he didn't love Mackensie less; it meant he loved her enough to say no.

Allie waited two days before contacting her mother. She didn't know what to say, or even if she should say anything. All the way home on the city bus, ideas on how to comfort her mother ran through her mind, all of which she quickly rejected.

Her mother had worked the same schedule for years, so Allie let herself into the house, timing her visit so she'd be there before her mother arrived home from the hospital. She'd talked to Paul, hoping he had some suggestions, but he was at a loss about what to say, which was unusual for him. He'd sounded rushed and eager to get off the phone.

Not knowing what was best, Allie started opening and closing cupboards until she found what she was looking for. It was a soup mix, and one of mother's favorites.

The water was at the boiling point when the door off the laundry room opened.

"I'm in the kitchen," Allie called, not wanting to give her mother heart palpitations.

Her mother came into the room. She looked exhausted.

"I made you chicken noodle soup," Allie told her cheerfully.

Blinking, her mother gave her a curious look. "I'm not sick."

"Yes, you are. Sick at heart."

"It's no big deal, but thank you, honey. That was thoughtful of you."

The best part about this chicken noodle soup mix was that it needed to cook for only four minutes. The timer went off and Allie got two bowls from the shelf and filled them close to the brim. She wasn't sure she'd ever grow accustomed to these new dishes. She decided that now, however, wasn't the time to mention it.

"Sit," Allie ordered as she carefully set the hot bowls with spoons on the counter eating space.

"Allie, honestly, I'm fine."

"No, you're not. I can see it in your eyes. You're miserable. Have you talked to Dr. Lancaster since . . . ?"

"No, and I'd rather not."

"I'm not convinced the story Mackensie told me about her dad is completely true. You should talk to him and get his side of the story."

"Not interested."

Her mother could be stubborn, often to her own

detriment. Allie tried another tactic. "What did Maureen say you should do?"

"Nothing. I haven't mentioned it to her."

This was odd. They talked about everything. "Why not? She's your BFF."

Her mother smiled. "Maureen's in love and sees everything through rose-colored glasses these days."

"Maureen's in love? Mrs. Zelinski? That Maureen?" Allie couldn't imagine her mother's friend in love. "What have I missed?"

To Allie's surprise, her mother laughed out loud. "She met someone at the library and she's head-over-heels falling for this guy. I'm happy for her."

She could see that her mother wasn't faking it; she was genuinely pleased for her friend. That made Allie even more determined to find out the truth about Mackensie and her dad. The things Mackensie had told her weren't ringing true. She'd transferred from Santa Monica to Seattle for a reason. As much as Mackensie had denied it, Allie was convinced the reason was her father.

Chapter 27

Maureen

The night of the ballet had finally arrived, and I was as excited as a five-year-old waiting for her friends to arrive for her birthday party. I was convinced that once Logan had the chance to absorb the beauty and elegance of the talented performers, he'd appreciate this art form as much as I did.

"Mom," Tori said, "are you sure about this?"

I could tell she thought that taking Logan to the ballet was the worst idea I'd ever had. It disappointed me that she'd even ask this question. She'd unexpectedly stopped by the house as I was looking through my closet for an appropriate dress.

"Of course, I'm sure," I insisted, not taking her seriously. She was a fan of both opera and ballet herself. From the time she was five years old, I'd taken her to both. Her husband, Jonathan, had never joined us, insisting this was a mother-daughter thing.

"Logan likes sports," Tori felt obliged to remind me. "*Manly* sports like hockey and football. Watching men leap into the air and lift women over their heads most likely is not his thing."

"You've misjudged Logan. Yes, he does appreciate sports, which is my point. Ballet dancers are every bit as athletic as those macho football players he admires so much." I'd like to see one of those linebackers dance on his toes. The image that flew into my mind was enough to make me squelch a laugh.

"Help me decide what dress to wear," I said, not wanting to argue with my daughter. She didn't know Logan as well as I did. He might work on a construction crew, but he was cultured. The books he chose to read assured me as much.

Sitting on the end of my bed, Tori crossed her legs and leaned back, resting her weight on her elbows. "You genuinely like this guy, don't you?"

Immediately I opened my mouth to deny it, and, to my amazement, I found I couldn't. Ever since the dinner at his house, he'd dominated my thoughts. The beautiful, romantic words he'd said had filled my heart. All these years, I'd hoped to fall in love again and had naturally assumed it would be with a teacher or maybe a researcher. Instead I'd fallen for a plumber.

A plumber, for the love of heaven, one who had taught me things about myself that I'd never suspected.

A smile so wide broke over me that my mouth hurt. Over the years, I'd been around only highly educated men. Several had Ph.D.s, and of those men, I was forced to confess, most had the emotional IQ of a slug. Logan was far more than intelligent. He was socially adept, with a well-adjusted personality. His peers admired him, and the company owner trusted him. I did, too, and I wasn't afraid to admit it.

"You don't need to answer me," Tori said, satisfied by my reaction. "The look on your face says it all." She stood up from the bed and gave me a hug. "I'm happy for you, Mom. I've been hoping you'd find someone for a long time."

I didn't want her to leave just yet. "You have?" I questioned. It wasn't like there'd been a parade of men in my life. It'd been more like a slow leak from an old faucet.

"It took someone like Logan to draw you out of your shell," Tori continued. "It's been fun to watch your relationship with him unfold." Finally taking my request to help me select a dress seriously, she walked over to my closet and shuffled hangers back and forth. Now and again she'd pause to examine an outfit before scooting it to one side to consider the next one in line.

When it came to evening wear, my choices were limited. I'd been toying with the idea of wearing the black silk dress but was uncertain if it was appropriate.

"This one," she said, holding up the very dress I'd had in mind. It was my favorite dress, and Tori had given it to me. The skirt reached mid-calf and swirled around my legs, which I considered my best asset. The matching dark silk jacket had silver threads woven into the fabric. I'd hesitated, thinking it might be overly dressy for the night. Having Tori's approval was all the confirmation I needed.

"I had the same outfit in mind," I said, taking it from my daughter and laying it across the bed.

Tori kissed my cheek on her way out the door. I was concerned about her; she still didn't look well, and I knew that deep down she was grieving her lost child from the miscarriage. It'd been hard for Tori and Jonathan. I'd cried with her; the disappointment had crippled her for some time, but she had appeared to be recovering until recently. The last I'd heard, Tori and Jonathan were talking about trying to get pregnant again soon. Maybe it was too soon. Tori needed to give her heart time to heal, not only her body.

"Call me in the morning. I hope you know what you're doing, Mom."

Once she was gone, I went about getting ready for the evening. The closer the time came for Logan to pick me up, the more antsy and excited I got. When putting on my makeup, my reflection in the mirror said it all. I couldn't seem to stop smiling. Tori was concerned about this evening, and her doubts had raised a few of my own. All I could do was hope that Logan would enjoy the experience as much as I'd enjoyed seeing the Seahawks play football.

One of the many things I liked about Logan was that he was punctual. He arrived five minutes early to pick me up. He took one look at me in my black silk dress and released a low, appreciative whistle.

"Wow. You polish up good."

His comment pleased me, enough to make me blush. I twirled around to give him the full view of my outfit, unable to hide the effect his compliment had on me.

"You look great yourself," I told him, and meant it. He'd outdone himself by wearing a suit and tie. He eased his finger around the collar and stretched his neck. He might not be accustomed to wearing a suit, but he made for a fine figure in one.

Ready to depart, he held his car keys in his hand. "My guess is we aren't headed to a car show."

"And your guess would be right."

"When do you plan on breaking the news?" he asked, eager to uncover my surprise. "I need to mentally prepare myself for this evening."

"You're going to love it, I promise."

"Okay," he muttered, but didn't sound convinced.

I reached for his free hand and a shiver of excitement raced up my arm. "We're going to the ballet. Orchestra seating, fourth row from the front in the very middle. Our view of the stage couldn't be any better."

"The ballet?" he repeated, blinking in a futile effort to disguise his disbelief, and possibly his disappointment.

"Yes, the ballet." These tickets were premier seats, and expensive; I certainly hoped he'd appreciate this gesture on my part.

He stared at me blankly, as if he needed a translator. "Have you been before?" I asked, guessing he hadn't.

"Never." He made it sound as though I'd asked him if he'd ever been stung by a thousand wasps. Or swum in crocodile-infested waters.

I refused to let his lack of enthusiasm discourage me; I decided to make the best of it by showing him my own passion for the art form.

"You're in for an amazing experience." The last time I'd

attended, the sheer beauty of what I'd seen on the stage had brought tears to my eyes. I wasn't the only one affected, either. At the end of the performance I'd noticed other audience members dabbing their cheeks, the same as me.

"Do they serve popcorn or hot dogs?" Logan asked hopefully. "What about beer?"

Surely, he was kidding. "No, silly. There's wine available during intermission."

"Wine," he repeated, obviously disappointed.

"You like wine." He wouldn't have served it with dinner if he didn't enjoy it.

"I prefer beer."

"Give it a chance, Logan, please? It's something new and different for us to experience together." Tori's concerns started ringing in my ears.

Beaming him my brightest smile, I reached for my evening bag and coat.

Logan continued to look skeptical.

Looping my arm around his elbow, I eased him toward the front door. "This evening is all about new adventures. These performers are going to blow your mind." I hoped he would soon remember our conversation about football athletes and ballet performers. It surprised me that he hadn't made the connection yet. I'd remind him later, once he'd had the chance to see the dancers in action.

Logan drove, as he was more familiar with parking downtown. We walked a couple blocks to McCaw Hall and went inside. I gave the attendant our tickets and we were escorted to our seats.

After settling in, I looked at Logan. "Aren't these great seats?"

He didn't answer.

He must not have heard me. He appeared to be checking out the exit doors. I had to admit he didn't look anywhere close to excited. I hoped that once the ballet started, he'd feel differently. Reaching for his hand, I entwined our fingers.

Logan took several minutes to read through the program. I had the impression he wasn't looking to educate himself on the performance. I was inclined to think he was avoiding conversation. Perhaps I'd overdone the enthusiasm part.

I hoped by explaining a bit about what was about to happen would help. Leaning my head close to his, I said, "Ballet dancers study and practice for years to be skilled enough to become part of a company."

No response again, so I continued: "The reason I mention this is because of something you mentioned about the football players. You said several of them had been involved in the game since they were in their teens or even younger."

He turned toward me, his eyes rounding as he remembered the comment I'd made at the end of the football game we'd attended together.

"So *that's* why we're here. You wanted to prove your point."

I held my breath. "Not at all. I wanted to show you that these performers are every bit as athletic as those involved in other sports."

"You honestly believe these dancers are in the same category physically as football players?"

"I do," I said. "You'll recognize the truth soon enough."

He appeared to relax, his hand holding mine. It wasn't long before the lights dimmed and the music from the orchestra filled the theater. Soon the dancers were on the stage. The beauty was everything that I'd remembered. Leaning forward, I let the sheer wonder of the experience surround me.

Logan leaned forward beside me. "What's happening?" he whispered loudly.

I shook my head, trying to explain nonverbally that it would be rude to the people around us to speak during the performance. This was different from a football game, where he was free to explain each play. Because he was intelligent, I didn't think it would take long for Logan to pick up on the storyline. What I hoped, more than anything, was that he would give himself over to the beauty and to the wonder of the performance itself.

At the intermission, I breathed in a deep sigh, caught up in the splendor of it all. I held on to the feelings, wanting to linger in the moment. Before I could ask Logan his thoughts, he leaped to his feet.

"I'll get us wine."

"We can't bring it back here."

"We can't drink at our seats?"

"No food or drink is allowed in the theater," I explained.

His disappointment was evident. He waved his hand, as if the audacity of that was beyond understanding.

Knowing that the crush at the bar would steal away my

enjoyment of the evening, I said, "I'll stay here. I'd rather do without wine."

"I need a glass," he said, and started to exit the row, excusing himself as he passed each seated person.

Perhaps getting seats in the very center hadn't been such a great idea after all. From his reaction and his sudden need for wine, I got the impression that he wasn't enjoying the performance. I wanted to talk to him, sound him out.

As much as I would have hated to leave early, I decided to make the offer. However, when Logan returned it was just half a minute before the ballet continued and there wasn't time to leave without making an unwanted statement and without upsetting everyone in our row who had already taken their seats.

Logan sank down in the seat, acting like he was ready to be strapped into an electric chair.

As best I could, I sent him a look of apology, hoping he could read the message in my eyes.

The second half was even more compelling that the first had been. I was mesmerized. Tears flooded my eyes at the emotion being portrayed through dance. I clenched my hands against my chest, swallowed up by the moment. I quickly glanced over at Logan, hoping this half of the performance had given him a change of heart.

To my absolute horror, I found he was asleep. His neck was braced against the back of the seat so that his head was tilted upward toward the ceiling. A soft snore escaped his partially opened mouth. Horrified, I elbowed him in the ribs.

Logan jerked awake and looked around as if trying to

remember where he was. His expression seemed to suggest that he'd been kidnapped by aliens and dropped nude into the middle of the theater. He straightened and rubbed a hand down his face.

At the end of the program, the audience rose to its feet in a standing ovation. My applause was louder and more enthusiastic than most. Ignoring Logan, I reached for my handbag.

He buried his hands in his pant pockets and mumbled, "I'm sorry, Maureen."

"And I'm sorry you didn't enjoy it," I said, stating the obvious.

"I tried," he returned, sounding terribly guilty. "The ballet isn't for everyone. In the same way, football isn't, either. You understand, don't you?"

It took me a while to accept what he said as fair. "I do."

Logan's face relaxed as the tension eased from his eyes.

It'd do no good for me to be upset with him. He'd given it a try. I couldn't ask for anything more than that. Next time I'd ask Jenna to accompany me instead of Logan.

"I didn't mean to fall asleep; I was more tired than I realized," he said as we exited the row and joined the throng leaving the theater.

"It's okay," I said, willing to overlook his lack of appreciation.

"It must've been the wine," he added.

"One glass shouldn't have done that."

He looked away and slowly cleared his throat. "I had more than one glass."

"More than one?" Knowing how crowded the bar got, I couldn't imagine him waiting in line again for a second glass.

"I talked them into letting me buy the entire bottle," he confessed.

That did it. I couldn't help but burst out laughing.

Logan placed his arm around my shoulders and brought me close to his side. He kissed the top of my head and I wrapped my arm around his waist.

"Thanks, Marian."

My smile widened, and it was understood that it wasn't the ballet tickets he was thanking me for.

Chapter 28

Jenna

It'd been a long, hectic day with a construction accident on the I-5 overpass that brought in five workers, three of whom landed in the ICU. At the end of my shift, I was more than ready for a soak in the bathtub. I'd done my best to put Rowan out of my mind and heart, with little success. He'd made himself scarce, I'd noticed. We were at an impasse. I refused to get involved with a man who would turn his back on his daughter, especially if all he had to offer me were excuses, laying the blame elsewhere.

Letting myself into the house, I was frightened out of my wits when I saw a man making himself at home in my living room. It was an even bigger shock to realize that the man was my son, Paul.

The last time I'd seen him had been late summer, when he'd spent a weekend at home before returning to school. He'd been around for only a handful of days over the summer break because of his job. When I last saw him, his dirty-blond hair had been long, and he'd sported a neatly trimmed beard. He'd worn tattered jeans and a T-shirt of some band I'd never heard of. Today was a stark contrast. He was clean-shaven, and his hair was neatly trimmed. He had on tan pants and a crisp button-down shirt with a tie. He looked more like a college professor than a student. He bounded up from the sofa to give me a big hug.

"Paul," I cried, overjoyed to see him. "Wow, you look great." The changes were impressive. Somewhere in the last three months he'd turned into a mature adult. I'd always been proud of my son, but I was astonished by the outward changes I saw in him now. Proud and pleased.

"You approve?" he asked.

"Very much. You look like a responsible adult."

"I *am* a responsible adult."

And that he was. Even as a teenager, he'd never caused me any worry. Young as he'd been when Kyle and I split, Paul seemed to understand that he had a new role in the household.

That he would arrive home unannounced was an immediate cause for concern. There could be only one reason. He'd come to tell me something and wanted to do it face-to-face.

My heart was pounding as I rid myself of my coat and dropped my purse in the hallway, where I kept it. Evidently, I didn't need to worry. Dressed as he was, it told me he hadn't dropped out of school and turned into a drug dealer. To even think such a thing was ridiculous, I know, but my thoughts naturally went to the worst-case scenario.

Following me into the kitchen, he said, "I stopped off and saw Grams earlier. She looks great."

"I suppose she fed you?" My mother's joy was finding an excuse to feed someone, especially if it was one of her grandchildren.

"Of course. My favorite." Whatever was left over in her refrigerator instantly became Paul and Allie's latest favorite. It'd become a big joke in the family that Grams considered the grandchildren her private garbage disposal.

"What was it this time?" I couldn't help but ask. "It wasn't broccoli with macaroni and cheese, was it?" Paul detested broccoli.

"She had a leftover pork chop and pan-fried potatoes with corn."

I smiled. "You were lucky."

"Don't I know it." He scooted onto the stool at the counter while I brewed us coffee. "She told me you're throwing her a big birthday party."

I glanced over my shoulder as I pulled down two mugs. "You didn't get the invite?"

"When did you email it?"

"A few days ago."

"Guess not. I haven't checked my inbox in the last couple days."

That didn't sound like Paul, but it also confirmed to me that he'd been working too many hours.

I handed him the mug, filled with steaming hot coffee. Standing on the other side of the counter across from him,

I leaned forward and braced my elbows against the edge, my hands cupping my own mug.

"I've suspected for some time now that you've been keeping something from me," I said, choosing to confront the problem rather than ignore it. "Whatever it is, I appreciate that you want to tell me personally rather than over the phone."

"Yes. I thought it'd be better if I did."

Right away I noticed that he had trouble making eye contact. He expelled his breath and squared his shoulders. "I guess I should start off by telling you that I've moved off campus."

In the past, this would've been something he would have discussed with me. Because he'd chosen not to, it told me that there was more to this than changing residences.

"It was a good move for me."

"Okay. Is there a girl involved?" He hadn't mentioned that he was dating, but he tended to keep his dating life to himself. Allie probably knew about her, but not me.

"No, Mom," he said with a laugh. "I'm too busy to get involved in a relationship."

I knew it. All the hours he was working were ruining his academic and social life. "Paul, it isn't necessary for you to continue working. What's the use of having spending money if you can't enjoy life? When was the last time you were out on a date?"

He grinned like I'd told him a joke. "It's been a while."

"See what I mean? Now please, give the restaurant your two-weeks' notice."

"I can't," he said.

I refused to believe that. "You mean you won't."

"Okay, I won't."

This conversation was frustrating me at a time when I already had enough frustration in my life to drown a whale. "What is it about this restaurant that you love so much?"

"I like the work, Mom. I'm good at what I do."

Recently I'd bragged to Rowan that my son would be excellent at whatever he did, but this wasn't the point. "Do you want to wait tables for the rest of your life?" I asked him pointedly.

"No. I'm hoping for more responsibility at the restaurant in the future. A lot more."

"What?" It sounded as if he was trading his engineering degree to work in a restaurant.

"The owner likes me," Paul explained. "He's taken me under his wing."

I was quickly losing my composure. "Oh please," I cried sarcastically. "Don't tell me you're being swayed away from school because some restaurant owner wants to take advantage of you and your hard work ethic."

Paul's eyes flashed with irritation and his mouth tightened. "I came home to tell you I've dropped out of college."

"You did *what*?" I burst out. "Paul, tell me you didn't."

He stiffened, his stubbornness on full display now. "It's a done deal. I realized that I chose to go into engineering because of Gramps. I made an emotional decision after he died, and I've regretted it. I wasn't enjoying my classes, and I could see that a career in that field was going to bore me. I know you had big aspirations for me, Mom, and I'm sorry to disappoint you, but this is what I want."

"Paul, think about what you're saying," I pleaded, doing my best to keep my voice level. "Are you seriously telling me you want to make a career of working in the restaurant industry?"

His eyes narrowed, and he waited several moments before he calmly said, "You make it sound as if the work is beneath me."

"It *is* beneath your intelligence. You're *so* much better than that."

His mouth dropped open, my response appearing to shock him. Stepping away from the counter, he placed both hands on top of his head as he paced. I could almost hear him counting to ten before he responded.

"Are you hearing yourself?" he challenged. "Do you sincerely believe people choose to work in the restaurant industry, or any service industry, for that matter, because they aren't intelligent?"

"I . . . I didn't mean for it to sound like that." And I didn't. "I wasn't talking about anyone else. I was talking about *you*. Paul, *please*. Think about what you're doing. If you don't want to be an engineer, choose another major."

"I have chosen a different career path, one that gives me real-life, on-the-job training." He looked at me straight on and added emphatically, "And I'm not changing my mind."

I could see he was getting ready to leave and I didn't want us to part like this. "Don't go, Paul. Let's talk this out. I apologize if I overreacted."

He hesitated and shook his head. "It's better that I leave now before we both say anything else we'll regret. I wanted to tell you before, and I didn't because I was afraid of your reaction. I have to say you didn't disappoint me. I'd hoped that of all people you would encourage me to do what makes me happy. Working in the restaurant does that. I'm good with people, with seeing the bigger picture of the business, and Mr. Owen is a great mentor. He's been more of a father to me than my own father ever was."

I felt dreadful. "Paul, please, don't leave in a rush."

He shook his head. "It'll be better this way. You need time to accept what I'm telling you. If I stayed, you'll just try to convince me to go back to college. That's not happening, Mom. I'm sorry if you're unhappy with my decision. I truly am. Talking any more will only create a greater rift between us, and I don't want that. We've always had a great relationship, and I'd prefer to keep it that way."

Stunned, I stood frozen as my son walked out of the kitchen. A few moments later I heard the front door open and close. The knot in my throat was so big I couldn't swallow. After several seconds I released a long, hard sigh and noticed that my hands were trembling.

I hated that my son had dropped out of his classes without discussing it with me first. I wanted so much more for Paul. I yearned for us to talk this through. It felt as if our close relationship had changed overnight, and all over a lousy job.

Leaving the kitchen, I went upstairs to my window on the bay, practically throwing myself onto the ledge. Tears fell down my cheeks in rapid succession as I mentally reviewed our conversation. It felt as if my life was falling apart. First Rowan, and now my son.

When my legs started to cramp, I took a hot bath and then dressed in yoga pants and a sweatshirt. I stuffed my feet into fuzzy slippers and grabbed a box of tissues as I continued to sniffle.

When the phone rang, hope leaped in my heart as I prayed it was Paul. Instead, it was Allie.

"Hi, honey," I said, sniffling and trying to hold the emotion at bay.

"I heard from Paul," she said.

Knowing that they had talked did my heart good. "Is he terribly upset with me?" I asked, holding in a sob. Looking back, I realized that I'd reacted instinctively, angry and hurt that he'd made these major life decisions without talking to me. The shock of what he'd done had overwhelmed me. I hadn't had time to take it all in, to absorb everything.

"He knew you'd take it hard," Allie said. "That's why he didn't say anything before now."

"Did you know?" I asked, because it sounded very much like she did.

"Yes," she admitted, and I could hear the regret in her voice. "I promised on my life not to tell you, but it was hard."

"How long have you known?" I asked. While I was happy my children were confidants, it saddened me to think they were comfortable keeping secrets from me.

"A while."

Her answer was vague enough to raise my suspicions. "How long?" I repeated.

"Okay, I'll tell you, but don't let Paul know you found out from me."

This didn't sound good.

"He dropped out of college the end of September."

"September." He'd been back to school for only a month at that point. I gasped. "He's kept it a secret that long?" My heart hit rock bottom and I felt the sudden need to sit down.

"He wanted to tell you, Mom. It's been hard for him not to. He was planning to talk to you about it when Grandma fell. Then her surgery and rehab . . . you were dealing with so much. Paul didn't want to add to your burden. We've talked a lot in the last few weeks. He might have waited until Christmas, if it wasn't for Mr. Owen."

That was twice now that I'd heard the restaurant owner's name. "What about Mr. Owen?" I asked, doing my best to disguise my suspicions. I hadn't met the man, and already I disliked him. I was afraid that he'd used his influence to convince Paul to leave school and work for him full-time. My hand tightened around my phone.

"I've never met him," Allie added, as if reading my mind. "Paul talks about him a lot. It was Mr. Owen who insisted it was time Paul told you he'd dropped out of school."

I should probably be grateful, but I wasn't. My immediate dislike and distrust of the man overwhelmed any hint of gratitude.

"What did Paul tell you about him?" The more I knew about this Mr. Owen, the better. I'd do my own online research as soon as we got off the phone, but I already had a strong feeling nothing would change my mind about him.

"Paul has nothing to say but good things. He's grateful Mr. Owen believes in him."

"No doubt," I muttered.

"He's taken Paul under his wing, Mom."

I clenched my jaw so tightly that my teeth made a clicking sound. My father had been the only male role model in my son's life, because Paul's father had failed him. It made sense that since my father had passed, my son would look to emulate another man he admired. This restaurant owner must have recognized that in my son and played on it.

"Mom, you aren't saying anything."

I couldn't, and furthermore, I wouldn't, for fear that anything I said would be repeated to Paul.

"It's better that I don't."

"You're not upset with Paul, are you?"

"Of course not." Every bit of my anger was directed at his boss.

"Good. He's changed a lot since this summer."

I couldn't help but notice. "When did he shave off his beard?" I asked.

"When he was hired on full-time. Mr. Owen suggested he cut his hair, and Paul decided to shave his beard off as well."

I laughed, which was far from a mature response, but again, I couldn't seem to disguise my feelings.

Either Allie didn't hear me or she chose to ignore it. "It'll all work out, Mom. Just wait and see. It's going to be fine."

All at once it sounded like my daughter was the mature adult in this situation.

"I hope you're right."

"I am. Give Paul time. That's what he's doing with you. He wants you to think about what he said. You'll do that, won't you?"

"Of course."

I slowly sank into the sofa, in the very spot my son had been sitting when I'd arrived home. My heart was heavy, and for the first time as a single mom, I didn't know what to do. I didn't know how to fix this, or even if I should try.

Chapter 29

Maureen

"Oh Tori, a baby! This is the best news ever!" I was about to become a grandmother. We sat in my kitchen drinking herbal tea and it was all I could do to hold still. That I hadn't guessed earlier was a testament to how involved my head and heart had been over Logan. I could hardly wait to tell Jenna and Logan, who was a grandfather of four.

"We didn't tell anyone until I was through the first trimester, and I'm sorry about the timing," she confessed.

"Why would you even think such a thing?"

"Mom, the baby is due in June, just when you have planned your trip for Paris. You said nothing was going to stop you this time. After waiting all these years, I refuse to let this baby ruin your plans with Jenna."

My heart sank. Tori knew how much I'd been looking forward to this trip. This would be disappointing news to Jenna, on top of what she'd learned recently about Rowan.

Plus, her troubles with Paul. It seemed she was getting hit from all sides. She didn't need another disappointment, only this wasn't something I could avoid. I knew she would understand.

"We'll change the dates," I told Tori. No question. I knew what was important. "Paris has waited this long; a few additional months isn't going to make a difference." It wasn't every day that I would welcome a grandchild into the world.

"Mom, Paris is a big deal and you know it," Tori insisted. "You and Jenna have been talking about this trip since you were in college. You *have* to go. I insist."

"We will—no question about it. Just not in June. There's plenty of time to reschedule our trip for later in the year. Autumn in Paris is sure to be just as lovely as late spring." I'd been looking forward to becoming a grandmother. I knew a lot of women worried that a grandchild would make them feel old, but not me. My heart was ready to burst. "Now, don't concern yourself with any of this. I'll talk to Jenna and we'll sort everything out. Don't you worry; your focus should be on that precious baby."

"Speaking of Jenna, did you invite Logan to her mom's birthday party?" Tori asked.

I wasn't fooled. This was my daughter's less-than-subtle way of asking how my relationship with Logan was progressing. I'd let her know she'd been right about him attending the ballet. We were fine—better than fine, really.

"It isn't my place to invite him to the party," I said.

"He's your 'plus one,' Mom."

I had talked to Logan about the party, but I just didn't want Tori to know, in case he decided against attending.

Following his lack of appreciation for the ballet, I'd downplayed him attending the birthday party with me, uncertain how he'd feel, as he wouldn't know anyone other than me. More than anything, I wanted him to go. He had yet to meet Jenna, or Tori and Jonathan. To introduce them at the birthday party would be ideal. It would be casual enough so that he wouldn't feel any pressure or that he was on the spot.

"I've already asked him," I finally admitted.

Tori couldn't have looked more pleased. "Good. You don't ever say much, but I can tell how crazy you are about him."

"Crazy?" I repeated, and for effect I rolled my eyes.

"Enthralled?" she tossed out with a laugh. "Oh Mom, it makes me feel so good to see you happy."

"You and Jonathan make me happy, especially now, with this wonderful news!" I hugged my daughter, feeling her excitement and my own.

We broke apart, and Tori held my look. "Seriously, I've seen changes in you since you met Logan."

"You have?"

"Oh Mom, Logan has been good for you. There's a gentleness in you, a tenderness. I love how quick you are to laugh these days."

"You're being silly." Her compliments embarrassed me, although I had to wonder if what she said was true. I didn't feel that I'd changed, but for Tori to mention it made me reconsider. Since meeting Logan, I'll admit that I seemed to have a happier outlook on life. The other day I'd caught myself singing in the shower. I'd giggled like a schoolgirl when I realized what I was doing.

Tori and I talked for several more minutes and made plans to get together soon. After she left, I called Jenna right away.

"I have good news and bad news," I said when the call connected. "Which do you want first?"

"You decide." Jenna remained depressed. Couldn't say I blamed her. She'd been in the doldrums ever since she'd learned that Rowan was an absentee father. He'd gone from green light to red in record time. It would take her heart time to mend. I hated that I was going to give her disappointing news about our trip, in addition to all of this.

Rather than drag it out, I decided to spill it all at one time. "Tori's pregnant. That's the good news. The bad news is that the baby is due in June."

"Tori's going to have a baby? Oh Maureen, I'm so happy for her—and for you—that's such great news." She hesitated for a moment, slowly coming to a realization.

"But . . . June?" Jenna repeated. "We're scheduled to leave for Paris in June."

"I know. I told Tori that you'd totally understand why we'd have to cancel the trip for June. We'll need to postpone to either September or October." I didn't want to leave too soon after the baby's birth. Those first couple months Tori would need my help, and I wanted to be available.

"We can do that. I'll ask for a change in dates at the hospital; just let me know what works best for you," she said, without giving it a second thought. "Being with Tori and Jonathan for the birth of your first grandchild is too important to miss, especially when we can see Paris anytime."

I wanted to ask Jenna if she'd heard from Paul but decided against it. If she had, she would've told me. I knew that the situation with her son had been eating at her. She didn't need a reminder from me.

"You okay?" I asked, giving her the option to talk or not.

"I heard from Rowan. He sent me three text messages, asking me if we could talk this out."

"Are you going to give him a chance to explain?"

"I . . . I don't know. I'm afraid he's going to try to place the blame on someone else and I don't know that I can accept that. I was falling for this guy, Maureen. Falling hard." Some part of me had been waiting for this. Irrational as it sounded. Deep down, I knew there was something . . . only I hadn't expected it to be this.

"If you don't feel you can trust him, then cut your losses and be thankful you learned what you needed to know before it was too late."

"I wish I could stop thinking about him." I could see that her heart was in turmoil. The situation with Paul wasn't helping. I knew she'd tried to reach Paul, but he wasn't ready to talk. The irony was that Rowan had been trying to talk to Jenna, too, and she'd turned her back on him, refusing to answer his texts.

My heart hurt for Jenna. I wished there was something more I could do other than be her friend and listen when she needed to talk.

"I'll be fine," Jenna said. "These things have a way of working themselves out. Isn't that what you always say?"

Hearing her repeat one of my life themes didn't resonate,

as I could tell she was close to tears. I simply didn't know what to say or even if I should say anything. "Paul will come around." As close as they were, I couldn't imagine him not wanting to set matters straight with his mother.

"I wanted so much more for my son," Jenna continued. "I was desperate enough to consider asking Kyle to reason with him. I thought if I couldn't get Paul to hear that, maybe he'd listen to his father."

"Please tell me you didn't involve Kyle." This was a desperate move on Jenna's part. I could remember only a handful of times over the years that Jenna had reached out to her ex-husband. The last time had been when Allie had badly broken her arm and the teenager had wanted her father to know. Because the break required surgery, Jenna felt Kyle should be made aware of the seriousness of the situation. He politely thanked Jenna for telling him. Then his pseudo-wife at the time had mailed Allie a get-well card, which Kyle had signed. That was the end of it. The man didn't deserve to be called a father.

Jenna's response was half laughing, half weeping. "No. Common sense reigned; I knew it would do no good. Kyle would come back and claim this would never have happened if I'd been a better mother, a better role model."

No doubt she was right. My friend needed me. "I'm coming over. My shoulder is dry, and you can cry on it."

Jenna managed a weak laugh. "Thanks but no thanks. It was a long day at work, and I need to relax and put all this out of my head for one night."

"Let me know if you need me."

"I will," she promised, "and don't worry about Paris. France is the last thing on my mind right now."

"On a positive note, this will give us a few extra weeks to hone our French," I said.

By the end of the workday on Friday, I was ready to explode with the news that I was going to be a grandmother. I could hardly wait to tell Logan, so I decided to surprise him. Heaven only knew why I'd return to the sports bar to do this. Maybe it was my way of proving that I was willing to make compromises in our relationship. Despite him being most comfortable at events that involved drinking beer and eating overpriced hot dogs, he'd been a good sport about the ballet. So I decided I could do something fun for him.

After my initial experience at the bar, I knew that I'd need to dress appropriately, so I'd brought a change of clothes with me to work. At the end of the day, I escaped into the ladies' room and changed into my skinny jeans. They were tight across my butt, but I knew they showed off my assets to the best advantage.

I'd purchased a new Seahawks T-shirt, too. This was no ordinary cotton T-shirt—it had bright, colorful beads of blue and green outlining the shape of the hawk's profile. It was flashier than what I'd usually choose, but I knew Logan would approve. I changed clothes and let my hair down. Logan once mentioned that he liked it that way.

As I suspected, the pub was packed by the time I arrived. I could see it was the usual Friday-night crowd. I managed to find a table in the far corner of the room with a good view of the door. I wondered how long it would take Logan to notice me. I'd give him a few minutes before I'd surprise him.

When the server came by for my order, I asked for a diet soda and relaxed in my chair. I didn't need to wait long before Logan showed. A cheer rose when he entered the room. What stunned me was seeing a woman with him.

My immediate reaction was anger. As ridiculous as it sounded, I wanted to shout out to her that he was my man and she couldn't have him. I'd never had such strong feelings of jealousy before. If her attire was anything to go by, the woman was a coworker of some sort, and they appeared to be familiar with each other. A little too familiar, in my opinion. I was about to stand up and let him know how I felt about seeing him with another woman when I overheard one of the men sitting at the bar.

"Hey, what's this I hear about you going to the ballet?"

Logan shrugged and pretended to ignore it, but I could tell he was embarrassed. He stepped up to the bar, and the bartender slid him a cold mug of beer. He seemed to be trying to find a way to escape the question. I noticed he didn't answer one way or the other.

"Yeah, Logan. You went to the ballet?" a second man chimed in, sounding incredulous.

Logan took a big gulp of his beer. "I went as a favor to a friend."

Friend? That's what I am to him? A friend? Furthermore, this wasn't a favor he'd done for me. I'd paid top dollar for those tickets.

"Did you like watching all those pretty women in pink tutus on their tippy-toes?" One of the guys raised his arms above his head and did a pirouette. The crowd laughed like it was the funniest joke they'd ever heard.

Logan included.

"It wasn't my thing," he explained. He took another sip of his beer. "I can tell you this much—there won't be a repeat."

"Why'd you go in the first place?" someone hollered out.

"No choice. Got roped into it. Like I said, never again. A ballet is the last place you'll catch me."

My heart was pounding so hard my ears rang with the heavy thud of the beat.

"I bet it was that prude librarian who took you."

Prude? I couldn't believe my ears, and I waited for Logan to defend me, to silence the one who'd referred to me in such unflattering terms.

"Come on, guys . . ." Logan pleaded, without getting the result he wanted.

"You still seeing her?" the woman who came into the bar with him asked. "I thought you said you were finished with her."

If he was finished with me, he'd failed to tell me. Maybe I was too dense to realize what was happening. My chest tightened, and I found it hard to breathe.

Unwilling to listen to any more of this dreadful, disrespectful conversation, I placed money on the table and grabbed my purse. Hurt and angry, I walked directly over to Logan and his friends.

"I don't know if Logan is finished with me or not," I said, loud enough for those in the vicinity to hear. "But I think you'll all be happy to know that *I* am finished with *him*."

A shocked silence followed. I gave the group my best stern-librarian look and walked out of the bar, holding my head high and my shoulders straight. Twice now I'd made an idiot of myself in that same sports bar. Would I never learn? It felt as if my entire body was trembling with the shock of what I'd seen and heard. I hurried away, speed-walking as fast as my feet would take me.

I hadn't gone far when I heard Logan call my name and saw him racing after me. This had happened last time, and he apparently seemed to think a quick explanation would change the outcome. That had worked once, but it wouldn't again.

"Maureen, wait up."

I wasn't listening and picked up my pace.

"Maureen, please."

It didn't take him long to catch up with me. He stuffed his hands into his pockets as he walked alongside me.

"Don't be upset. It's just the guys razzing me about the ballet. It's stupid stuff, and I apologize."

I pinched my lips together, holding on to the hurt because I didn't know what else to do with it. Lashing out at him wouldn't help me, and so I said nothing.

"This wasn't about you."

Those jokes might have been directed at him, but they hurt *me*.

He sighed heavily. "I guess this is what's known as the silent treatment. Don't you know that I love you, Maureen?"

How could he say this when he'd just allowed his friend to talk about me like that? Why hadn't he corrected the woman coworker when she'd said that she'd heard he was finished with me? I wanted to demand answers, but my throat had closed up tight.

"All right." His voice was full of frustration with my lack of response. "If that's the way you want it, so be it."

That he was so willing to let me walk away spoke volumes.

His steps slowed, and with a determined voice, he added, "I'll tell you what. When you're ready to take back that part about being done with me, let me know. Until then, it's over."

Over. I blinked hard. I was angry now. Good and angry. If that was the way he wanted it, then fine. Just fine.

Chapter 30

Jenna

It felt as if lately I'd been on a roller-coaster ride. I sat by my window on the bay and looked out over the city and the water. The sky was steel gray with the threat of a storm; the waters were dark and turbulent, much like my thoughts.

Rowan had stopped texting me, and I should've been grateful. I shouldn't want to hear from him, as each message had torn at my heart. I'd read and reread each one a dozen times, and each time I struggled with giving in and listening to his excuses. Excuses, explanations, and justifications. He probably had any number of reasons why he'd stayed out of his daughter's life. The same as Kyle had. I was afraid to listen, afraid if I did that I would give in and believe him because I so badly wanted him to have a valid excuse. Where he was concerned, I was weak and I couldn't allow myself to fall in love with a man it would require me to put blinders on to respect him.

One blessing was that I hadn't run into Rowan while at

the hospital, and for that I was relieved. I don't know what I would have said or done if I had, and, frankly, I didn't want to find out.

My son's decision to leave school weighed heavily on my mind. The shock of his confession had thrown me off guard, and I'd overreacted. Now I was paying the price. If Paul didn't want to continue his engineering studies, I could understand and accept that decision. When he'd said he wanted to go into the same field as his grandfather, I'd been pleased. My dad would have been so proud. In retrospect, I realized that had been an emotional decision and one he now found unsuitable for his skill set. Although he was a junior, changing majors shouldn't be that difficult.

If Paul decided to go into the hospitality industry, I wouldn't stand in his way. This was his life, and while the career choice wasn't what I wanted for him, he had to be his own person.

After checking online, I saw that Washington State University had an excellent program in that field. While on-the-job training was all well and good, a degree in his chosen field would be helpful in the future, especially if the relationship with this Owen person changed. Now all I had to do was get my son to listen to reason.

My phone rang, and I recognized the number. It was Rich Gardner. I wasn't in the mood to talk. For two rings I debated if I should answer or not. I didn't feel much like talking to him, but in the end I gave in and answered.

"Hello."

"Jenna. Glad I caught you. How are you?"

"I'm doing fine." No need to mention my current troubles.

He sounded upbeat and happy. "I got the invite to your mom's birthday party and thought I'd RSVP personally. How's she doing?"

I switched the phone to the other side of my head and leaned back, bracing myself against the wall. "Mom's doing great. She's getting back into her old life; thanks for asking."

"She showed real determination while at Parkview and inspired others around her during her stay with us. I am using your mother as an example of what can be achieved when properly motivated."

Mom would be happy to hear that. "If you're able to come to the party, you can tell her yourself."

"I hate to miss the party, but I have a previous engagement."

"I'm sorry. Mom wanted to personally thank you for the excellent care she received while at Parkview."

He hesitated for a moment. "I have a question for you."

"Sure, go ahead." I had a feeling there was another reason for his call but didn't want to be presumptuous. He was going to ask me out again. This would be the third time, and if I declined, the message would be crystal clear.

"I don't want to step on anyone's toes here, so if I am, please let me know."

"Of course." This was his less-than-subtle way of asking me if there was someone else.

"There's a charity art gallery event tomorrow evening, and I would very much like for you to go with me." He mentioned the name of the artist, William Benson. I'd recently read an article about him and his work and was interested.

"No pressure, Jenna."

Viewing the work of the man I'd heard so much about strongly tempted me; still, I hesitated, not wanting to lead Rich into believing I was interested in dating him. On the other hand, if I wasn't at the art show, I'd be sitting home, feeling sorry for myself, weighed down by my thoughts of Paul and Rowen.

When I didn't immediately respond, he added, "It's going to be a formal event with champagne and appetizers. It starts at six. I need to make an appearance, but it isn't necessary that I stay long."

"I've read about Benson's work," I said, hesitating still.

He waited patiently while an internal battle waged inside me. The thought of spending another night home, stewing and stressing, was what led to my decision. "I think I'd enjoy the art show, Rich. Thanks for thinking of me."

He paused, as if I'd surprised him.

"Wonderful," he said enthusiastically.

He went over the details of when he'd pick me up, and I told him I'd look forward to the evening.

The night of the charity event, I put on my little black dress that I reserved for more formal dates. I spent extra time on my makeup, hoping to conceal the fine lines around my eyes from lack of sleep.

Rich was punctual, arriving at the house on time.

"You look beautiful, as always," he said, greeting me with a huge grin.

"You don't look so bad yourself." He was a fine figure of a man, tall and debonair.

He led me out to his car and opened the passenger door for me: the perfect gentleman. It'd been raining on and off all day, and the evening chill had set in. Not unusual weather for this time of year, although my spirits would have appreciated a sunny day.

The art gallery wasn't one I recognized, although, to be fair, I didn't frequent a lot of galleries. My budget didn't have any wiggle room for expensive art. And when I say expensive, I'm not joking. The first piece I saw was listed at twenty-five-thousand dollars. I stared at it for a long time, seeing nothing more than swirling colors with no distinguishable pattern, which was what Benson was best known for creating.

"It's a masterpiece," Rich said, coming to stand at my side. He handed me a champagne flute.

Tilting my head to one side and then the other, I tried to see it through his eyes. Perhaps it was my mood, but I got nothing out of this painting. From my perspective, the artist had been having a bad day and took his mood out on this innocent canvas.

"You don't agree?" Rich asked.

"You apparently have a more appreciative and knowledgeable eye than I do."

"Art is one of my passions."

"You collect, then?"

"I do. I've purchased several investment pieces through the years. Some have escalated ten times in value and others not so much. I don't always make the best decisions. I buy what appeals to me most and hope for the best."

"It's sort of a retirement fund, then?"

He thought about it and nodded. "I guess you could say that."

He led me to another part of the gallery. The work there featured lesser-known artists, those less modernist and more to my liking.

"I've never married," he said casually, "and have more discretionary funds for such investments."

"You've never married?" This surprised me, seeing how attractive and successful he was. I'd imagined women flocking to him and suspected my appeal was that I hadn't. "Have you never been in love?"

Sadness bled into his eyes. "Yes. It's years ago now. I met an artist soon after I graduated from college. Jeannie was talented beyond anyone I'd ever met before or since. Unfortunately, she died in a freak accident when the space she rented to paint in was hit by a tree in a windstorm and the roof collapsed."

Oh my. "I'm sorry."

"Thank you, Jenna. My one regret was that I never told her how much she meant to me. How much I loved her. I was young and foolish, and I assumed we had all the time in the world. It was a painful lesson. Afterward, I never found anyone I could love who was her equal."

"I imagine her artwork hangs on your walls."

"It does. It's worth far more to me in sentimental value. I'll never sell it, although I could probably retire early if I did."

Regrets. We all lived with them. I know I did.

"Your glass is empty. Let me get you another."

I would have normally declined, but he didn't give me an option. He briskly took the flute from my hand and disappeared. Telling me about the one love of his life seemed to have brought a barrage of painful memories.

The crowd was growing, moving from one part of the gallery to the next. To my surprise, I recognized several faces. Rich hadn't mentioned the name of the charity, and I had to assume it had something to do with the medical field, as several of those attending were physicians.

How had I been so oblivious? Nearly everyone in attendance came from local hospitals. Rowan could be right around the next corner. My pulse accelerated. Right away, I decided I would look for Rich and suggest now might be a good time to leave. Earlier, Rich had mentioned that he only needed to make an appearance. As it was, we'd stayed nearly forty-five minutes.

I went to find him and came face-to-face with Rowan.

He seemed as shocked to see me as I was to see him.

"Jenna."

I took a deep breath and froze. "Hello, Rowan."

His eyes steadily held mine, full of questions. He looked from left to right, as if seeking out my companion.

It was getting harder to breathe normally. Every part of my heart longed to reach out to him. I couldn't. He was right, I'd made my choice, painful as it was.

"You're here with someone?"

I nodded.

He stiffened and said nothing. Really, what was there to say?

Unable to maintain eye contact, I looked down.

Rich reappeared then with two champagne flutes. "Here you are," he said cheerfully. "Rowan," he greeted. "Good to see you. I didn't know you'd be here."

"It's a worthy cause."

"Yes, and like I was telling Jenna, art is one of my passions." He placed his arm around my waist.

Rowan's gaze went to his arm, then to my eyes and back to Rich. He nodded once to Rich. "Have a good evening," he said as he turned away.

I didn't think I'd ever be able to forget the pain in Rowan's eyes as he left me standing next to Rich Gardner.

Chapter 31

Jenna

"Mom?" Allie's voice rang through the house. "Where are you?"

I stuck my head out my bedroom door. "Upstairs, getting ready." My head was buzzing with everything I still needed to do for Mom's party. I'd taken today off for the party, and Tom and Louanne were in town and had stayed overnight at my place. They'd given me a helping hand all day yesterday to prepare. They'd left to head over to Mom's place, as their kids were about to arrive from Oregon. Tom and Louanne needed to get back in time for work in the morning and planned to leave before the cleanup began. I'd appreciated everything they'd done to make this party a success.

Allie raced up the stairs. "I had a long talk with Mackensie. You need to hear what she said."

"Now?" I cried. "It's Grams' birthday party this afternoon." Allie knew that as well as I did.

"Not right this minute," she said, as if I was a dunce, "but soon, okay? It's important."

"Okay, I will. I promise." I'd hoped to talk to Mackensie about her relationship with her father. I'd hesitated, unwilling to put Allie's friend in the middle of what was going on between Rowan and me.

"When you talk to her, you'll see that not everything is the way it seems," Allie insisted. "Just hear her out."

"I said I would, only I can't do it today." I had enough on my mind. This party had turned into a lot more work than I'd thought it would be.

I noticed the time, and a sense of panic took hold. "We need to leave," I said, while mentally reviewing the list of what had to be done once we arrived. "Do you want to ride with me?" I wasn't sure who'd dropped her off at the house, but assumed it was either Wyatt or Mackensie, probably Wyatt.

"Sure."

When we arrived, I found Tom and Louanne busy following Mom's instructions. My mother wanted everything to be as perfect as she could make it when hosting company. I sequestered myself in the kitchen, getting the appetizer and snack trays ready.

When the doorbell rang, I glanced at the clock. I wasn't expecting anyone to arrive this early. I stiffened when I heard Mom greet Rowan. Although I knew he'd received an invitation, I hadn't expected him to come. Seeing how early he was, I had to assume he'd stopped by to give Mom a birthday greeting and then leave.

"Rowan," Mom cried out. "How good of you to come."

You'd have thought Rowan was her long-lost son by how excited she sounded. I could only partially hear their conversation after Mom introduced him to my brother and sister-in-law. Next, I heard Rowan ask about me, and then Mom explaining that I was in the kitchen.

My first thought was to remain exactly where I was, but I couldn't hide in the kitchen for the entire party. It was ridiculous to try to avoid him, and I refused to do it. Taking the filled trays with me, I came through the swinging door, forcing myself to smile.

He looked my way and I looked his. Seeing him again so soon after the scene in the art gallery left me feeling like I'd walked face-first into a brick wall. It took a moment to right myself emotionally before I could manufacture a welcoming smile. It'd been foolish on my part to think he no longer affected me.

Rowan spoke first. "Jenna."

"Rowan," I returned in kind. I turned my back to him while setting down the trays, and briefly closed my eyes as I steadied my heart.

My evening with Rich had been pleasant. I'd enjoyed our time together at the gallery. The contrast between Rowan and Rich was striking. Rich was entertaining and interesting. Polished and charming. Rowan was quiet and intense. Thoughtful and introspective.

"Jenna, please offer Rowan something to drink."

"Coffee?" I said, doing as my mother asked.

"Please." I wanted to ask him why he'd come, and

suspected he intended to confront me, seeing that I hadn't answered any of his text messages.

As I turned away to pour Rowan's coffee, I heard the doorbell ring, and Tom began to greet other guests. Trying to gain control of my pounding heart, I dragged in a shuddering breath and headed toward Rowan with his coffee.

"Did you enjoy the charity event?" he asked.

"It was a lovely evening."

When I went to give Rowan the coffee, he put his hand over mine. "Was it, Jenna?"

As much as I wanted to, I couldn't lie. "I had a knot in my stomach the entire time."

"I did, too," Rowan said in a near whisper. "Will you be seeing Rich again?"

While it was none of his business, again I found I could only speak the truth. "No."

Rowan released a tight breath and offered me a small, grateful smile. I briefly closed my eyes because I found it hard to resist this man who had become so very dear to me.

"Allie tells me there's a problem between you and Paul," Rowan said next.

"You talked to Allie? When? Why?" I hadn't realized my daughter had dragged Rowan into this.

"I'll tell you about that later. I want to know what's going on with Paul." His concern was genuine.

Part of me wanted to refuse to involve him in a matter that was none of his business. Another part yearned to seek his advice. "It's nothing . . . I'm sure it will all work itself out in no time."

The concern on his face told me he wasn't going to accept that. "Jenna, tell me." He gripped hold of my hand with both of his, refusing to let go, his eyes imploring mine. "What's happened?"

At his touch, my entire body felt like a bolt of electricity had shot through me, and I automatically stepped back, withdrawing my hand, although he was reluctant to release it. I didn't know what Allie had told him. As soon as I was able to corner her, I most definitely intended to ask.

"Paul isn't speaking to me at the moment."

The doorbell again. I could hear Mom's guests greet her. While this was her birthday party, I was the host, along with my brother. Tom was busy talking with an old friend from high school. Ted and Tom had been on the football team together.

"Excuse me, please. I need to greet the guests."

"You can explain everything later."

Concern and worry clouded his eyes, and I sensed his unwillingness to delay our conversation. I hadn't intended to tell him anything. This was my problem, not Rowan's. My son and I would find a way to resolve it together.

After I finished delivering the food trays to the dining room table, I saw that Maureen had arrived. I was disappointed to see that she'd come alone, without Logan. I was looking forward to meeting him. Something must be wrong, especially if the sadness radiating off her face was any indication. I'd sensed when we briefly chatted the day before that things were amiss. I'd asked about Logan and her answer had been vague. Because I'd been wrapped up in my own troubles, I'd let the subject slide. Not only had I failed as a mother—now I'd apparently hit rock bottom as a friend, too.

I hurried back into the kitchen for more mints and nuts, and when I returned I saw that Mrs. Torres from next door was sitting next to Mom, involved in conversation, chatting and laughing.

"Jenna, honey," Mom said, stretching out her arm to waylay me. "Would you make certain Mr. Bones has food in his dish?"

In the middle of her seventy-fifth birthday party, my mother was concerned about that cat. Unable to refuse, I did as she asked, and noticed that Allie's boyfriend, Wyatt, had made an appearance. I didn't expect he'd stay long but was pleased when he took a seat. I grinned when I saw that he filled his plate twice and caught him looking longingly at the birthday cake.

Mrs. Torres left Mom's side to help herself to the appetizers and returned with a plate for Mom. Then I noticed Rowan and Allie seated next to each other in the corner of the room, their heads together. Whatever they were discussing seemed to be of a serious nature.

I knew Allie was anxious for me to talk to Mackensie, and seeing her talking so intently with Rowan had me wondering, until I caught sight of Maureen making small talk with Louanne. My sister-in-law got up to replenish her coffee, and while she was away, I strolled over to Maureen.

"All right, girl, what gives?" I said, sidling up to her.

"What's happening with you and Logan? You said he was coming. What's the deal?"

"We . . . We had a parting of ways."

I frowned, curious as to what had changed. To this point, their relationship had sounded promising. Green lights all the way.

She stared at the wall, her back straight and her features grim. "I won't be seeing him any longer."

"What?" I cried, attracting the attention of nearly everyone. Lowering my voice, I added, "Isn't this all rather sudden? Something must have happened."

"Not here," Maureen insisted. "Not now." Her voice trembled as she spoke. I could see that while she'd tried to make light of their split, she was hurting.

"Okay, I'll agree that now probably isn't the best time, but you will tell me everything after the party." No way was I letting her escape without explaining what had happened. Yes, I had my own troubles and they were weighing heavily upon my heart, but I couldn't bear to think that Maureen had been hurt, especially when everything had seemed to be going so well between her and Logan.

"Not today," Maureen said, shaking her head. "I don't intend to stay much longer . . . I'm here to wish your mom a happy birthday and that's it."

"You sure? I don't think the party will go on too late."

"I'm sure. Besides, I want to check on Tori. She's suffering with morning sickness that is lasting far longer than morning."

As I recalled, it'd been the same when Maureen was pregnant. She was sick every morning and well into the afternoons for the first five months of the pregnancy. I hoped it didn't last that long for Tori.

"Once I'm home I want to find a big, fat hole where I can bury my head."

My friend needed a hug, and I gave her one. "I'm so sorry."

"No sorrier than I am," she said.

"Are you sure you won't stay?"

"I'm sure. I'm not in a partying mood. Besides, I see Rowan is here. Looks like you have a story to tell, too."

"I'll call you later," I said, before returning to the kitchen.

For the rest of the afternoon, I sensed Rowan watching me. He made polite conversation with Mom's neighbors and friends, but I knew parties didn't much interest him. Yet I knew he came because he genuinely cared for my mother. And the only reason he stuck around was because of me.

I knew it. He knew it. And my mother knew it.

By the time the festivities were winding down and the cake dished up and served, I could see that Mom was exhausted. The guests seemed to notice, too, and said their good-byes. My brother and his family had already departed for the drive home to Oregon. While Allie helped Mom into her bedroom to rest, Rowan joined me, collecting the dirty dishes and carting them into the kitchen.

"You don't need to do that," I said.

"I know."

"Mom," Allie said, calling into the kitchen from the living room. "Wyatt and I are leaving now."

With Mom in bed and Allie leaving with Wyatt, that left me alone with Rowan. I started to battle a sense of panic. I silently pleaded with my daughter to stick around, but my entreaty was ignored.

Allie hugged me and whispered close to my ear, "Paul wants me to call him."

This was welcome news. Allie knew how much I regretted the last conversation I'd had with Paul. "Give your brother my love," I whispered back.

"Everything is going to work out, Mom—don't worry."

She seemed confident, and I could only pray she was right. I knew how hard it was for Paul to tell me of the changes he wanted to make, and I hoped he'd forgive my overreaction.

I saw Allie to the door and watched her race to where Wyatt was waiting in his small Honda. When I returned to the kitchen, Rowan had the dishwasher open and had rinsed the cake plates, stacking them inside.

"You didn't need to do that," I repeated.

"I believe we've already been over this, Jenna."

"Please, you can leave. I've got this covered." His presence made me uncomfortable.

"I don't fully understand what's going on with you and your son, but what I do know is that you could use a hug. Come here. This isn't about what's happening between you and me. This is about you."

He held open his arms. I should have resisted. I should've sent him on his way. I found I couldn't. I walked into his embrace like a homing pigeon heading to where it knew it belonged. Right away I was engulfed in warmth and love.

He didn't speak. Didn't ask for an explanation. He didn't offer me reassurances. All he did was hold me.

That was more than enough. It was all that I needed. All that I craved. I had missed him more than I was willing to admit. More than I realized. I felt more at peace than I had since that last conversation with my son. With Rowan's arms around me, the heaviness that had weighed down my heart lifted. I clung to him like he'd rescued me from a raging fire.

Burrowing my face against Rowan's chest, I breathed in the woodsy, citrus scent of his cologne. It felt like heaven in his arms, yet I mentally resisted, fearing what it could mean. I tightened my grip around him and he rubbed his chin across the top of my head, mussing my hair. Nothing could have made me break away from him, even a nuclear bomb threat and loudspeakers blaring to immediately seek shelter.

When I realized what I was doing, how firm my grip was around him, I eased my hold and said, "I don't know that I can trust you."

"You've made that clear numerous times."

"Have not," I insisted. More likely, the truth was that I wasn't sure I could trust myself. I wanted to believe he was everything I thought he was instead of the deadbeat father.

His body shook with a silent laugh. "Oh, but you have."

I buried my face in his chest, savoring his comfort.

"I'll go, if that's what you want."

"I think you should," I said, and then added, "But please don't."

"All I ask is that you hear me out. I know it sounds bad. I admit I've made mistakes and I could have been a better father. But I have always loved and supported my daughter and done everything I knew how to be a part of her life. If you can't believe that, then believe this: I love you, Jenna Boltz."

I desperately wanted to believe him. Fighting my feelings for him was nearly impossible. Repeatedly he'd asked me to hear his side and I'd put it off. Now it seemed that Allie, my own daughter, was ready to defend him.

"Please, don't say that."

"That I love you?"

"Yes."

"Is it so hard to accept?"

"Yes," I said, and then quickly changed my answer. "No."

I wanted to tell him not to talk of his feelings for me. I couldn't deal with what was happening between us, and between Paul and me at the same time. I didn't want him to care, didn't want to see this tender, gentle side of him. That made everything ten times more difficult.

"Your daughter knows how deeply I feel about you, otherwise I don't think she'd be willing to help as much as she has. Mackensie and I are talking, and that means the world to me."

Allie had done that? I didn't know what to say—it was hard to think straight when Rowan was looking at me with his heart in his eyes. Slowly, he leaned down and kissed me. I'll say one thing about this man. He knows how to kiss. The way his lips moved over mine made me weak in the knees. The electricity we shared was magnetic. I'm sure there's a technical term for this, but I couldn't think of it. All I knew was that with that one kiss, I felt like we could light up an entire city block.

"You do this to me every single time," I whispered.

He gave me a puzzled look, not realizing what I was saying.

"You rock my world."

His smile was huge. "I could say the same about you. You rock mine."

I bounced my forehead against his solid chest. "Please tell me what Allie said about Paul."

"Nothing she hasn't already told you."

"You two chatted a long time."

"We did," he agreed. "She also gave me some good advice about Mackensie."

Sometimes I didn't give my daughter the credit she deserved.

"You've done an excellent job raising your children, Jenna."

I hid my face and wanted to cry all over again. If I was such a good mother, why wasn't my son willing to talk to me?

Chapter 32

Jenna

"Thanks for meeting with me, Ms. Boltz," Mackensie Nelson/Lancaster said. She sat at my kitchen table with her hands neatly folded in her lap. Allie sat next to her. After seeing Rowan at the party, I'd become eager to meet with Mackensie, as Allie had asked me to do.

"I'm not sure where to start?" Mackensie asked, looking to Allie.

"Start at the beginning," Allie urged her friend.

Mackensie nodded. "This fall, I transferred to the University of Washington from Santa Monica and met Allie the first week in a class I needed. We hit it off right away. We were both new and seemed to share a lot in common."

"We've had a lot of fun together," Allie threw in.

I gritted my teeth. "You mean like frat parties and tattoos?"

"Mom," Allie said and groaned. "You're distracting Mackensie from what's important."

Personally, I considered my daughter inking her body to be significant, but she was right. Now wasn't the time to discuss that.

"The reason I wanted to change schools was because of my father," Mackensie explained. "He hadn't been a part of my life, and I wanted the chance to see what kind of person he was."

I bristled just thinking about fathers abandoning their children.

"I sent him text messages and . . . and I was manipulative. I didn't let him know I was living in the area. I intended to but didn't. I'll explain more about that later."

"Okay." I could see that Mackensie was nervous. I noticed that she had Rowan's eyes.

"Allie's friendship has meant a lot to me." Mackensie brushed her long hair out of her face. "Allie mentioned you were a nurse at the same hospital as my dad. I thought I would learn more about him through you and her, and I did."

From the look on Allie's face, this information came as a surprise to her.

"It wasn't until later that I learned that both Allie and I were raised without our fathers being part of our growing-up years. Allie's experience was different from mine, though."

"Different?" I asked.

Mackensie nodded. "My mom had men drift in and out of our lives for as long as I can remember. Allie said you were always there for her and her brother, and that you put them first. It was never that way with my mom."

I was astounded that Allie had paid attention to the choices I'd made to be sure I was there for my children.

"I watched how my mom dealt with each new relationship," Mackensie continued. "When the breakup came, and it inevitably did, Mom got vindictive. She would do everything she could to make that man sorry for leaving her. If she thought being spiteful would win them back, it didn't work."

I wasn't sure what to say.

"I have long suspected that she deliberately kept my father out of my life. I can remember packages arriving on my birthday and Christmas, thinking they were for me, but Mom never let me open them. She would throw them in the trash."

Allie looked over at me.

"Once, when I was around eight or nine, before she woke up, I dug one of those packages out of the garbage and opened it. Inside was a beautiful doll and a letter from my dad, saying how much he loved me."

"Did you keep the doll?" Allie asked her.

Mackensie nodded. "I did. Mom never said anything, but after that, no other packages arrived. At least none that I saw."

"Didn't you ever ask about your father?" I asked.

"Sure, lots of times, but her answers were always the same. She claimed he was a selfish bastard and wanted nothing to do with me."

"And you believed her?"

"Yes, except every time I looked at that doll, I had to wonder. Which is why I'm in Seattle. I needed to find out for myself."

"But why . . ."

Mackensie hung her head. "I know what you're going to ask. You want to know why I didn't let him know I was here."

"Why didn't you? And why did you change your name?"

"Mom changed my name to her maiden name. I didn't even know my surname was Lancaster until I saw my birth certificate when I was eighteen. When I asked Mom about it, she said my father didn't deserve for me to have his name."

"But why not tell him you were in town?"

Mackensie kept her eyes lowered and nervously picked at her nails. "I was afraid."

"Afraid?"

"Afraid that he might be everything my mother claimed he was. I sent him the first text message and he sounded pleased to hear from me, but I wasn't sure I should believe him, so I asked him for money. Not a lot . . . you know, sort of a test."

"Did he give it to you?" Allie asked.

She nodded. "It's how I was able to pay for my tattoo."

I wondered if Rowan knew this, and suspected he must. More than once I'd seen him staring intently at his phone and frowning. He must've been reading text messages from his daughter.

"You texted him a picture of your tattoo, didn't you?"

Mackensie's head shot up, her face full of surprise. "He showed you?"

"No, just speculation on my part."

"He gave me whatever I asked for, until I insisted if he loved me and wanted to be part of my life, then he'd buy me that new BMW." Mackensie looked away, embarrassed to make eye contact.

Rowan had mentioned that to me. "He refused."

"He did, but then, I expected he would. What I didn't know was that he'd paid for the car I'm driving now and all my college expenses. My mother had made me believe she was sacrificing to scrimp the funds together for my college education. It's only been since I bumped into my dad that I've learned that he was the one who's been paying for my studies through a trust fund he had his attorneys manage."

Rowan's ex sounded like a real piece of work.

"It's taken me this long to realize the only person my mother truly cares about is herself. Only now do I understand that my mother didn't care who she hurt along the way, me included. Nothing and no one else mattered."

"I'm sorry, Mackensie." It couldn't have been easy growing up with a mother like that.

"Looking back," she continued, "I think it's sad; I think she's sad. I don't ever remember a time my mother was ever genuinely happy."

I'd met women like Rowan's ex who lived selfishly, seeking to find their happiness in material things and in shallow relationships. I felt sorry for Mackensie's mother, and sad for Rowan's daughter, who had been deprived of a father's love for all these years.

"Allie has been a good friend," Mackensie went on to say. "She's been instrumental in helping me come to terms with a lot of things. She might be younger than me, but she's smart. Allie didn't defend my dad or criticize me. She simply asked me what demanding a fancy car was all about, and I told her."

A smile crinkled the edges of Mackensie's mouth. "You know what she did? She laughed. I mean, she laughed so loud it was embarrassing. When I wanted to know what was so funny, Allie explained that by refusing my demand, my father had proved his love in ways I didn't realize. She pointed out that if I was looking for confirmation that he loved me, he'd given it to me."

She looked down at her hands, clasped in her lap. "I didn't appreciate Allie laughing like that; it wasn't until later that I thought about what she said, and it started to make sense. I've never had a friend like Allie before: She's direct, honest, and fair. I know she truly cares for me as a person, not for the material things I own."

Mackensie focused her attention on me. "It would have been the easy way out for my dad to give me what I wanted. Others have. After what Allie said, I understood that it took far more love for my dad to tell me no. Buying me a car would've proved that I could manipulate him whenever I wanted, which was why he'd refused. She explained that my dad wanted to be more than a Santa Claus in my life. She was the one who urged me to go to him."

"You and your dad are working all this out?" This was why Allie had wanted me to talk to Mackensie.

"You have a wonderful daughter, Ms. Boltz, and I have a good friend."

"Please, Mackensie, call me Jenna. All of Allie's friends do," I insisted. I had no idea my Allie could be so wise.

"Allie and I have talked a lot, especially after my father and I met face-to-face for the first time. I have only a few memories of him as a little kid. These weren't easy discussions with my dad, or with Allie, even. More than once I was ready to walk away and end our friendship."

So much had been going on behind the scenes that I knew nothing about.

"Like I said, Allie told me her own dad had been an absentee father for nearly her entire life." Mackensie shifted her attention to me now. "She said how lucky I was that I had a father who really loved me and who wanted a relationship with me, and that I was a fool if I turned my back on him for my own selfish reasons."

"Allie is right," I reiterated. "Your father is loyal, generous, caring, and kind." I could only hope she'd someday appreciate the man he was.

"When she finally met with her dad," Allie interjected, "Mackensie learned that her father had always wanted a relationship with her. Several times he flew to California for visitation, but he wasn't allowed to see Mackensie."

"I learned that my dad spent thousands of dollars on attorney fees. I don't know what my mother said or did that prevented him from seeing me. I could be angry and bitter at her, but what's done is done."

"You're all he has, Mackensie," I said.

"I know, but I hope that won't be the case for long."

"What do you mean?" I asked.

"Mom," Allie jumped in, "don't be silly. She's talking about you and Dr. Lancaster. He loves you, Mom. When you broke up with him, it devastated him."

I hadn't exactly been singing songs and skipping through

the park myself. This misunderstanding had been hard on me, too.

"When did you finally get the courage to speak to your dad?" I asked Mackensie.

"Soon after I unexpectedly bumped into him here." She turned to look at Allie. "That night I got stupid drunk. I was lucky to have Allie there to keep me out of a bad situation. Once I sobered up, she had a come-to-Jesus meeting with me."

I smiled. That sounded like something Allie would do.

"And I've talked with Mackensie's dad, too," Allie added.

I'd seen Rowan and Allie with their heads together at my mother's birthday party. "I know. I saw."

"And before then, too."

"Before?"

"You were miserable, and don't try to tell me you weren't. Mackensie felt much better after the talks she had with her dad, so I decided to have a talk with him of my own."

I couldn't believe my daughter's audacity.

"If you were going to give Dr. Lancaster the green light, then I wanted to make sure he was worthy of my mother."

"Was this another come-to-Jesus meeting?" I asked.

"No. Dr. Lancaster already knows Jesus, so no introduction was needed," Allie clarified, then continued, "I like this man, Mom. Of all the men you've dated over the years, Rowan's the best. And better yet, he loves you. A lot. If you let him go, you'll be sorry."

After all these recent revelations, I had no intention of letting this man go. The bond we shared seemed to be growing stronger and deeper each time we met. Almost from the beginning, I'd felt this draw to him, one I didn't completely understand.

"Maybe one day Allie and I can be stepsisters," Mackensie piped in.

They were getting ahead of themselves. One thing was for sure: I'd made a terrible mistake when I'd refused to hear Rowan's side of the story. Now it was my turn to reach out to him. And seeing how instrumental Allie had been in patching things up between Mackensie and her father, I might do well to go to my own daughter for wise advice in the future.

Chapter 33

Maureen

Tori and I met for a little shopping therapy. It'd been her suggestion, and I was more than willing to indulge in anything that took my mind off Logan.

"I need to ask you something," I said to my daughter, as she held up the cutest onesie that I'd ever seen. Baby clothes had surely changed since Tori had been born. So, so cute and clever. If I wasn't careful I would be tempted to buy out the entire store.

"Sure, Mom. What is it?" she asked, as she checked a price and added it to her cart.

"Am I a prude?"

Tori cocked her head at an angle. "Someone called you a prude?"

I swallowed hard and nodded.

"Who?"

"A . . . friend of Logan's. Logan didn't defend me, so I have to assume he agrees with his friend's assessment."

Tori wheeled her cart closer to mine. "I knew something was troubling you. You tried to hide it, but I can tell. Let's get tea at the Starbucks, and then I want you to tell me what's going on."

I didn't want to talk about Logan and me, especially in a crowded store, even if the Starbucks was tucked away in the corner. My concern wasn't that someone would be able to listen in on our conversation but that I'd embarrass myself and tear up. I remained upset and angry, even though the incident had happened a week ago. Irritation, however, was the best defense I had, and I held on to my outrage with both hands in a death grip.

"No, it's fine," I said, dismissing her offer. "I'd rather not discuss it."

"It's not fine," Tori insisted. "Tell me what happened."

Somewhere between the baby aisle and Starbucks, I relayed the events of that horrible Friday afternoon, sparing none of the details, including my flashy Seahawks T-shirt. I'd been tempted to burn it, and would have if I wasn't too frugal to waste the thirty-five dollars I'd spent on it.

"To make it worse," I concluded with the final details, "Logan hardly said a word in my defense. He suggested that I take the guys' teasing with a grain of salt. It was more like a teaspoon of arsenic, if you ask me."

"Mom," Tori said, looking serious, "I'm not around construction crews much, so I don't know how they talk, but I do know that men can be insufferable, especially when it's just them hanging out together and drinking beer. My guess is that Logan is mortified that you heard any part of that conversation."

"Well, I did." My spine stiffened, thinking about what had been said. To his credit, Logan had made a pitiful effort to put a stop to it, but it had been too little too late.

"And you told Logan you were finished because of what his friends said. Oh Mom, that must have been dreadful for you."

She set down her tea at one of the small tables outside the Starbucks stand before pulling out a chair and taking a seat. I reluctantly put my own tea down and sat beside her, as I could tell this wasn't going to be a short conversation. I began to regret mentioning what had happened.

"You never answered my question about me being a prude," I said, before she got into how I'd mishandled the situation.

Tori looked at me with all the wisdom of her years. "I'm not going to answer it, because whether or not you are a prude isn't the point."

I suppose she was right, although it wasn't what I wanted to hear. I had told Jenna most of what had happened, and, being the good friend she is, she'd quickly sided with me. When I thought about it, I couldn't count on Jenna to be totally objective with me—she was my dearest friend and would defend me to the end. My daughter was more likely to speak the truth.

"You haven't seen or heard from Logan since then?"

"No." Nor had I expected I would. When we'd parted I'd seen that stubborn glint in his eyes. He was standing firm on his pride, and, admittedly, so was I. If he was content to let others ridicule the woman he claimed to care for, then he wasn't the one for me.

"You satisfied with the outcome?" Tori asked.

That wasn't a question I was prepared to answer. "Satisfied?"

"Is this what you want?" she asked, rephrasing the question. "Did you expect him to come back and apologize, to beg for your forgiveness? He did that once, didn't he?"

"I . . ." My tongue seemed to tie itself in a knot. "I don't know what I expect anymore."

"Pride will take you only so far, Mom."

"It's more than pride." I hadn't allowed myself to dwell on that heaviness I carried in my heart for all this time. From the beginning, I'd believed this relationship between Logan and me wouldn't last. I had failed in all my relationships with men, and I couldn't see that this one would be any different. All along I'd been waiting to be proven right and it'd finally happened.

"It's because of Dad, isn't it?" Tori asked, her eyes dark with concern.

"Your father?" What a ridiculous question. "Don't be silly."

"Face it, Mom, you're afraid of giving your heart away. A wonderful, intelligent, and caring man has finally been able to break through that brick wall you've erected around your structured life. Once Logan got close, you froze and had second thoughts."

I dismissed the statement quickly. "I don't remember you taking psychology in college."

"I don't need a psychology class to know my own mother."

"You're wrong, Tori."

"You may not recognize it, but you've been looking for

an excuse to break up with Logan almost from the first. Admit it."

"Wrong again." I had no idea where Tori got these ideas.

"I don't think I am." She shook her head like she was the adult and I was the child, as though she knew my inner thoughts better than I did.

"I bought a thirty-five-dollar T-shirt for that man," I reminded her in protest. "I was the one willing to bend, not him. He didn't even pretend to enjoy the ballet."

"That's because Logan chose to be honest and genuine with you. You're faulting him for that?"

Putting it in those terms made me sound hypocritical. "No."

Tori held up her hand. "I won't say anything more. This is your life, and if you want to live alone, that's your choice. But, Mom, I've seen the light in your eyes when you talk about him. That light isn't there any longer, and it hurts me to stand by while you refuse to acknowledge what the real issue is."

My daughter had certainly given me something to think about.

We finished up our bargain shopping, and with my mind spinning, I returned home after we said our good-byes. Jenna and I were meeting later to rework our Paris plans. I had a couple errands I needed to run before I headed her way, and I was on a tight schedule. I'll admit it: I did like order. It was comfortable to me.

However, as I unloaded the car, my head was caught up in my talk with Tori, and now I was restless. While I'd rejected her theory when we were talking, I had to accept that there was some truth to what she'd said.

I'd forced myself not to think about Logan, to put him completely out of my mind since the blowup. It wasn't easy, but I'd accepted that he was gone. Now, all at once, he was back in the forefront of my thoughts, front and center, and he wasn't moving. I could no more follow the rest of my schedule today than fly to the moon.

If I was thinking of Logan, and I was, it made me wonder what might be going through his mind. I'd probably never know.

My head filled with questions. Was he still upset to the point that he wanted to wash his hands of me and move on? Did he miss visiting the library and seeing me? Did he still think of me?

By now I was standing in the middle of my bedroom, with my shopping bags and their contents scattered across the top of my bed. The weight I'd felt in my heart sank lower and ended up in my stomach. It was as if I'd eaten something sour. I recognized that distasteful feeling for what it was: regret.

Tori was right. Pride would carry me only so far. My pride appeared to have run its course, and now I was left to deal with the truth. And, more important, the reasons why.

I covered my face with both hands and exhaled. I didn't know what to do. If I were to ask Tori, I knew she would suggest I contact Logan so he and I could talk this out. A chill moved slowly down my back. The look in his eyes when he last spoke to me had been cold and unyielding. My hands trembled, and I reached out to grip the edge of my dresser, needing something to brace myself and keep me from falling.

For some reason, Logan's daughter, Misty, came to my mind. The night we'd met when Logan had me over for dinner, Misty had given me her phone number. She was close to her dad. I could ask her the best way to approach Logan, or even if he'd accept my call.

Before I lost my courage, I reached for my phone, found her contact number, took a deep breath, and touched the call symbol.

The phone rang several times. My throat tightened, and just before the call went to voicemail I heard Misty's voice.

"Hello?"

"This is Maureen." My voice was small and came out sounding more like the squeak of a mouse than anything human. The independent, strong woman who'd been so sure of herself hours earlier had completely vanished.

"I wondered if you'd call," Misty said, as if she'd been waiting to hear from me all along.

"I . . . I was hoping to talk to you about your dad," I said, faltering because she seemed to know I'd connect with her first before reaching out to Logan.

"What do you want to know about him?" she asked.

"How is he?" My voice continued to quaver.

"You mean health-wise?" she asked. "He's doing great. Never better."

That told me everything I needed to know. "Oh . . . that's good. Thanks for telling me." Deeply discouraged, I was ready to disconnect until she spoke again.

"However, if you were to ask me about his mental state, that's a different story."

My heart leaped with anticipation.

"You did a number on him."

"I . . ."

"I shouldn't even be talking to you. If Dad knew, he'd be furious."

"I . . ."

"I don't know what happened between you two. Whatever it is, I hope you intend to fix it, because Dad is miserable without you."

"Really?" It was probably wrong to be so happy to hear this.

"My dad is one of the greatest men I know."

"I think so, too," I said, grateful to get a chance to speak.

"He wouldn't talk about what happened, but I'll tell you this: He misses you. What went wrong, anyway? One day Dad was walking on cloud nine and the next he was in the dumps."

"I have issues," I said, rather than go into the details.

"You have issues. Dad has issues. Doesn't everyone?"

I snorted a laugh. She was right. Everyone did, in one way or another. The key was working them out instead of running away.

"So now that we've come to this point, I'm guessing you called for more than an interest in Dad's health."

"I did," I readily confessed. "Do you think . . . he'd respond if I sent him a text?"

"Why would you text him?" Misty asked. "From what little Dad told me, you said you were finished with him. Have you changed your mind?"

"I regret saying that." I'd been hurt and angry and stupid, but I was willing to admit it now.

"In other words, you've had a change of heart?"

"I have."

She considered my words, then said, "Don't toy with my dad, Maureen. This is the second time you've pulled the rug out from under him. The first time was bad enough. Either you're in or you're out. You need to decide what you want, because I refuse to stand by and let you stomp all over his heart."

His heart wasn't the only one that felt like it'd been caught in a stampede. "I know what I want, and that's Logan. He said I should let him know when I was ready to take back what I said. I'm ready. More than ready."

"Good," Misty asked, and sounded pleased. "But why are you talking to me and not to my dad?" she asked, which was a perfectly legitimate question.

"I wanted your take on how receptive he'd be." The request floated in the air like a balloon tossed about in the wind.

"At this point, I don't know," Misty said, and exhaled loudly. "If you had asked me a few days ago I'd say it was a lost cause. Now I'm not so sure. He's been low. I don't think you have any idea. Dad was head over heels for you."

"Was?" Past tense observed, and my heart sunk.

"He's moving on as if you're out of his life. If you do this thing—reach out, call, text, whatever it is you decide to do—great. But like I said, be sure this is what you want. This yo-yo thing isn't working. Understand?"

"I do."

"You say you've got issues. Deal with them."

"I intend to do exactly that." My heart felt lighter than it had been in a long time. Funny how it was that two women, my daughter and Logan's daughter, had been the ones to set me straight.

"Thank you," I told Misty. "I mean that. I'm sincerely grateful."

After Misty and I ended our call, I stared at my phone, considering how best to approach Logan. My head searched for the words that might get him to respond to me. I toyed with several ideas, some funny, some apologetic, but nothing I came up with felt right.

Finally, after a lot of thought, I started moving my fingers.

It's said the truth will set you free. So here it is: the truth. I love you, Logan.

Sucking in a calming breath, I pushed the send button. The words disappeared, and the message delivery notification came back. I held on to my phone with both hands as I waited for a response.

For a full ten minutes I stood in my kitchen, staring at the face of my phone, waiting.

None came.

Chapter 34

Jenna

We had plans to meet at my home later in the day to discuss the trip. It simply wasn't in Maureen's DNA not to show up on time. I had wonderful news to share after this morning's conversation with Mackensie and Allie. I had plans to meet Rowan later and could hardly wait. I would have canceled lunch with Maureen, only I knew she needed to talk. Besides, Rowan had early duty at the hospital. Over the years she'd had unavoidable delays, but each time she'd called to let me know. Not so today, which made me more than a little concerned.

Five minutes passed beyond the time Maureen was due. When it was ten minutes, followed by fifteen, I was convinced something bad had happened: a car crash, a fall that left her unconscious, or some other unavoidable disaster. Just about the time I was ready to call Tori in a panic, I saw Maureen's car pull up and park in front of the house.

Even before she had climbed out of the vehicle, I was out

the front door. The day was full of dark clouds, and Maureen looked as if one of those very clouds hung over her.

"What's up?" I asked, as we met partway up the sidewalk.

She shook her head, telling me she didn't want to say anything until we were inside the house. This could be one of those subjects not open for discussion, so I kept quiet. Once in the warmth with the door closed, she removed her coat and tossed it over the chair. I'd never seen Maureen toss her coat. She always hung it up in a neat, orderly fashion.

"Does this require alcohol?" I asked.

"What do you have?"

"RumChata and an open bottle of pinot noir."

"Wine," she said without hesitation. She followed me into the kitchen while I brought down two wineglasses and poured us each a generous glass.

"Okay, spill."

Maureen took a gulp and set the glass down on the kitchen table, where we both took a seat. I don't know what it is about this room of the house. My mother and I had the most serious conversations of my life in the kitchen. It'd been the same with my kids and me. Perhaps it was the familiarity of gathering around the table that welcomed confidences. Whatever the reason, Maureen and I both were the most comfortable sharing our hearts and our hurts in this very room.

"I texted Logan to tell him I loved him."

This was big. More than big. It was huge. Maureen had always kept her feelings and emotions close to her chest. She would never say what she didn't mean. If she'd been willing to tell Logan that he had her heart, then this was as real as it got.

This should also be a reason to celebrate, only Maureen wasn't smiling. She wore the same look she'd had the day she'd come to tell me that Peter had moved out and they'd decided to divorce. It was that lost, pained look that made my heart ache for her. I noticed how pale she was.

"And his response?"

"He didn't return my text. I thought he felt the same. He . . . must have changed his mind."

I took a slow sip of wine to give myself time to think this through. I wasn't convinced this was the case. "Maybe he didn't read it."

"He saw it."

"How can you be so sure?"

"My screen said it was delivered."

"Delivered, yes, but that doesn't mean he read it."

"It doesn't?" Hope came alive in her eyes. "You're sure?"

I nodded. "What is it about love that makes everything so difficult?" I asked, not expecting an answer. Relationships between men and women never seemed to be crystal clear. Most of the time it was like looking into a muddy puddle and expecting to see a Picasso painting.

"What's going on with you and Rowan?" she asked.

Leaning forward, I braced both of my elbows against the tabletop and covered my face with both hands. "I met with his daughter earlier, and she explained a lot. You were right to tell me to hear him out. I would have saved us both a lot of angst if I'd listened to you."

For the first time since she'd arrived, Maureen smiled. "I knew he was the one. Told you so, didn't I?"

"I don't know how you can say that. If I were to make a list of everything I didn't want in a man, it would be the description of Rowan. He's a physician. He works at the same hospital as I do. He's divorced and, until recently, estranged from his daughter; he wasn't allowed any access to her since the divorce. You, of all people, know that these are all big issues with me, and yet he's the one I fell in love with. Can you explain that?"

"Nope," Maureen said. "Life is strange."

"You're telling me. I knew almost from the moment I met him that I was going to fall for this guy. And when I say fall, I mean as in leaping off the Golden Gate Bridge—that kind of fall. My head keeps telling me it's crazy for us to get involved, and yet my heart refuses to listen."

Maureen's eyes showed understanding. If she had any more words of wisdom, she was keeping them to herself.

"It all started with that walk along Gold Creek Lake," I murmured. "When I felt his arms around me that first time, I'd been lost. From that point forward it was all over for me. Some part of me had known that there was no going back. I'd stumbled along the way—more than once. But Rowan wasn't like other men. He wasn't ruled by his ego. He was patient beyond explanation, content to wait me out. He seemed to believe that if he waited long enough, I'd eventually accept that we were meant to be together, as he had."

Maureen took another big guzzle of her wine. "I met

with Tori earlier. She forced me to look at myself and confess that I have issues. Don't you hate it when our children are right?"

"Don't look so glum. We all have issues. Some are bigger than others. I have my own, as you well know."

"No!" Maureen feigned shock.

"Paul still isn't speaking to me." I'd reached out again, and no response. This was killing me. More than anything, I longed to resolve this issue between us. I knew he was upset with me. We'd had disagreements before, but never any that had lasted more than a day or two. This had gone on long enough, and I was desperate to set things right.

"What are we going to do about Paris?" Maureen asked, bringing up the original reason that we were meeting today in the first place.

"We'll do what we always do," I assured her. "Yes, we can travel to Paris in September or October, but I've always dreamed of seeing the city in the spring."

"I know. I have, too."

"Then let's put it off for another year."

"Just as long as we set a date that doesn't interfere with my grandbaby's first birthday."

"It's a plan." I clinked the edge of my wineglass against hers. Some dreams simply had to be postponed. We'd put Paris off this long. An extra year wasn't going to be that difficult to accept. Our plans were set, but I remained concerned about Maureen.

"You going to be okay?"

"Nothing more I can do. I laid my heart and my pride on the chopping block. The next move is up to Logan."

We finished our wine, and before Maureen left, we hugged.

About fifteen minutes later, I got ready to meet Rowan.

Chapter 35

Maureen

After I left Jenna, I headed home; my heart felt like a boulder was pressing against it. It seemed Logan was going to need more than a text from me. I'd hoped he would respond to my declaration of love. He hadn't. I'd lost count of the number of times I'd checked my phone. Nothing.

This only meant that I would have to swallow even more of my pride and reach out to him in person. I had to ask myself how willing I was to admit I'd made a mistake. The answer was easy: I wanted Logan in my life. I wanted this relationship. As I looked back on the years since Peter and I had divorced, I recognized that I'd sabotaged every chance I had to build a new life with another man. I didn't want that to happen again. Logan was someone I wanted to start a new journey with. Obviously, something was wrong with me that I would continue to push away the very man I had come to love.

As I turned onto my street, I noticed a truck parked in front of my house. One of the neighbors, I assumed, until I got closer. My breathing stalled, and I gasped for air when I realized that it wasn't the neighbor's vehicle.

It belonged to Logan.

He sat in the cab and was looking down at something. I had to assume he was either snoozing or on his phone.

Once I parked in the driveway and got out of the car, the truck door opened and Logan climbed out.

"Did you mean it?" he hollered to me from the curb.

No need to pretend that I didn't know what he was talking about. We both knew he was referring to the text I'd sent him. I nodded.

"Then say it."

I glanced around, certain that by now I had the attention of every neighbor on the block. I became convinced when Mrs. Olson's draperies moved and I saw her looking out the living room window.

"May we go inside and talk about this?" I pleaded.

"No."

I shuffled my feet, kicking at a brightly colored leaf on the edge of my driveway. "I care about you."

"That wasn't what you said in the text." His voice seemed to vibrate in the air as loud as a sonic boom.

"I texted that I am in love with you," I said in a low voice, keeping my head lowered.

"I didn't hear that. What was it you said?" He cupped his hand around his ear, even though I knew he'd distinctly heard every word.

He was going for blood now. "Okay, okay," I all but shouted. "I'm in love with you."

Satisfied, a big grin spread across his face, and he started walking toward me. His smile was bright enough to rival that of the summer sun. When he reached me, he wrapped his arms around my waist, lifted me off the ground, and whirled me in a circle. I brought my arms around his neck and held on to him, smiling in return, almost forgetting that the entire neighborhood was probably watching.

"It's about time you admitted it," Logan said, hugging me close.

I hugged him back, kissing the side of his neck.

"Guess that text was your way of telling me you weren't finished with me, after all."

"I'm not anywhere close to being finished with you."

"Good to know."

"You can put me down now," I said, certain we were causing a scene that would be the talk of the neighborhood for months to come. "Please?" I was embarrassed enough, and convinced my cheeks were beet red, and not from the November chill.

Logan reluctantly did as I asked. Taking his hand, I led him to the porch and into the house.

"I have some news, and it's the reason I showed up at the sports bar in the first place," I said. "I'm going to be a grandmother."

His smile was wide and genuine. "Congratulations!"

We sat close together on the sofa and Logan reached for me, bringing me into his arms, kissing me until the room was spinning out of control. I'd never thought of myself as sensuous. I was too staid to get caught up in the physical aspects of being a woman. Logan's kisses, however, were awakening me to an entirely different aspect of my nature. Winding my arms around his neck, I practically climbed into his lap as I brought his lips to mine. I loved the smell of him, the taste of him . . . I loved everything about him.

"No more of this, Maureen."

Oh my, I was just getting started, I thought to myself.

"You don't like kissing?"

"I was talking about the thing you do when you're upset with me. It's like you can't wait to get me out of your life when we face a bump in our relationship. I can't live that way, walking on eggshells around you. I need to know that you'll stick with me . . . that you'll work through things and not run away."

"I couldn't agree with you more." I was making myself a promise, and Logan, too. From this point forward, I wouldn't run away; I'd run toward him. And I'd avoid the sports bar at all costs. That went without saying.

"Good."

"I was jealous, you know." This part wasn't easy to admit. "I saw you with that woman."

"What woman?"

"That night in the sports bar. She . . . She looked like she worked construction."

"Sally?" he barked a laugh. "That's no woman. Okay, I guess she's technically a woman, but I don't think of her that way. We've worked together for ages. She's like one of the guys."

"You had your arm around her."

Logan twisted his face, as if reviewing his memory. "I did?"

"Her shoulder," I amended.

His smile slid back into place. "And you were jealous?"

I nodded.

"I like that. I'll let you in on a secret: I'm a one-woman man and I have my woman—you."

I smiled at his comment. "Good to know." He was saying all the right things—all the things I needed to hear.

"I have a question for you," he said, drawing me close and kissing the top of my head. He put his arm around my shoulders and I laid my head there, enjoying the warmth and the closeness.

"Okay."

"I feel like we both need a bit of clarification moving forward. Where do we go from here?"

Tilting my head back, I looked up at him, unsure how best to respond. "I . . . Where would you like us to go? I mean . . . we could continue the way we've been, getting better acquainted, sharing time and experiences together, that sort of thing."

Logan nodded his head in agreement, but his eyes were thoughtful, unsure. "What would you say if I asked for more than companionship? After all, if I needed someone to pal around with, I'd just go down to the sports bar and ask my buddies to hang out."

His question was becoming clear. He wanted, needed, more from me.

I held his look. "Do you love me, Logan?"

"More than I have the words to say. You center me, help me to understand what's important in my life. At the same time, you challenge me with these books you have me read. And you calm me, although not as much as I'd like, especially in the last couple weeks. When I'm with you, the stress from work lifts right off my shoulders. To me, that's love."

He might not have the gushy words, but this was the most genuine declaration of love that I'd ever heard in my lifetime.

"I look forward to the day when I come home from work," he continued, "and you're there to listen to my day and to share yours with me. My children and grandchildren are eager to meet you. You've already met Misty. I'm pleased that you're about to become a grandma yourself. It's a joy that you'll find hard to compare to anything else."

With my arms around his middle, I hugged him. "Tell you what," I said, "I'm happy to follow this road wherever it may take us, and I know where it's headed—to a life together. But there's just one small concern," I added.

"Which is?"

"I still need to go to Paris, though who knows when it will happen at this point. Jenna and I have been planning this trip since we were teenagers. I can't disappoint her."

"Paris," he repeated.

"You've been?"

"Never."

"I'll tell you all about it when we return," I promised.

"You do that," he said, and, pulling me back into his arms, he picked up where we'd left off minutes earlier, bringing his lips back to mine.

Chapter 36

Jenna

Rowan had suggested we meet in a bar close to the hospital. I knew a few of the staff frequented it. The location didn't matter to me. Being with Rowan did.

He was sitting at a table when I arrived, and stood as I approached. He held out his hands to me and I gripped them in my own. Leaning forward, Rowan kissed my cheek.

We sat next to each other, and Rowan again reached for my hand. He waited for me to speak. I wasn't sure where to start, and then remembered Allie's advice to begin at the beginning. So simple. So smart.

"I met with Mackensie this morning. She had a lot to say about what it was like growing up with her mother."

Rowan nodded. I wasn't telling him anything he didn't already know. "I was foolish. You tried to tell me, and I refused to listen. I'm sorry, Rowan. I was wrong for not giving you a chance to explain. I'm embarrassed at what I've put us through because of it. I hope you will forgive me."

His gentle smile was the sweetest I'd ever seen. "You have no idea how much I love you. I can forgive you most anything, only promise me you won't ever date Rich Gardner again. I don't think my heart could take that."

"You were jealous?"

"Insanely so."

I would have felt the same if I'd seen him with another woman that night. "You have no worries. You're the only one I want."

"We're good, then?" Rowan asked.

"More than good," I assured him. This was Rowan. He didn't use flowery language, didn't declare his undying love on a funeral pyre. He simply asked if we were ready to put the past behind us and move forward.

He lifted my hand and pressed his lips against the back of it. "I love you, Jenna."

"I know, and I love you back."

"Now that this is settled, can you explain to me what exactly a green light means?"

"You know about red light/green light? Who told you?"

"Allie."

I should've known. I was about to explain when Rowan looked past me to a well-dressed man who appeared to take the dress-for-success mentality to heart.

Rowan stood and extended his hand to the other man, who shook it. I had to assume the other man was a colleague.

"Bill Janacek, this is Jenna Boltz. Jenna, Bill.

"I hope you don't mind, Jenna. I asked Bill to meet with us this afternoon."

"I don't mind at all," I replied, but I was curious.

We exchanged small talk, and I could see why Rowan and Bill were friends. Bill didn't look to be more than thirty-five years old, if that. He was charismatic and likeable. In many ways he reminded me of my own son. We talked for a while, exchanging pleasantries. Both men had mixed drinks, while I asked for coffee. I'd already had one glass of wine and didn't want to drive home with two in my system.

"So, how long have you known Rowan?" I asked Bill.

"Not long."

This must be a new friendship. "Are you in the medical field?"

"No," he said, leaning forward slightly. "I own and operate five restaurants in Washington state."

"Five," I repeated. That was impressive, especially for someone so young.

"When I first got into the restaurant business, I was wet behind the ears and didn't have a dime. The man who became my mentor saw potential in me and trained me. Later, when he felt I was ready, he loaned me the money for my first restaurant. When it was successful, I paid him off and purchased a second. It's grown from there, as I've added a new restaurant almost every other year since."

"That's amazing." I began to sense there was more to this meeting than Rowan introducing me to a newfound friend. "And you're in town because . . . ?" I asked.

"I'm here for a number of reasons, but mostly to check into purchasing another restaurant."

I glanced over to Rowan, who had remained quiet while Bill and I conversed.

"I was barely twenty when Walter, my mentor, saw that I had an entrepreneurial spirit. He's done this with other college students before and after me. He's rarely wrong about those he chooses to mentor."

I stiffened. "Walter's last name wouldn't happen to be Owen, would it?"

Bill grinned and glanced at Rowan. "I wondered how long it would take her to catch on."

"You set this up?" I asked Rowan, unsure how I felt about him interfering.

"No, Mom, I did." Without me knowing, Paul had come into the bar and stood behind me. "I asked Rowan if he'd be willing to help me, and he agreed. If you're going to be upset, be upset with me."

"Paul." I was so grateful to see my son that I leaped up from the chair and grabbed hold of him in an uncomfortably tight hug. It felt as if my heart was about to burst wide open.

When we broke apart, I wiped tears from my eyes. Paul joined the three of us, claiming the fourth chair. "Rowan reached out when he heard what happened between us," Paul explained.

Rowan took hold of my hand again, and I squeezed his. I found it hard to believe he'd done this for me. My gratitude made it difficult to take my eyes away from him.

"I couldn't bear to see you heartbroken," Rowan explained, "not if I could find a way to make things better."

Paul picked up the conversation. "I only knew of Rowan

through Allie, and, to be honest, I wasn't that thrilled about talking over family problems with him."

"But you did."

"He didn't give me any choice. He drove to Pullman and confronted me."

My head swiveled back to Rowan. "You drove to Pullman?"

He shrugged, as if the ten-hour round-trip drive was a small thing. Then I turned to Paul.

"And you listened?"

"Yes, because he had an idea that he felt would help you understand my position."

"This man," I said, and looked pointedly in Bill's direction.

"Yes." Again, he agreed. "Rowan and I had a good, long discussion. I expected him to argue your case, to try to convince me to return to college. I wasn't too thrilled to be talking to him, until I realized that he wasn't trying to influence me in any way. He only asked for the details of what had led to my decision."

Details. I'd neglected to ask Paul for those before rushing to judgment. All I heard was that Paul was no longer in school, that he had misled me for months. My willingness to listen had shut down after those two facts.

Rowan added, "Paul managed to convince me that Walter Owen was offering him a great opportunity, one where he was going to have to work hard if he was going to succeed. From everything I've seen so far, Paul has what it takes to make a go of this, Jenna."

"Rowan did a bunch of research on Mr. Owen, too," Paul added.

"This is where I come into the picture," Bill interjected. "I had met Paul through Walter, and Paul asked me to meet you. Rowan arranged the rest."

All this information was overwhelming.

"So, Mom, what do you think? I'm working my way from the bottom up in the restaurant business with on-the-job training. Mr. Owen has great hope for me. The bottom line is that I love every minute of it. It's more than waiting on tables. It's about managing people, meeting customer expectations, and food costs . . . keeping employees satisfied at work, creating a great dining experience for the customers . . . I'm dedicating myself to something far beyond a simple job. I want to make it a career, and I know I have what it takes to be an owner and to be successful at it. And yes, I'll enroll for classes next semester and change my major to hospitality. Rowan convinced me that it was the right thing to do."

My throat was tight as I smiled at my son.

"Mom, can you forgive me for not letting you know what was happening in my life?"

I nodded. "I think you're onto something, Paul."

His smile was gargantuan. "I had a feeling that once you heard the details, you'd see things my way. I wanted to explain all this when I came home the last time, but we got into it and lost our tempers."

"I know. I'm sorry. I should have been willing to listen."

Bill looked at the time. "Sorry to break up this lovefest, but I need to leave now if I'm going to make my next appointment."

"Mom, if you don't mind, I'd like to accompany Bill as

he checks out his new investment opportunity. I'll be learning something new."

"Of course," I said, hugging him again.

"I'll be by the house later. Oh, and Allie is stopping by. I thought it would be great if the three of us had some time together." He hesitated and looked to Rowan. "That is, unless you'd care to join us and make it four, Rowan."

"Another time," Rowan said.

Paul left with Bill. Rowan didn't say anything, so I spoke first. "You did this for me?"

"It's the kind of thing someone does for a person they love, Jenna."

His eyes met mine, and it felt as if my heart was in a vise. I was so in love with this man.

Chapter 37

Jenna

"What's the matter?" Rowan asked, giving me an odd look.

I stared back at him blankly. After Bill and Paul had left the bar, Rowan and I stayed behind. I reached for my coffee, which had cooled considerably, and took a swallow, needing to lubricate my throat. A hundred different emotions came flying at me from as many directions. I found it difficult to breathe, and knew I needed to get away and process everything. My emotions had been on a trampoline, bouncing up and then down, only to be repeated.

"You look like something is troubling you. Is it Paul?" He didn't wait for my response. "I'd hoped this meeting would reassure you."

"It has," I said. "Very much so. I feel worlds better about Paul and his decision, and that he's agreed to return to school and switch his major."

"Then what is it? I don't think I've ever seen you look this intense."

It took everything I had in me to attempt a weak smile. Leaping up from the overstuffed chair like a jack-in-the-box, I grabbed my coat and purse. "I . . . I need time to think." Not bothering to explain further, I headed for the exit.

I should have known Rowan wouldn't leave it at that. He followed me out the door. "Jenna, hold up. What is it? Talk to me."

I shook my head, afraid that if I tried to speak, I'd do something silly like burst into tears, which would be even harder to explain. This moment at the restaurant had somehow brought it front and center that we were meant for each other. Although Rowan had felt this much earlier on in our relationship, it now hit me square in the chest, terrifying me. I longed to run and hide, to bury my head in the sand.

Sleep. That was what I needed most right now. Sleep. It'd been several nights since I'd had a decent night's rest. These thoughts ran in my head. My window on the bay was beckoning to me.

"I thought you'd be happy," Rowan said, matching his steps to mine as I headed down the sidewalk. My steps were rushed.

"I am happy," I said, and to my embarrassment, a sob erupted at the tail end of the sentence.

We reached the corner of the sidewalk. Pausing, I looked at Rowan, whose face was a blur from the tears floating in my eyes. His features swam before me in undulating waves. "I need time alone," I pleaded, wanting nothing more than to sort through the tangled messages floating around inside my head.

Rowan silently agreed, turned back and headed to the bar. Disappointment, or it might have been sadness, radiated from him. I stood in the fading light of the afternoon, frozen, and watched him go.

I loved this man, and it'd hit me like a wrecking ball that true love isn't static—it must grow or it will die. Our future was staring me in the face and I didn't have a clue where it would take us, but I had to trust.

Before I could stop myself, I hurried after him, calling his name. "Rowan, wait up!"

He turned around, his look curious. He stood outside the entrance of the bar while I retraced my steps.

I was breathless by the time I joined him. Breathless and uncertain of how to explain myself.

"Thank you for what you did for Paul and me."

"You've already thanked me, Jenna."

I kept my focus on my feet. "Would you mind walking with me?"

"Okay."

I linked my arm through his elbow and moved close to him. Our steps matched as we continued slowly down the sidewalk, neither of us speaking.

Rowan broke the silence. "What's going on inside that beautiful mind of yours?"

I felt self-conscious and less inclined to talk now that I was by his side. I basked in the comfort he offered, the breeze buffeting against him as he protected me from the chill it brought. "Everything hit at once today: talking with Mackensie and Allie, comforting Maureen, meeting with Paul, and acknowledging in my heart and mind that I've fallen in love with you. It's more than I can absorb in a short amount of time. All these emotions are rushing at me and I don't know how to deal with them." I probably sounded like an overacting drama student, but I couldn't help myself.

For the longest time he said nothing.

"I can understand why."

This sounded just like the Rowan that I'd come to know and love. He was incredibly patient, insightful, and warm.

"You've been through a lot in a short amount of time."

As I was no longer worried that he saw me as a basket case, I quickly added, "And then there's Allie, who doesn't like my new dishes and . . . and she doesn't want me to make Paul's room into a guest room. I . . ."

Turning me in his arms, Rowan smiled broadly and kissed me. I wouldn't have considered this a kissable moment, with my nose threatening to run and me babbling nonsense.

"I think I fell in love with you the first time you kissed me, or the second."

"*You* kissed *me*," he insisted.

"I beg to differ. You intiated that first kiss."

"Okay, I'll admit it. You're right," he agreed reluctantly.

"This may be one of the first times in my life I've heard a man admit that he was wrong and I was right."

I didn't know where we were headed, walking against the wind with the light fading as dusk settled in. What hit me was the peace I felt being with Rowan. It was hard to understand why I had wanted to run away only minutes earlier. He completed me, and I realized the most natural place in the world for me was at his side.

"You've grown quiet," Rowan noticed.

"Most men would appreciate the silence."

"If you haven't noticed, I don't fit into the typical 'man mold.'"

"In that case, I'll count my blessings."

His hand covered mine. "Want to tell me what's on your mind?"

"Well, mostly I was mulling over what my coworkers are going to say at the hospital."

"Do you honestly think anyone will be surprised how we feel about each other?" Rowan asked, grinning with the question.

"Probably not. I'm certain the gossip has made its rounds. If anything, I'm going to be eating a lot of crow. Especially after all the times I emphatically insisted that none of it was true."

Rowan chuckled. He sighed and asked, "So how do you feel about asking Allie and Mackensie to be sisters?"

We were nearly to Pike Place Market, the lights from the waterfront shining before us. I had to stop and think about what he was asking me. When it hit me, my eyes widened. No fancy words of romance or undying talk about love. Just a simple question.

"Rowan Lancaster, is this a roundabout way of proposing to me?"

"Yup."

"Allie would love it. She and Mackensie get along great. They will keep each other in line. How do you feel about being a surrogate dad to mine?" I asked, turning the tables on him.

"Confident. I've already asked Paul for your hand in marriage. He asked a few hard questions, but he's happy for us."

"You talked to Paul already? You were that confident?"

"No, just hopeful."

"What about Allie?"

"Not yet. I will as soon as you agree that we belong together."

I didn't need to be convinced. Joy simmered up inside me like tiny champagne bubbles.

"I've always been fond of holiday weddings," Rowan said.

"Me, too. Just as long as you know in advance that I've got plans to fly to Paris with Maureen, and I'm thinking we're going sooner rather than later."

"I'd never keep you from that trip."

"Wonderful. It's a deal."

"A deal."

And, as if to seal it all under the light of the lamppost, Rowan turned me in his arms and cupped my face on both sides, his fingers tangling with the hair at the base of my neck. With his eyes holding mine, he leaned down and kissed me like there was only today and no tomorrow. Somewhere in the background, I swear I heard the melody from the theme song from *Casablanca*, "As Time Goes By." Or maybe it was all in my head. Whoever penned the line "a kiss is just a kiss" hadn't been kissed by this man.

"I love you, Jenna."

"And I love you back, Rowan."

Sighing, Rowan leaned his forehead against mine. His eyes were closed as he whispered, "It took you long enough."

"Are you complaining?"

"Nope. Just savoring the moment."

And then he kissed me all over again.

Epilogue

Jenna

Five years later

Early Thanksgiving morning I snuck out of bed, careful not to wake Rowan as he had returned home late after performing emergency surgery on a car accident victim the night before. I lovingly looked down at my husband, my heart filled to overflowing. Although I was tempted to wake him with a morning hug and kiss, I'd let him sleep as long as he needed to.

Once I had a cup of coffee and did my morning reading, I brought the turkey out of the refrigerator to let the bird sit at room temperature while I prepared the stuffing. It was this time of year that I missed my mother the most. She'd passed away the year before, at the age of seventy-nine, going quietly in her sleep. When we found her, she'd had this wonderful look of contentment on her face. In my heart, I knew the happy look on her face happened in the short space between life and death when she first saw my father. The instant she'd recognized him, she was complete again, and he'd reached across time and eternity to draw her close.

I remembered all those early Thanksgiving mornings I'd spent with Mom in the kitchen, working together to stuff the bird. I was grateful for all those lessons in cooking and in life that she'd shared with me over the years. I could feel her presence with me now as I added the chicken broth to the dried bread and the sautéed onions and celery.

The front door opened with Allie and Mackensie making a surprise entrance. They were as close as sisters, and by marrying Rowan I'd gotten a bonus daughter. They each had men in their lives, and I suspected I'd be planning weddings soon. I looked forward to that. As I believed, Allie had gotten her degree and now worked for the state of Washington as a social worker, and Mackensie had gone to graduate school to become a physician assistant. I knew how proud Rowan was to see her excel in the medical field and to follow in his footsteps.

"Why are you two here so early?" I asked, although I'd guessed.

"We came to help you with the turkey," Allie said, as she pulled open the bottom drawer and brought out two aprons. She handed one to Mackensie.

Mackensie tied it around her waist. "Let me do that," she said, using her hip to gently bump me away from the large bowl where I'd placed the dressing ingredients.

"We want to watch you put in the spices the way you used to watch Grams," Allie explained. "One day we're going to be doing this on our own, you know."

"Not for a very long time," Mackensie was quick to add.

"Hopefully not," I said with a laugh.

"Hey, what's going on down here?" Rowan asked, joining us in the kitchen. He wrapped his arms around my waist from behind and kissed my neck before helping himself to coffee.

"I thought you'd sleep longer," I said, surprised he was up this early after such a late night.

"And miss out on all the fun?" he joked. He finished with a yawn. It went without saying he'd be the first to succumb to a nap following dinner. Carrying the mug with him, Rowan wandered into the family room and turned on the morning news. "What time are Paul and Katelyn due to arrive?"

"Around three." Paul and Katelyn had met at college. They married after graduation and gave us our first grandchild, Drake, now two years old. Paul was the proud owner of a restaurant in the Seattle area. Busy as he was, I didn't expect him to stay longer than two or three hours, as the holidays were hectic at his establishment.

I'd always believed my son would be a success at whatever he undertook. He'd done as he'd promised and graduated from college with a degree in hospitality. Walter Owen had been a mentor and champion to him. I'd come to appreciate Walter and was grateful for the guidance and training he'd given Paul, and he'd become part of our extended family.

"Are Maureen and Logan stopping by?" Rowan asked.

"Yes, later. They're having dinner with Misty, Matt, and their families, and then stopping by to have dessert with us."

"Great." Rowan plopped down in front of the television with his coffee. He liked to ease into mornings, something I'd learned after we'd married. I gave him his quiet time the same way he did me.

While the girls watched, I assembled the poultry seasoning, sage, and other spices and added them to the bread mixture and tested the moistness. They gathered around me, as if it was a science experiment. It was the same way I had once stood close to my mother when she added the final touches to the stuffing.

Putting on a disposable glove, I stuffed the bird, bathed it in butter, and had Rowan place the twenty-pound hen in the oven to slowly cook to a golden brown.

The girls left with the promise to return at about two o'clock to help with the final preparations.

Rowan had his coffee and the morning newspaper when I sat down next to him on the sofa to relax for a few minutes.

"There's an ad here for discounted airfare to Paris," he said, glancing over at me.

"Paris," I repeated. Before either of us married and before Tori delivered her daughter, Maureen and I had found last-minute bargain airfare and on the spur of the moment flew to Paris with barely twenty-four hours' notice. We feared if we kept putting it off we'd never go, and so we threw caution to the wind and went. It was crazy and wonderful. Paris was everything we always knew it would be. And with Maureen's list in hand, we toured every site we'd originally planned. Truly the trip of a lifetime.

For our honeymoon, Rowan and I had visited Italy, and I'd fallen in love with Florence. We'd spent three glorious days there, and another three in Rome. While I loved Paris, I would return to Florence in a heartbeat.

"Would you like to return to Paris, this time with me?" my husband asked, placing his arm around my shoulders and bringing me closer to his side.

Leaning my head against his shoulder, I thought about his question. "No, the trip with Maureen satisfied the promise we'd made to each other back in our college days. There are other locations I'd like to visit."

"Like?"

"How about New Zealand or Australia?"

"That can be arranged."

I grinned, suspecting that was exactly what Rowan had been hoping to hear. His inquiry made all the more sense when opening my Christmas gift the following month.

The aroma of the cooking turkey filled the house, and the quietness that Rowan and I had grown accustomed to was soon filled with the laughter of our combined families. Drake clung to his mother's leg, holding tightly on to the yellow blanket that I'd knit him.

The house was full as Allie and Mackensie worked in the kitchen, laughing and chattering as Christmas music played softly in the background. Paul and Rowan had the television on, watching a football game, while Katelyn kept Drake busy.

I remembered the days when the house had felt so empty— when I could hear the echo of loneliness shortly after Allie left for college. At that time, I'd look out from my window on the bay, unsure of how I'd fill my days, uncertain of my future.

My nest was no longer empty. These days it was filled with a loving husband, our children, a grandson, laughter, and plenty of love. I wouldn't have wanted it any other way.